CHURCH
BURNING

CHURCH BURNING

TIM LOWE

TL

Published by Tim Lowe

ISBN: 978-0-6484833-0-4 (paperback)
ISBN: 978-0-6484833-1-1 (ebook)

Cover illustration by Sabina Hopfer
Cover design and typesetting by Ilura Design
www.ilurapress.com

Printed and bound by Ingram Spark Australia

With thanks to the patients who told me their stories

1

Early in the morning, Chapel Street is recovering. The air seems stiller, the traffic muted, the occasional pedestrian exposed and uncertain. The first shift coffee-drinkers, only two thirds awake, blankly watching the flurries of shop staff. The footpaths are hard and reflective, jarring with ugly imprints of the previous night's heroics, broken bottles and spattered vomit. The thrumming begins with a lemming-like migration from the flats of Windsor and Prahran and the high-rise colonies of the marginalised. There is a gravitational pull to the great strip which is long enough, between its ethnographic margins of Dandenong Road and Toorak Road, to make it feel limitless. It greets its flock with a nourishing blast of canyon air, an essence of youth and history. The mood shifts and lightens as determined shoppers weave between brunching tables and muttering crazies. Clusters bunch up at pedestrian crossings and cars toss gobbets of music. An arterial tram zings and dong dongs its importance. By mid-morning on a Saturday, Chapel Street is starting to come alive, like a great serpent which has dragged itself onto a rock in the sun, it is now starting to pulse and writhe.

Justin held back as the other passengers left the train at the Windsor station. Arrivals were important for him; he wanted to feel the contact his feet made with the platform. The timeless bustle of humanity at a station rendered the Windsor Station almost anonymous but he smiled when he saw the tuck-pointing on the newly-cleaned bricks. He was the last passenger to touch off with his Myki card.

At the top of the ramp the weight of his own history pulled him up as he entered Chapel Street. It was fifteen years since he had been there, more than thirty years since he had lived there and developed that sense-of-place consciousness that young people form when they leave their childhood homes. The Victorian facades were reassuringly familiar but the shops had changed. Justin resisted an urge to feel disappointed by these changes and felt excited. A new tribe was in place; a tribe which like all previous tribes, had been generated by the economic forces that fed the great beast that was Chapel Street. A tribe which recognised this connection in its need to meet and spend and watch itself.

'Grungey' was the word that was used in the past to describe this end of Chapel Street, the part where Justin had lived. It had been a place where students mixed with the homeless and the desperate, a strip of pawn shops, ops shops and eccentric second-hand stores. A place where stolen property insinuated itself into the economy and drug addicts squeezed out cash. Where shoppers from the north cruised for a whiff of the exotic. Justin noticed the modern offices and the eating places spilling out onto the street but was delighted to find a few remnants of grunge, an Op shop and an adult book shop.

He started walking north along Chapel Street, he wanted to walk slowly to absorb the street's ambience but was immediately caught in its rapid stream of humanity. Inevitable. Young people with white earplugs, an elderly woman wearing a shocking blue dress, beards, tattoos, exposed bra-straps. An old Greek woman wearing black, Justin realised he wanted to see that woman, a living testament to the area's history. She would have come to Melbourne during the 'time of the colonels', experienced prejudice, raised a family, buried a husband. She would have witnessed the exodus of the Anglo Australians to the outer suburbs during the sixties, then their gentrifying return during the eighties leaving her washed up, a cultural sand bar before the tide. She and her husband would have struggled to buy a house which, with the passage of time would have added two noughts to its real estate value.

Rosenberg's shoe store, unchanged! The ageless specialist shoe store for big-footed ladies and transvestites. Next, Justin walked over the place where he knew that, beneath the concrete, the soil type changed from ancient Silurian siltstone to the more common sand that was deposited throughout the area when it was submerged millions of years ago. He conjured up a memory of a geological map showing the various soils in different colours and the excitement it gave him, the strange pleasure he felt when he paced out the street to determine where the soil transition lay.

He remembered chip in a curb stone where he found the exact place. Was he still anything like that serious young man who wanted to understand his environment in such depth?

There were too many things to look at, the shop fronts, the traffic, the rich diversity of people walking past him. He would have been content to just stand and watch but that would have set himself in conflict with the spirit of the street. To enjoy the passing parade, you must sit at a street cafe and become yourself part of the scene, an observer who gives meaning to those who want to be observed. He permitted himself to be intoxicated by the visual over-stimulation. He wondered if it would ever be possible to measure the essence of a place like Chapel Street, the feeling of excitement that comes from being amongst an anonymous body of people where conversational connection is unnecessary.

Justin crossed High Street and had to modify his pace in order to move with the crowd. There was an informal notion of keeping left in the crowded conditions, something that probably stemmed from Australia's left-side-of-the-road driving but so many individuals stopped to talk or gaze in windows that the flow of people was turbulent. Justin felt relieved when the throng spread out in the space in front of the town hall where the down-and-outs sat in clusters on the benches, watching but not talking. Then he was in amongst the monumental buildings near Commercial Road. He loved those buildings and recalled his grandmother describing shopping expeditions to the emporia, The Big Store, Love and Lewis and Read's Store, during the nineteen twenties when the Prahran shopping strip rivalled Melbourne's central business district. They were converted to flats now but their preserved facades of Edwardian baroque and Art Nouveau architecture and their critical bulk lent gravitas to the junction.

He crossed Commercial Road and felt suddenly uplifted by the smell of roasting coffee. The smell intensified when he reached Elizabeth Street, the lane that leads to the back of the Prahran Market. He couldn't resist the smell and followed it, like a dog sniffing the air and that was how he found his way to the coffee house called Market Lane.

Outside the shop men were grilling large mushrooms and selling them in buns, like vegetarian hamburgers. The shop was crowded, attractive with its coffee smells, the fug of bodies and the space and light created by its high ceilings but the architecture was otherwise unappealingly industrial. Justin moved into a short queue and noticed the large coffee roaster dominating the left side of the building, the epicentre of the magic. A young woman with several piercings served him, he had almost forgotten how to order coffee, 'flat white' was the expression he recalled. It was shockingly expensive since the last time he bought coffee many years before. He was lucky to find a vacant space at a bench against the window.

It was a busy, noisy place vibrant with the atmosphere of Saturday morning shopping. Many of the patrons had shopping bags around their feet, filled from the market. They carried with them a sense of reward for a job well done, delayed gratification after their shopping. They mostly young adults but with a scattering of grey heads and families with young children. The staff fascinated Justin, they were obviously very busy but they all looked calm. There was a beautiful Japanese woman, doll-like with her bobbed hair, pouring water from a kettle with a look of blissful devotion over a drip filter container. A tall, thin man of North African appearance worked at a coffee machine, his head tilted slightly to one side and a sense of focussed serenity. It dawned upon Justin that he had chanced upon a very special coffee shop. He noticed that there were newspapers scattered around the tables, some being read, some idle as if they had been supplied by the shop. They were all the same newspaper, *The Age*. There were no copies of the other two main newspapers, *The Australian* and *The Herald Sun*. What did that mean? Did the shop owners only provide *The Age* because they saw their clientele as educated and slightly left-of-centre? They certainly looked that way. Or had there been changes in the character of the big three newspapers since he last looked at them? He picked up a copy to see what *The Age* was like now. The frontpage story was about a politician who had chartered a helicopter, at tax payers' expense, for the short trip from Melbourne to Geelong to attend a party fund raising meeting. Justin smiled. The only time he thought about politics now was at election times and then only because voting was compulsory. The article reinforced his view that politics was not worth thinking about.

The barista brought over his coffee which smelled unctuous and strong. Justin sipped it and was surprised by the dimensions it held. There was the strong coffee flavour but there was also a variety of other flavours and length and mouth-feel. He sipped again and wanted to describe it to himself but did not have the vocabulary so he analysed it the way he would have dealt with good wine, decades ago. The coffee had honeycomb and a type of nuttiness, possibly walnut. There was citrus on the rear palate. The mouth feel was big and creamy with a gentle buccal bite, like the tannin of a red wine. It had great length and lingering acidity. Justin was drinking a truly wonderful cup of coffee and lost himself in the delight of the experience. He felt guilty almost; this was the cup of coffee that a coffee connoisseur should spend years searching for after reading books and websites and tasting coffee at a hundred other coffee shops before eventually finding this coffee heaven. Was this Justin's reward for emerging from the place he called his hermitage?

He flicked through *The Age* and found an article about a man who suffered horrific abuse as a young boy in a Catholic orphanage. There was apparently a Royal Commission into institutional responses to child sexual abuse. As he read the article, Justin experienced a variety of feelings he hadn't felt for a long time. He had a process, automatic now, for dealing with emotions; he allowed them to rise like bubbles and gently pushed them away while at a cerebral level acknowledging their importance. He wondered if reading the article would prove to have the impact of an experience he had three weeks earlier, an experience he now defined as a message.

The message was beautiful. He was sitting on a train opposite a mother and her young son who looked about six years old. Justin had been gazing out of the window of the train for a while and turned to find the boy staring intently at him, perhaps he was interested in Justin's beard. The boy had a broad, freckled face and red, curly hair. When Justin's eyes met the boy's, he broke into a beautiful smile which lit up his whole body. The smile was brief and he then seemed to shrivel with embarrassment at being caught out for starring. Justin smiled back to reassure him.

The image of the smiling boy stayed with Justin for weeks and the boy appeared in his dreams. He investigated what was happening in his subconscious through focussed meditation and dream analysis. The outcome was a powerful message that it was time for him to re-enter the 'real world' and that is what had brought him to Chapel Street that day.

Justin left Market Lane with a sense of exhilaration and purpose, that forces were moving through him. He enjoyed the monastic simplicity of his life but he always had the sense that it was preparation for something more. He did not know what, but was sure that an important change was about to occur.

He continued his walk north along Chapel Street, now in the fashion section dominated by clothing and shoe stores. There were lots of 'sale' signs, reductions of up to 70% and closing down sales. So, there was a retail recession in Melbourne. The people he passed were less diverse in their appearance and he noticed that many of the women were wearing black. Melbourne women still wore black as they had when he was young! On impulse, he decided to calculate the proportion of women wearing black. He reached Toorak Road, crossed to the other side and started his survey as he walked back towards Dandenong Road. He simultaneously counted the total number of women he passed and the number of women wearing predominately black. He had the sort of mind that could manage two separate counts at once and enjoyed the mental challenge of it. He passed a total of 375 women of whom 221 were wearing black, about 60%.

As he approached the Windsor Station, Justin saw in the distance a shape, a figure, a memory. There was a man standing with his back to Justin and it was his posture that triggered the memory. The shoulders were slightly hunched and the left leg tilted inwards. He turned his head, which was balding and grey, but Justin had recognised him before he saw the face, which was strange because he had no memory of ever noticing the posture before. It was Peter McBride, a friend from his school days. When Justin saw people from his past he usually went to great pains to avoid meeting them but on this day, he had no hesitation about walking up to greet him.

"Hello Peter."

Peter looked at Justin but didn't recognise him and the confusion that animated his face made Justin laugh,

"It's Justin, Justin Collins from St Crispins. How are you Peter?"

Peter only slowly emerged from his fog of confusion to say,

"So it is. The beard tricked me. You look like Sir Roger Casement."

"Other people have said that."

They both sized up the physical changes the other had gone through. For Peter, it was harder to match this bearded, short-haired, grey-haired man with the handsome school boy he remembered. For Justin, Peter was softer and rounder. They both had an overriding sense of good will, this was an important meeting, something to be nurtured. They would discount the physical changes and reach for connection. Their conversation was superficial but drew deeply on the memories and feelings of the bonding years of their adolescence; their struggles in the classrooms and on the sporting fields and their early forays into adulthood. Peter was a history lecturer at Melbourne University, living in Eaglemont. He was sorry to hear about Justin's post-traumatic stress problems, Justin's sister had told him. Justin was evasive about his life but agreed to visit Peter soon. Peter slumped and the tone changed.

"Did you hear about Kevin? He died four weeks ago, hanged himself. They tell me the Royal Commission stirred him up."

Justin knew what he was referring to but neither of them mentioned the black history they shared with Kevin and many other boys at St Crispins. They sorted out the difficulty of Justin not owning a phone and arranged their meeting.

Justin walked to his home but barely noticed the surroundings because he was so overwhelmed by that encounter, another message.

2

In the hours before Justin's visit, Peter cleaned and tidied his home. He rattled around in his kitchen thinking about what to offer Justin and which crockery to use. There was something defining about this behaviour, something tragic. His life had led up to this moment of unease; here he was, a divorced, childless, scruffy academic getting flustered about a visit from an old school friend.

Justin had been in his thoughts since the chance meeting on Chapel Street, he had even looked at photos in old school magazines. At school Justin had been likeable, lovable even but strangely remote in the hustle and bustle of schoolboy life, as if he was merely drifting down amongst them from a higher plane. He attracted people with his warmth and wit and was devoid of the status consciousness and bullying that was so common at the school that it was normal. His athleticism showed itself best on the football field where he was fast, graceful, brilliant at ducking and weaving but at the same time he was a team player to the point of self-effacement, hand-balling and short-passing so that others scored the goals. He captained the First XVIII and did so brilliantly and yet Peter remembered a despairing coach failing to instil in Justin the fierce sense of competition which everyone thought he should have. "He's more like a gentlemanly cricketer than a footballer," he overheard the coach saying.

Peter wondered if he himself had been influenced by the aura of significance that attached itself to Justin. Justin's grandfather was a cousin of Michael Collins, that charismatic Irish hero who had led the Irish in the war against the British and helped to win for Ireland her independence. Their school was infused with a romanticised and tribal sense of Irish history and Peter remembered the sense of awe with which the priests spoke of Michael Collins. It was said that Justin's grandfather had escaped to Australia to avoid being murdered by the British and had brought some of his cousin's glory with him. And now Peter was one of those historians who collected Michael Collins memorabilia and had made a pilgrimage to Beal na mBlath to pace out for himself the ambush site where Michael Collins was killed by the anti-Treaty forces during the Irish Civil War. Was it that indirect contact with Irish history at an impressionable age that sent him down the pathway to his professorship of Twentieth Century History?

Their relationship had always been a bit one-sided. At school he wanted to be close, everyone wanted to be close with Justin, but Justin didn't have best friends. Perhaps that was why he was now so excited about Justin coming to visit. Justin had spent several years overseas and their communication had gradually waned but he disappeared completely when he returned to Melbourne. Justin's twin sister Maureen's story of post-traumatic stress disorder from military service had surprised him because he couldn't see Justin joining the armed forces.

*****

During the three weeks since that chance meeting with Peter, Justin's sense of purpose had become focussed on one task, to arrange a meeting with his school mates, those who had been traumatised by the drama teacher Father Stephen O'Dwyer. He wasn't sure how to make this meeting happen but his mission became such an overwhelming preoccupation that he felt the need to use one of the mental containment techniques he had taught himself. It was the exercise of 'living with the opposite'. Instead of thinking about the meeting, he dwelt upon reasons for not arranging the meeting and came up with dozens of reasons to support that view. The technique worked to the extent that he was now prepared to let other forces do the work, he would go with the flow rather than push.

Justin's interest in visiting Peter was genuine. He enjoyed thinking about the meeting, he had not felt like that for a long time. They had been fairly close friends at school and Justin recalled Peter's eagerness and enthusiasm as a student. At sports he was very determined, good at football and tennis. In the classroom, a hard worker and keen to do well, always winning one of the form prizes that were awarded each year to the top three students. But there was also a vulnerability in Peter, damage that showed before they completed their schooling. Justin would raise the delicate topic with Peter but he would need to be very honest, and giving of himself. He wanted to make the visit important for Peter.

When Justin left the station, and stepped into the Eaglemont shopping centre, he had an image of arms opening out to greet him. He was at the junction of the two streets which made up the shopping centre and the panoramic view greeted him like a warm embrace. He could see all the shops at once, traditional ones such as the post office, butchers shop, fish and chip shop and a scatter of more discrete offices. It was very peaceful with no traffic and few people about. For Justin, it was an unexpected blast of nostalgia, like the shopping centre of his childhood, or the cosy film set of a black and white movie, or an imagined Enid Blyton landscape. He walked through the shopping centre amongst the solidity of two-storied chocolate brick buildings and time-softened Art Deco facades. On the grocer's walls were painted murals of the street in the days of horses and carts, a feature which expanded the ambience out into the surrounding streetscape. Justin realised that he had never been in Eaglemont before and he wanted to explore.

He walked past architecture which varied on the theme of genteel security; Spanish Mission, Californian Bungalow, Federation, mock Tudor. The gardens were well-tended but relaxed with many gently disciplined shrubs. Flashes of stained-glass, elaborate brick work and columned verandas underlining the wealth behind the initial building plans. Justin followed a curving road up a hill. The land blocks became bigger but the houses more discrete, set back behind trees or nesting above terraced gardens, houses which had no need to demand attention. There were lych gates and hedges with feminine contours. Along the nature strips were long-established plane trees shaped into cups around the telegraph wires. Having lost their leaves for winter they were statuesque. He was used to the shaping of branches around wires and had thought of it as normal, inevitable until he visited Japan and saw men clambering amongst the trees putting protective guards over the wires so that the trees could grow as they wished. Justin had grown up in a street with similar trees during an age when people burnt the autumn leaves in the gutters making the whole neighbourhood smell of the acrid smoke. Just thinking of it made him recall the smell.

"This suburb is beautiful," he thought. "Why haven't I been here before?"

He wandered further. There were a few people in the streets and front yards but they looked as understated and discrete as their houses. Highly polished European cars in driveways were more obvious indicators of wealth but, Justin thought, their purpose was to display their owners' wealth in other places.

He came to a house which jarred with its surroundings, it was newly built and enormous, filling the block so that there was no room for a front garden. The block had been dug out deep to allow underground parking for many cars and the house tapered to three stories, symmetrical with a balcony in front of the upper floor. He wondered why the local council had permitted the building of such a discordant house, it was like a pipe band amongst string quartets.

Justin found Peter's home in The Eyrie, a rendered brick duplex with a neat garden. It was like a smaller version of the rambling old house in Auburn where Peter grew up with his seven brothers and sisters, a house Justin used to love visiting because of the sense of happy chaos that the large family spawned. Their greeting was warm and Justin found himself enthusing about Eaglemont. Peter had an explanation for why Justin had never been there before.

"No main roads go through Eaglemont. Welcome to Sleepy Hollow."

They had coffee and easily mixed decades of catching up with school memories. The last time they had met had been at Justin's mother's funeral seven years earlier. Peter was too polite to ask but Justin felt the need to explain his failure to keep in contact. He said,

"I owe you an explanation and an apology actually. You know how my sister Maureen told you I had been in the SAS and had post-traumatic stress disorder? That's not true, that's the story we agreed upon to explain my disappearance from society. The truth is, I'm a sort of a hermit. I lead a monk-like existence and hardly communicate with anyone. At Maureen's insistence, we email each other every Sunday but I haven't seen her for years and I don't own a phone. But I'm glad I ran into you; it's been great to meet like this."

Peter felt deeply Justin's sincerity, then his usual discomfort when entering emotional territory. He laughed,

"You always were a bit remote."

He changed the topic to a more comfortable one.

"I've often wondered, did your grandfather ever tell you why he had to leave Ireland?"

Justin lit up.

"Yes. I challenged him about that not long before he died. The myth of his heroism during the Anglo-Irish war pervaded my childhood but I was always told that he didn't want to talk about it so I just exaggerated the whole business in my imagination. I think he was embarrassed when he told me what really happened. He lived in County Cork where there was plenty of conflict with the Black and Tans but he was never an active member of the IRA. He sheltered active service unit members on a few occasions but he had a sick wife and three small children and never got involved in the fighting. During the civil war he was Pro Treaty, as were most people, but kept out of the conflict. What happened was, he had an enemy, a character he had known all his life named Dinny O'Toole who was an Anti-Treaty gunman and he threatened to kill my grandfather. During that dreadful time a lot of personal settling of scores went on and he took the threat seriously. So he borrowed money and fled to Australia where he already had a brother living. I think he always felt ashamed and cowardly about what he did and that's why he didn't want to talk about it."

"Well, he made a good decision, coming to Australia. Did he have much to do with his famous cousin Michael Collins.?"

"No. Michael lived in another part of the county. He only saw him on a few occasions."

They paused. Peter felt the rising sense of excitement he experienced whenever he dwelt on a favourite aspect of history. He said,

"Civil wars are dreadful. Ireland's was particularly nasty with often brother fighting against brother. De Valera, who came to dominate Irish politics in the 1930s had a personal mission to restore Ireland's morality. As part of that he gave the Catholic Church unprecedented power. It dominated education, public morality and social services and that power has only really been challenged in the last ten years. That power of the Church is important to us in Australia because it's what we got, we got the Irish priests and the authoritarianism of the Irish Catholic Church which is quite different from the Italian Catholic Church. So our experience of our Catholic childhoods stems indirectly from Ireland's traumas in the 1920s."

Justin smiled, enjoying Peter's obvious enthusiasm for his historic interpretation. He said,

"It must be great teaching history. I used to love reading history books, I read a lot of history until I was about thirty. I used to get this great sense of connection from the knowledge it gave me, even a sense of power. Irish Catholicism really dominated our childhoods didn't it. I remember the reverence my mother used to show whenever a priest visited our house."

The time was right to introduce what he wanted to talk about with Peter.

"And that's why Father Stephen O'Dwyer got away with it for so long. I was upset to hear that Kevin died and I'm feeling guilty that I had cut myself off so effectively that I didn't hear about it. Can you tell me about him?"

Peter too wanted to talk about Kevin. It was a challenge he was ready to face and one of the reasons he was so glad he had bumped into Justin.

"I ran into Kevin about twenty years ago. You know that after he left school he got into drugs and was in and out of jail. I met him by chance and he opened up over a cup of coffee. He was off drugs and on the methadone program, on a disability pension and living in one of the high-rise flats in Prahran. He had a son who he never saw. He was doing casual work with a builder and I paid him to come and do some work at my place, he did a good job. He wanted to do some Uni subjects and I helped him get into Arts at Melbourne Uni. With several breaks, he eventually got his BA and I went to his graduation. He was very damaged by Father Stephen; he had a phobia about the names Stephen and O'Dwyer and would have palpitations and start sweating whenever he heard them. If there was a football player with either of those names, he had to watch football on TV with the volume turned down. As the years passed, he seemed to be improving. He had caught hepatitis C when he was injecting drugs and a few years ago he had this special treatment to clear himself of the virus. The treatment made him sick but he went through with it. The last time I saw him, he told me he had got worse since the Royal Commission came to Melbourne. The police visited him and asked him if he wanted to talk to one of the investigators and that caused him to have a break down. He couldn't listen to the news or read newspapers in case the Royal Commission was mentioned."

"So that's four of us now," said Justin. "Four out of twelve from Father Stephen's drama class who have killed themselves."

In the silence that followed both Peter and Justin bowed their heads, a mourning reflex and a desire to avoid eye contact. They became aware of background sounds, the clock ticking in the next room, the neighbour mowing the lawn. Peter broke the silence,

"I've been thinking a lot lately about how it affected me. I'm not good at relationships, I neglected my wife. I used to think that it was just me and that I deserved to be alone but I think it goes back to the terrible sense of shame that I had. I couldn't talk with my parents about it, I felt so dirty."

He grimaced and Justin experienced with him the sense of shame. Peter continued,

"I think I lost something, the ability to be open and honest with women, the ability to be intimate. My parents couldn't cope and wanted to blame me. They were limited emotionally and I saw them as sucking up to the priests, but ..."

He couldn't continue, his hands were shaking and he looked away. Justin suspected that this was to hide tears. It was Justin's turn.

"That was a dreadful time, and we were all about 13 years old, an age when we were all so vulnerable. Then there was the horror of Danny hanging himself and the trauma with our parents when it all came out. I was so ashamed when my mother found out about the pornographic films he'd been showing us. It took me a long time to understand how Father Stephen had been abusing us so that I could get angry with him. I can't remember much about what he did so I think I suffered less than others, but he made me feel isolated and "not a good team member" for resisting him. Remember how he wheedled and tried to coerce me and Frank in front of the drama group?"

Peter managed to gasp a weak, "Yes."

As Justin spoke, Peter had the sensation of being choked. His heart was racing and he felt hot and clammy. He couldn't look at Justin, he wanted him to continue but was fearful of him continuing at the same time. Justin said,

"I think my parents handled it as well as they could. I didn't want to talk about it with them but they kept telling me that Father Stephen was a monster and they spent a lot of time with me, taking me to films and on great holidays. They left the church which must have been devastating for them. Their old friends stopped visiting. Later they told me they went to the police but the local sergeant, who was a Catholic and a member of their congregation, convinced my parents that it would be too traumatic for us to appear in court and that the bishop had made sure that Father Stephen would never offend again. They were so angry when he went to trial and they read how he had continued to offend at two more schools

My sister Maureen thinks I was damaged, and I can't blame her because I live like a hermit. I'm not convinced; I think I was destined to end up living the way that I do now and I'm quite content. I had a healthy heterosexual life when I was younger and some good long-term relationships."

Justin lapsed into silence. Peter had passed his low point and wanted to change the topic.

"Would you like to go for a tour of Sleepy Hollow?"

Justin recognised Peter's need for a change and was enthusiastic about a walk. He mentioned the new house further up the Eyrie which had bothered him. Peter flared,

"I hate that monstrosity, the whole neighbourhood hates it. It's got ten toilets, six bathrooms, two kitchens and near the pool there's a barbecue section which is like another kitchen. It was built by a Russian who made his fortune as an importer/exporter and he lives in that enormous house with his wife and one grown up daughter. I know Wayne who lives in the house on this side of that phallic symbol. He took the Russian to VCAT to try to prevent him building the third story. He had sound evidence about the way it would block the sunlight from most of his property but the Russian's lawyer convinced the magistrate that the tapering would allow plenty of sun in. That third story consists of an enormous master bedroom, a living room and a home theatre. And now the bastard has abandoned the whole floor because he got sick of walking up the stairs!"

They walked up The Eyrie, a transition from an affluent but fairly typical streetscape to a different zone at the top of the hill.

Here, Peter explained, the architect Walter Burley Griffin had designed a housing estate which was revolutionary at the time. Instead of the usual square grid of streets with houses backing onto each other, the streets were curved with communal parks tucked away behind the houses. Here the houses had a greater presence than the roads. Justin and Peter glimpsed grand houses squatting snugly at the ends of curved drives. There were bluestone embankments and terraces dividing roads. Decades of loving attention had draped foliage over walls and thrown up enormous hedges. Some homes were cocooned by dense canopies of mature, exotic trees.

Peter's excitement grew with the ascent and he bubbled with snatches of local history and architecture; the Hollywood house, the Walter Burley Griffin designed house with its fat chimneys. His joy peaked as he walked Justin past three Arts and Crafts buildings designed by Harold Desbrowe-Annear.

They visited three of the secret parks, public spaces which felt like extensions of backyards, a possessiveness expressed by gates which announced 'Private. No through road'. An aboriginal canoe tree, long since fallen but respected with a plaque and a support summoned up an alternative ambience, a sense of history and loss.

As they walked back down The Eyrie to Peter's home he said,

"Now back down the hill to where the poor relations live near the station."

The mood changed and Peter felt the need to fill in his tour with another layer, a dark side of this urban magnificence. He said,

"People love their houses and their gardens here. Once here, no one wants to leave and the houses rarely go on the market, but when they do, they are usually bulldozed and monstrosities like the Russian's house go up. It's as if the people who can afford to buy here are out to demonstrate their wealth but have no feeling for the neighbourhood. But this appalling damage to the neighbourhood really comes back to the vendors. They go for maximum sale price, which means selling by auction. They don't have to, they could sell privately and carefully weed out the grandiose thugs but they never do. It's as if they are declaring to their neighbours, 'I've loved living here but now I'm leaving and I don't give a stuff about what happens to the neighbourhood'. I've spoken about this with some of my neighbours, people who hate the phallic symbols as much as I do but they look at me as if I'm mad and you can see them thinking, 'When I sell, the money will be all that matters.'"

When Justin left, they both felt the pull. Their conversation had subsided to a level of irrelevance as they waded together in a pool of easy compatibility, something that amongst men usually requires the deep roots of shared childhoods. Peter spontaneously walked with Justin to the station. It was during this short walk that Justin introduced his idea.

"I've got this idea of getting the drama group back together again, the eight of us surviving, to talk about how Father Stephen affected us. What do you think Peter?"

Peter felt the choking return but it was if the idea was his own. Beneath layer upon layer of defences there was a part of him that wanted this challenge. The answer spilled out of him before he was even aware of forming the sentence,

"That's a good idea Justin. We could meet at my place if you like."

Then he did something uncharacteristic because he didn't like touching people. He shook Justin's hand.

3

Every Tuesday morning, Justin walked to the Dandenong Market to buy food for the week. The journey of thirty kilometres took him six to seven hours depending on the route he walked because he varied it each time, wandering along suburban streets north and south of Dandenong Road. He always enjoyed the feeling that he was witnessing the history of Melbourne through its architecture. At the start of the journey he would pass Victorian buildings, grand mansions and crowded terrace houses, next he would be among Federation houses followed by Art Deco flourishes and frugal post war homes. By Huntingdale he would be in the vast expanses of double and triple fronted cream brick veneers then the more environmentally suited seventies houses of Mulgrave among established native gardens. There were architectural blips in the former country towns of Oakleigh and Dandenong where the wave of suburban spread had left older buildings isolated and now looking sadly out of place. Justin pictured the wave going even further beyond Dandenong in concentric growth rings moving ever outwards at a rate of about five kilometres per decade to Pakenham and beyond.

However, during the previous few years Melbourne had been changing. Instead of the relentless outward growth it was restlessly bursting upwards with multi-storied buildings appearing along the main roads, noisy with cranes and tradies who were always on the job at the noise-permitted time of seven o'clock in the morning. Justin had noticed the increase in traffic and with that the increased number of traffic lights. He had the vague idea that Melbourne's population was about three and a half million and was shocked to read a newspaper headline that it was in fact four and a half million.

Justin always started his walk at four o'clock which meant that in winter half of the journey was in darkness. He enjoyed the walks most at this time of year, dressing in warm clothes with coat and scarf, smelling pockets of wood smoke, feeling enclosed in his own little capsule when walking through fog or under an umbrella.

His shopping done at the market, he would indulge himself by watching the cosmopolitan crowd, the Central Europeans buying small goods, the Vietnamese carefully selecting whole fish, the banter between the stall holders. Then he would walk to the Dandenong Station and catch the train back to Toorak.

He always enjoyed the short walk back to his home in a court off Lansell Road. It was a street filled with mature trees, high fences and views of opulence down long driveways through arched wrought iron gates. It still amused him that it was here, in

Melbourne's most affluent suburb, that he finally found the place where he could live the way he wanted to live. His first attempt, on an island in the Outer Hebrides, had quickly failed when he became entangled with a local woman. His second attempt was in the Melbourne suburb of Broadmeadows, a poor outer suburb which he chose as a place where he would never encounter anyone who knew him. There, however, he was welcomed into the lives of his neighbours who were mostly Iraqi immigrants. They shared with him their food and company and he had the most social time he had ever had.

It was in Toorak that he could disappear. Here people lived their lives privately behind high walls with security gates and CCTV cameras. There were no parks and no one walked to the shops. The only people you ever saw on the streets were the employed gardeners who over-mowed the nature strips and pushed the odd leaf off the footpaths with noisy leaf blowers.

Justin lived in a single storied, two-bedroom, rear flat. It was an aberration for Toorak, an ugly nineteen sixties development that had snuck through the planning process when an older house was demolished. There had originally been four flats, two on either side of a central driveway but the two flats on the left side had been bought for five million dollars and then demolished by the neighbour on that side. In their place, he built a tennis court and a swimming pool. Justin could just see the top of the fence around the tennis court beyond the high boundary fence but would occasionally hear the pock and tinkle of tennis beside a fountain. On the other side of the remaining two flats was another high wall. There, it was rumoured that an organised crime figure lived and large vehicles with tinted glass windows would slink through the security gates at odd times.

In this rear flat, Justin had found the peace he wanted but there was one problem; Mrs Weissman who lived in the front flat.

When he first moved in, Mrs Weissman distressed him so much that he considered moving out. She would look out for him and pounce like a spider, coercing him to do chores for her. She had the waddling gait of a woman who has engulfed her body with fat and wore large rings on all eight fingers. She wore heavy, cloying perfume which inadequately covered some underlying unpleasant odour. She pleaded and whined, often referring to her dead husband "my poor Herman" and manipulated Justin into doing gardening and maintenance jobs for her, jobs which he was sure she could afford to employ someone to do. In time, Justin came to recognise that she was displaying the neediness of someone who felt unloved and accepted her role as a sort of gatekeeper, a gauntlet that he had to run as compensation for leaving the real world. He was always courteous and addressed her with the German pronunciation of her name. On this occasion, he saw her peeping out between her curtains because she knew the time he usually returned from his shopping. He gallantly refitted a loose fly screen for her.

*****

Justin had made an agreement with his sister Maureen that he would send her an email message once per week. 'I just want to know that you're alive,' she said. He kept this agreement, writing to her every Sunday night. He usually had very little to say, he might report what was happening in his vegetable garden or discuss some philosophical concept he had been reading or thinking about. Maureen would reply with longer messages about her daughter and grandchildren and of life at Barwon Downs with her partner Jacques; walks in the forest and activities at the cafe they had established in the village. On this occasion, Justin felt like writing at length about his experience of re-meeting Peter and his plans for getting his former school friends together. It became an exercise in trying to express for himself the strange but exciting currents which churned within.

Maureen was ecstatic to receive Justin's email. She read it three times, looking far beyond the words into the consciousness of the brother who wrote them. She found and felt his gentleness, his enthusiasm for life and his curiosity. With the joy came an ache, a realisation of how much she missed him, that her life was incomplete as long as it wasn't shared with him. She was surprised when Justin accepted her invitation to stay at Barwon Downs for the winter solstice. She was so distracted that she couldn't settle to do anything and put her energy into preparing the spare bedroom for him. Jacques was delighted, having never met Justin before and teased Maureen about "St Justin emerging from his hermitage". Her thoughts filled with conversations they might have and things they might do around Barwon Downs. She asked him to bring his viola and practised on her harp the tunes they used to play together.

Justin caught the train to Birregurra, the station closest to Barwon Downs. After Geelong, the train passed into the Western District. Justin looked through the window at green plains with reflected sunlight glistening on dams and patches of water lying on paddocks from the recent heavy rains. Rows of sugar gums beside roads made this a civilised landscape but more defining were the occasional edifices of bluestone; stations, houses and ruins. If he had travelled east from Melbourne it would have been different, the hills and forests of Gippsland were devoid of bluestone. He couldn't help but feel excited by the stimulus of revisiting a landscape. Now that he had re-entered the 'real world' he kept experiencing these surges of delight that accompanied his new visual experiences.

For most of the journey, Justin had been dreamily reflecting on his relationship with his twin sister Maureen whom he hadn't seen since his mother's funeral. She had always been the dominant one and he expected that characteristic would re-assert itself within minutes of him entering her company. Would that be irritating? Perhaps her years of trauma had changed her. The tone of her emails now was always one of contentment.

In their early childhood, they played together all the time, resisting the attempts of their parents to get them to play with other children of the same gender. In their play, Maureen would make the plans and the rules and Justin would comply, often getting into trouble while Maureen managed to wriggle out of responsibility. Justin had been very underweight as a newborn and Maureen was bigger than average for a newborn twin. As a child Justin learned from his mother that "Maureen had taken most of the food in my womb" and he accepted and was fascinated by this concept. In his teens, he read about placentas and twin-to-twin transfusions which gave him a physiological explanation for their different sizes at birth but that knowledge did not alter his deeper psychological understanding of himself. They had twin telepathy but Justin's was stronger than Maureen's; he would experience abdominal pain and anxiety when she was distressed. At its most extreme Justin started vomiting with abdominal pain when Maureen was suicidal and his abrupt appearance at her home at that time probably saved her life. Their childhood closeness started to change as they approached their twelfth birthday. This was led by Maureen with her intimations of bodily and mood changes and reinforced when they went to single sex schools for their secondary education, Justin to St Crispins and Maureen to Genazzano. Much to everyone's surprise, this transition went smoothly.

Maureen asked Jacques to stay at home because she wanted to meet Justin on her own at the Birregurra Station. She was on the platform for ten minutes before the train arrived and saw him first when he emerged from the carriage. At first, he looked vague and lost and Maureen had a gush of maternal feelings for him but then he saw her and beamed, seeming to grow in stature. He walked up to her boldly and hugged her, holding on for a long time. Maureen melted then found herself saying,

"You're thinner, and greyer," he replied.

"You're greyer and ... cuddlier."

"Fatter you mean."

Maureen did most of the talking as she drove them the short distance to Barwon Downs, calm now with a feeling that she would later identify as a sense of being complete; a part of her had been missing but now it was back in place. Justin was excited when they startled a hare, it ran along the road in front of them for a short distance, not with the erratic weaving and dodging of a rabbit but the majestic lope of a deer. Maureen had once given him a stuffed hare as a present because he often had dreams about hares. Through misty rain he noticed the dark hills beyond Barwon Downs marching up towards the Otways proper in the background. Here paddocks extended up to the forest like irregular bite marks where the land-hungry pioneers had finally run out of steam.

As they drove through Barwon Downs, Maureen pointed out to Justin the building that she and Jacques had purchased to run as a bar on the weekends, a weatherboard building with a veranda extending over the street which had once been a butcher's shop. It was painted a rich burgundy which matched the velvet drapes hanging inside the large front window. The curtains framed Maureen's Celtic harp which was on a raised platform in the front of the bar, a surprising sight for the drivers passing through Barwon Downs on their way to Apollo Bay. Painted in a flowing script high on the window was 'Clarice's.'

"What an appealing sight," said Justin. "No wonder you are so popular."

"Yes. We expanded six months ago and we still fill the room every Friday and Saturday night. We get locals, passers-by and now it's routine for the diners from Birregurra's flash restaurant to come to us after their all-afternoon degustations."

Near Maureen's home, Justin noticed a wooden church painted an irreligious bright scarlet set back from the road. There was a 'For Sale' sign in front. Maureen noticed Justin's inquiring look and said,

"That's the old Catholic church. It was closed for years before a couple from Melbourne bought it and started doing it up intending to live there. Then they got divorced and it's been for sale ever since. The colour doesn't help its sale prospects."

Justin warmed to Jacques immediately and found him to be almost a caricature of the jolly Continental. Jacques was from Belgium, he had a mane of silvery, grey hair and a moustache which he shaped to curls at the ends. He was effusively friendly and Justin could picture him wearing the red suit and white beard of the perfect Santa Claus. Jacques had been a chef in France and now, instead of raving about the qualities of French produce and cuisine, was passionate about Australian food. He served Australian wines and tasting plates of Australian cheeses and charcuterie at Clarice's. When he served people, he wanted to educate them and encouraged them to taste samples before purchasing. He knew the local produce and loved his weekly trips to the Melbourne markets.

Justin had been anxious about meeting Jacques, but having met him, felt able to relax and enjoy the ambience of Maureen's home on the edge of the forest, 'there's nothing but forest between us and Lorne' she said. He had disliked Maureen's husband Fraser from when first they met. On family occasions, they had evolved patterns of behaviour which allowed them to ignore each other as much as possible without any conflict or discourtesy and he was glad when they divorced.

That evening, Justin joined Maureen and Jacques at Clarice's. Jacques persuaded him to try a pinot grigio and he enjoyed a platter of cheeses consisting of a cheddar from Tasmania, a blue from South Gippsland and a washed rind cheese from nearby Timboon. The atmosphere of the bar was somehow jittery and Justin felt uncomfortable, a feeling he attributed to his habits of isolation because he could see that everyone else seemed to be enjoying themselves. At about nine o'clock Maureen started playing her harp and the ambience changed as the patrons listened to the delicacy of her playing and the haunting breathiness of her singing voice. Justin had brought his viola but, as he had explained to Maureen, it was so long since he had played in front of an audience that he might not be able to. As she sang and played her harp Justin remembered the times they had performed together. For him it was never about the audience, it was the way they connected with the music. He couldn't sing and he always thought of himself as 'second fiddle' to Maureen's harp playing but when they played together, they were expressing things they couldn't put into words, wonderful things to do with their family values, their cultural history and their twin-ship. He could feel the urge to join her building and when she played *Mna na h'eireann* and sang it in Gaelic, he reached for his viola and pulled his chair over towards her.

Maureen flashed him a smile, inviting him to join her with the second verse, Justin focussed on Maureen, playing as gently as possible while he gauged the correct complementary volume. He felt comfortably enfolded where he sat in a corner of the long room and the acoustics were good. He didn't notice that the background hum of the audience was diminishing because he was so intent on blending with Maureen's playing. Halfway through Maureen's second verse he began to feel in the body of his viola those magical secondary resonances which happened when he was playing near another stringed instrument, especially Maureen's harp; years fell away and he realised how much he had missed that feeling.

Maureen started the third verse with a slight increase in tempo and sense of approaching climax in her voice. Justin felt his body responding with a slight tightening of his grip on the finger board and exaggeration of his shoulder movements. As Maureen's voice dropped in the last bar he too faded as he withdrew the energy. Maureen nodded to him, he knew what she meant, he was to finish by playing a verse solo, something that they had determined long ago worked well for the slow Irish tunes. He didn't feel self-conscious because it was so natural, he turned towards the audience and cast his eyes just above their heads. He concentrated on the critical variations of timing which brought the tune to life holding on longer in parts than he could when accompanying. As he dropped to the final bar he felt tingles in his spine and relished the growly lower notes, not wanting to let them go.

There were a few seconds of absolute silence then a torrent of applause. Maureen, radiant but in command, thanked the appreciative audience and said,

"I'd like to introduce you to my brother, my twin brother, Justin. I haven't seen him for years and I'm so glad he's back."

Cheers as Justin looked over the crowd. He felt their enthusiasm and for the first time noticed what a mixed bag they were, with many manifestations of the rural and the urban expressed in clothing, hairstyles and facial hair. It was a warm and reassuring experience to be amongst them.

Maureen and Justin performed for about an hour; songs and tunes they had played together in their teens and early twenties. Maureen performed a few tunes and songs alone and Justin did jigs and reels which had some members of the audience stomping out primitive dance steps. Justin practised his viola every day and was constantly teaching himself new pieces but he always maintained his familiarity with these earlier tunes. He wondered if he had been doing that because he knew deep down that one day he would again perform with Maureen.

4

The next day was the winter solstice. Justin woke early to the sounds of gentle rain falling and currawongs crying out their domination of the wet forest. It was a pleasure to break his usual discipline of early rising and just lie in bed. He eventually rose when the house changed with the domestic bathroom and kitchen sounds of Maureen and Jacques starting their activities for the day. Jacques celebrated the winter solstice and there would be more guests arriving that morning. Justin joined the breakfast conversations; lingering excitement over the performance of the night before and concern that the rain might spoil the planned bonfire. Justin was drawn to the cosiness of the slow combustion heater in the large kitchen but even more so to the open fire in the small living room filled with books which they called the library.

The guests arrived, a couple from Melbourne, Steve and Mandy with their dog and soon after came Rob. They were all old friends of Maureen's but the arrival of Steve and Mandy made

Justin feel very uncomfortable. They were both strong characters and brought with them a need to impose their personalities on the domestic calm of the household. Maureen's behaviour in greeting them felt to Justin like the response to an assault. He couldn't take part in their greeting behaviour and resorted to playing with their little dog who was named Faecal, a surprising name that they explained they had given him because he was a 'Shit-Poo', a Shih Tzu-Poodle cross. Rob was a much quieter character whom Justin had met in the past but even with him he felt inadequate in his greeting behaviour and realised just how out of touch he was with normal human interactions. Since seeing him last, Rob had gone through a divorce and treatment for lymphoma. Justin was so overwhelmed by the collective excitement of this gathering that he felt like retreating to his bedroom for a while. Maureen sensed his discomfort and asked him to go for a walk with her. The rain was easing and it felt good to rug up and enter the forest.

Maureen chatted lightly about the visitors but they soon lapsed into silence as the hushed quiet and smells of the forest seeped into their consciousness. Justin felt the unease of city-dwellers, of getting lost in a forest when they can no longer see habitations or hear traffic sounds, but he knew that he was safe with Maureen. She commented on the fungi they saw, naming them and squatting down to take closer looks.

"I didn't know you were interested in toadstools," said Justin.

"I've come to love them and all the seasonal changes that happen in my forest. I call it that now, 'my forest'. Jacques and

I walk in the forest every day. Have a look at this, one of my favourites, a Slimy Yellow Cortinar."

They bent down to a cluster of bright yellow toadstools flecked with spots of soil, as if they had just burst out of the earth. Following her lead, Justin put a finger to the top of one of the slimy toadstools and stretched a strand of mucus from it until it broke. Maureen was delighted.

"Lots of the Cortinars are slimy like that. I think it is to stop insects and slugs from eating them."

As they walked deeper into the forest Maureen pointed out more fungi; some surprisingly purple Emperor toadstools, lime green Dermatocybes and rosy coral fungi. She picked a white-capped fungus and asked Justin to smell it.

"What can you smell?" she asked.

"Curry powder!" Justin answered, surprised.

"That's right. That's how I first identified that one. My fungus book says you can distinguish it from other white fungi by its smell."

They found some enormous fleshy fungi at the base of a large eucalypt.

"Notice where they are growing?" said Maureen. "They only grow at the bases of mature eucalypts. Their spores will only sprout on a thick layer of shed bark."

She became excited when she found some tiny blue fungi sprouting from the side of a log.

"Blue Pixies," she shouted. "I love them. They are incredibly old as a species. They are found in New Zealand and Chile as well, not because they were introduced but because they have always been there. They are Gondwanaland fungi and haven't changed in the hundred million years since the continents moved apart. How old are we as a species? A mere hundred thousand years or so. I feel humbled beside those little pixies."

In a wet gully, Maureen led Justin off the track to an area covered with damp moss. In the moss were several irregular white fungi which were growing in stacked layers.

"Pagoda fungi, like the Chinese pagodas. I like them because they seem to have an inner glow about them."

Justin squatted down and also noticed the intensity of their whiteness against the green of the moss. He looked up at Maureen, with her woollen cap and gloves and her puffy jacket and thought that she too was glowing.

They returned to the house along an unsealed road, a place and time that lent itself to the conversation that Maureen had been wanting to have with Justin. She started,

"I'm very happy now Justin."

Justin turned towards her and leant weight to her statement by pausing before replying.

"I thought so; your emails are so positive now. I enjoy reading about your life here with Jacques, he's a lovely man."

"You know you saved my life six years ago. I find it hard to believe now what a hole I was in."

They were both silent as they remembered that time. Maureen had been a middle level public servant in the health department. She was bullied by an administrator when she rejected his sexual advances. What followed was a drawn-out period of false accusations, demotion, stress leave, treatment for depression and treatment for chronic fatigue syndrome. Then her husband, Fraser, who was also a public servant, left her for another woman and there was a bitter divorce and the selling of their grand home at Gisborne. Their daughter Siobhan went through a rebellious phase causing more trauma for Maureen. She continued,

"I'm distant enough from that terrible time to have some perspective now. Wasn't I stupid to get caught up in that materialistic lifestyle?"

"Yes," Justin said bluntly remembering how he had teased her about her materialism since their teens.

"I put so much energy into having the big house and the expensive car and I mixed with people who wanted the same things. It was so competitive and empty. The friends I had in those days don't want to know me now. Fraser has continued down the same pathway, Siobhan tells me he drives an Audi TT now. I don't miss it in the slightest and I'm glad I'm out of it. Siobhan's like me when I was in my twenties. I cringe when I visit her McMansion at Point Cook.

The job was part of it, we had to have a certain look. I've come to hate hierarchies because of what they do to people. We spent so much time at meetings, committed to an ideology of good public service and thinking that we were doing good things but really, we were nurturing ourselves and our careers. We treated people badly and we wasted money. Then I found out how a hierarchy behaves when it is threatened and all these forces emerge to protect the slimy ladder that all the people in the hierarchy, myself included, have been aspiring to climb."

At that moment, Justin felt a familiar visceral discomfort as he slipped into a nearly forgotten role. People had always told him that he was a good listener. It was because when people told him their troubles, he would go quiet and his silence was perceived as sympathetic, so they felt free to ventilate their feelings. In fact, Justin was usually battling with feelings of despair at these recurring stories of frustrated egos. Maureen had done this from an early age, perhaps his adaptation to her was why he earned his reputation as a good listener. He was now able to define why he disliked these stories; they always boiled down to 'I was bad but now I'm good' without any sense of responsibility for the past behaviour. He didn't want to hear these stories, to be the good listener. It was one of the reasons that he chose to live apart from people.

About an hour before dusk, Jacques produced with a dramatic flourish, an effigy which he had constructed to burn on the bonfire. The others had past experience of Jacques' bonfires but Justin was amazed by the quality of the effigy. It was no mere scarecrow, not a quick construction of sticks and rags, Jacques had spent months making it; a solid wooden mannequin with articulated shoulders, elbows hips and knees. Its face was a carved wooden mask with a Pinocchio nose and it was dressed in a shirt, trousers gloves and shoes. It had been assembled and firmly attached to a long, solid pole. The men all wanted to admire it and explore its construction with their fingers, he was definitely male and

Jacques pulled down his trousers to show a wooden penis with fireworks attached. The women wanted to name him and giggled over politicians they identified him with. Jacques tolerated their game but closed with,

"He is just 'the bad goblin.'"

With a manual post hole auger, the four men dug a deep hole at the site of the planned bonfire and placed the effigy in it on his supporting pole, carefully packing the earth around it and making it perfectly vertical. Jacques had firewood which had been kept dry under tarpaulins and they stacked it around the base of the pole. The bad goblin rested high on his pole with his feet more than a metre above the ground. When they had used up all the dry firewood, Jacques instructed the others to get more firewood from the forest, which he assured them would burn well despite being damp and they soon had a wood pile to be proud of. Justin loved the camaraderie of this shared experience. It was as if he was re-living a childhood activity with old friends.

Jacques explained to Justin his family tradition of the bonfire,

"All through my childhood we had a bonfire on the winter solstice. It was always bitterly cold and there was often snow on the ground. My brothers and sisters and I would build up a pile of sticks and rubbish for weeks beforehand and my father would construct an effigy which had to look scary, it really was a bad goblin. Before the bonfire was lit, we all had to write on pieces of paper our sad thoughts and put the messages inside the bad goblin, then they would be consumed in the flames along with him."

"That's very pagan Jacques. Was that a local tradition?"

"No, no, no Justin. We were part of a devoutly religious rural Catholic community and my father was criticised for his bonfires. He was a very eccentric man. We couldn't invite other children to join us for the bonfire and we were meant to keep it secret, but we didn't and we were envied.

But the tradition pre-dates my father, it was my grandfather who started the winter solstice bonfires. We lived in an area where there had been many battles during the First World War and farmers would often find the remains of soldiers when working in their fields. There was an official process for dealing with recognisable skeletons but most farmers would ignore the small pieces of bone and military uniforms which they found. My grandfather was a very pious man and he would carefully store the material he found, the bone fragments, bullets, pieces of shrapnel and bits of rifles and then burn them as a ritual of respect. It was my father who made it a happier ritual, but that was after my grandfather died.

As children, we searched for and stored relics of the First World War to put on the fire. We were always excited if we found bone fragments imagining that they were parts of soldiers although most of these were probably animal bones. Many Australian soldiers died in the fighting where I lived and if we found a bone fragment we would say 'this is a piece of a brave Australian soldier'. I grew up with a wonderful impression of Australians, perhaps that is why I always wanted to live in Australia."

Justin loved Jacques' story and its tidal pull of family history. Like the others who had attended previous bonfires he now felt part of the ritual.

Soon after five o'clock it began to get dark and the group gathered by the bonfire. They set up a trestle table and put on it bottles of wine, glasses and nibbles. Jacques called for any last messages to go into the bad goblin and Maureen and Steve put envelopes up the bad goblin's trouser legs. Then Rob brought forward a cardboard box filled with files of paper and X-rays in brown paper envelopes. He emptied the box pushing the papers and X-rays through gaps between sticks deep into the base of the pile.

"The doctors can't give me a guarantee but I think I'm finally cured of my lymphoma and I want to get rid of all this stuff ..."

At that point, his voice faltered and tears came to his eyes. Maureen moved towards him and hugged him. He was making awkward gasps as he tried to suppress pent up emotions. Then Jacques too hugged him followed by Mandy and Steve and finally Justin and by the end of all this he was laughing.

With the light fading and the forest birds making their settling sounds, Jacques announced that it was time to light the bonfire. He pushed screwed up pieces of newspaper deep into the pile and reached in with a lighted match. A wisp of smoke struggled up through the branches sharp with the smell of newsprint. Jacques stepped back, watching, serious. Justin wanted to poke the newspaper, light other pieces, fan the fledgling flames but there was an unspoken etiquette that this was Jacques' fire, he had to be patient.

Slowly, tiny soldiers of flame colonised adjacent pieces of newspaper, then with much crackling and fizzing the dry tinder wood passed on the batons of flame. Rob's bundles of medical records fanned out of their clusters like black flowers bursting into bloom. The brown paper bags peeled away exposing X-rays which buckled and blistered sending out stinking black smoke. In clear view, the X-ray of a chest filled with bubbling metastases then melted with one last dying breath. Rob cheered.

Flames licked at the bad goblin's feet then ran up his trousers with surprising speed jiggling one foot in an unbearably realistic way at which the viewers made primitive sounds of awe and delight. The men stood close to the fire, less concerned than the woman about the smoke taint to their clothes and wanting to feel the heat. The flames opened the bad goblin's shirt exposing a rag-stuffed chest and evoking images of blood lust and mob violence. A bang as the cracker on the penis exploded and cheers as the wooden phallus partly erected, an accident of the contortions of the burning pelvis. More cheers as the left arm fell off then a spectacular flare as the bad goblin's heart, a plastic container filled with Little Lucifer Fire Lighters, ignited.

They watched while the bad goblin shed pieces of his skeleton from the supporting pole into the fire. The eye holes enlarged with horns of flame above the burning nose until the mask too dropped off. The men couldn't resist supporting the fire by kicking in logs and throwing new branches on the base while the central pole, staunchly vertical, flamed like an antenna to the stars amidst floating embers.

They eventually drifted inside for a dinner which Jacques called 'The Winter Solstice Feast' a comforting winter spread of pea and ham soup, roast lamb and apple crumble. They were all in good spirits from the bonfire and the alcohol and Justin, not used to alcohol, was amused to note how talkative he had become. It started to rain but the fire continued to burn on its bed of hot embers and the men would occasionally go outside to stir it up again and throw more wood on it, a pointless activity but a way of holding onto the communal spirit of the fire. It was just so good to stand around together staring into the flames and embers. The meal passed easily and when Maureen started to yawn suddenly everyone became involved in clearing the table and washing dishes in a distracted sort of way. By 11pm, smoky, mellow and tired they were all in their beds.

The next morning some early risers walked in the forest then the six met for a brunch of bacon and eggs, croissants and coffee. Maureen drove Justin to the Birregurra Station for his return to Melbourne, a gentle transition to the reality of his solitude. Both Justin and Maureen thought of things to say but opted for silence during the short car journey. It was only when they saw the train approaching the platform from Colac that Maureen raised one of the big issues which they hadn't spoken about,

"Do you still have the dream about the burning church Justin?"

"Yes. Perhaps meeting the men from school will put to rest that troubled part of my subconscious."

He said this with humour but also with a sense of resignation. Maureen hugged him and saw him onto the train then watched the train passing to the east until it was out of view.

Justin settled into his seat in a carriage which was filled with mostly young people engaged with their mobile phones. It would take him weeks to absorb the experience of that weekend at Barwon Downs. Spending time with Maureen had been delightful but the pagan bonfire had been a wonderful surprise. He thought about Maureen's description of hierarchies. There was probably some truth in it but he could not separate her story from his knowledge of the way Maureen thought. Maureen had been a conformist and loved working her way up a hierarchy. Because of her bad experience, she now condemned all hierarchies. The fact that her hated ex-husband was doing well in a hierarchy compounded her view. When he was young and working in the money market Justin had been part of a hierarchy but his experience had been different; he had been one of the young Turks, the clever young men who were using their imagination, taking risks and were respected for the way they earned money for the company. And Maureen had a capacity for self-deception; perhaps one day she would be living a more mainstream lifestyle and would speak dismissively of this phase in her life as, 'my hippy phase'.

Thinking of Maureen made Justin think about what would happen when he got his old school friends together. What did he expect? Would he dislike hearing the stories of their lives and find them egotistical and self-deceptive like Maureen? He was responsible for starting a process which might bring about a sort of comfort for the men, that was what he hoped, or it might have unexpected consequences. For the first time, Justin felt a terrible weariness and heaviness at the prospects of his unusual mission but he still had no doubts that it must go ahead.

5

Justin thought a lot about the men he wanted to re-meet and tried to remember what they had been like at school. Even though they had been together for six years, his memories were patchy. Forty years had passed but also, he realised that he had a different way of thinking about people during his adolescence. He had a few memories of what they were like in the classroom, such as Michael and Peter always sitting eagerly near the front of the class. Pat had the best acting skills. In his early years at St Crispins he was often bullied and sometimes called a poofter but by the later years he had the social and verbal skills to look after himself and command respect. Glen was very good-looking and would shock them with stories about what he did with girls, stories they didn't know whether to believe or not. Finn was always telling jokes and was fun to be with. His memoires of playing football with Frank and Gerard were clearer and he had been in teams with them right through his school years. Gerard was short but fearless, a great rover. Frank was solidly built and played rough.

He would target opposition players who were performing well and find ways to injure them. He was admired for his toughness and egged on by the rest of the team. By final year, he had become a liability because he gave away too many free kicks. He missed the finals because he had been suspended.

Justin was both nervous and excited about meeting his friends again and wondered if, when he met them, he would rediscover long-forgotten characteristics such as Peter's posture.

Justin communicated with Peter and the others and set a date on a Sunday afternoon in late July for them to meet. Peter offered his home for the meeting place. Contacting four of the men, Michael, Gerard, Pat and Glen was straight forward; Justin phoned them, had a brief conversation then visited them. In each case, he was well received because he had been popular and become a bit of a mystery with his 'disappearance'. By chance, he had arranged his meetings to households of decreasing social status; Michael was a married barrister living in Kew, Gerard a divorced printer/publisher living in Alphington, Pat a barman living with his male partner in a seedy, rented house in Collingwood and Glen on a disability pension living alone in public housing in Prahran. There was something quite beautiful about these visits, in each case they evoked happy memoires of school days together, especially incidents on the sporting fields. Justin encouraged these reminiscences then moved on to the idea of his meeting, triggered by Kevin's suicide, to discuss how their lives had been affected by the abuses of Father Stephen. He was surprised by their willingness to meet, it was as if they had all been waiting for someone to take the initiative. They all said the abuse had been on their minds because of the regular trickle of news about the investigations of the Royal Commission. Gerard had spoken to the commissioners and Glen had planned to but became so upset that he dropped out at the last minute. Michael was the only one who was reluctant to attend the meeting and that was because he thought he considered himself unaffected by the abuse and was a practising Catholic and hence might be out of place.

The fifth man Justin contacted was Frank, a businessman, apparently very wealthy now, living in Perth. Justin had a long phone conversation with him and he expressed a wish to attend the meeting but wasn't sure if he could make it. The sixth man, Finn, was the problem because none of the others knew how to find him. Glen said he had seen him about a year before in St Kilda. At the time, Finn appeared to be under the influence of drugs but Glen thought he had meals at the Sacred Heart Mission in Grey Street. Justin decided to walk over to Grey Street to see if he could find him.

Justin walked from his flat to St Kilda and it took him ages to get across the St Kilda Junction, a concreted confluence of roads that evolved without pedestrians in mind. As he waited for the fourth lot of pedestrian crossing lights to change he remembered a story his father had once told him about his father. Justin's grandfather owned a car in the 1930s but was nervous of driving in traffic. Whenever he had to drive through the St Kilda Junction he would start sweating in anticipation, something that Justin's father and uncles watched for in secret delight. Justin had a vague memory of Fitzroy Street as a cool place to go for gelatis and souvlakis in the seventies but wandered off into the side streets behind Fitzroy Street to look at the architecture. Here grand mansions had gone shabby and become rooming houses then a burst of building activity during the 1960s had scattered the area with ugly blocks of flats. Now, another wave of building was throwing up grander towers where fashionable architects had the opportunity to show off their styles in termite mounds of tiny apartments. There were some lovely flashes of Victoriana and Art Deco but it was an environment uncomfortable with itself. Justin heard the sounds of an argument behind closed doors and didn't like the way a man who was sitting on a front fence, stared at him. There were many blue stoned alleys, the former dunny cart lanes found throughout the inner suburbs which Justin usually enjoyed exploring but here they felt like places where bad things happened.

He emerged onto Fitzroy Street near its junction with Grey Street but even here the clean-lined coffee shops and young backpackers seemed subdued by an oppressive gloom, so different from the thrum of Chapel Street. By Grey Street all pretence of gloss was gone and Justin avoided eye-contact with the mutterers and predatory, thin men who spilled out from the charitable institutions which formed the centre of their world there.

Justin found the Sacred Heart Mission, a tightly-packed cluster of nineteenth century buildings with numerous practical signs stamping a functional nature on its grand appearance. At the front was a concreted area with seats occupied by people who looked like the types who might use a charitable service for their meals. Most of them were wearing newish-looking track suits, the tops not necessarily matching the bottoms. He followed arrows between buildings going past three 'Do Not Smoke' signs then a 'No Spitting' sign to where a man with a lanyard around his neck was standing purposefully at a door.

"Hello. Are you joining us for lunch today?" he asked in a bright and cheery manner. Justin couldn't help feeling embarrassed.

"No. I've come to see if I can find an old friend of mine, Finn Magee."

The man smiled,

"He often comes here for meals but I don't think he's been in today. Let's have a look."

The man took him through the door to the scene of a large, busy kitchen then around a corner to a dining room. It was simple but clean and inviting. Justin noticed that the man closest to him was eating a roast. The man with the lanyard seemed proud of the service and told Justin without any prompting,

"We serve about two hundred people here twice per day. Lunch is always a three course meal. It looks like Finn isn't here."

"Do you know where I might find him?"

"He lives in the Gatwick Private Hotel."

"Where's that? I'll see if I can find him there."

"I hope you're vaccinated," the man said and despite his big smile Justin didn't realise he was joking.

"Why? What against?"

"Bubonic plague, rabies, you name it. No, I'm only joking but the Gatwick is a pretty rough place."

He told Justin where to find the hotel and sent him on his way back to Fitzroy Street.

The Gatwick was a faded and chipped monolith with a timeless quality about it, a sense of separation from its environment. In front there were four people, all smoking, none of them interacting with each other. There were two aboriginal women sitting on the footpath curled up against the front wall and on a bench, two men, one obese and one very thin. Justin hesitated at the glass front door, not knowing the procedure of gaining admission, not even sure if he wanted to go in but then a man came up behind him and walked confidently into the building and Justin followed. In the lobby he felt disoriented, the dull lighting and custard coloured walls matched his expectations but the spaciousness and aged wood panelling gave a sense of old world grandeur and welcome. He made his way to an office, a cluttered cubby of wood and glass panelling where a motherly woman gave him a penetrating look and asked if she could help.

"I'm looking for Finn Magee."

"Are you a friend of his?"

The woman asked this in a light and kindly manner but he could tell that she was carefully assessing him and he also knew that she would have talents beyond his imagination in judging the sorts of people who came to her office. It was essential that he was open and honest with her.

"Sort of. We were friends at school and I've come to see if he would like to come to a type of class reunion I'm organising. I haven't seen him for more than twenty years."

"He's one of our regulars, been here for about fifteen years. But he's probably not in now, he goes to the Sacred Heart for lunch."

"No, he's not; I've just been there. They sent me here."

Justin laughed. The woman was warming to him.

"I've never been here before. I love the old wood panelling. When was the Gatwick built?"

Mary was her name and she was keen to tell Justin about the building. She had been there all her life. It had been owned by her father, a migrant from Malta and now it was still run by Mary and her sister. She was proud of its Art Deco character and the way the plaster ceiling features were different in every room. She left the office and showed Justin the grand dining room which was no longer used. She also showed him the functional communal kitchen but made the point that none of the residents ever used it. She told Justin where to find Finn's room on the third floor and directed him to the stairs.

Confident now, Justin indulged himself in the ambience of the Gatwick. He liked the original swirled plaster work, the broad stairs and landings and the former telephone boxes on the landings, now panelled shells with all electrical parts removed. It was patched but un-renovated, the carpets were stained and thread-bare in places, the paint work chipped. He glanced into a bathroom where the taps looked antique. There were some original dark panelled doors but most had been fully or partly replaced; suggesting untold stories of anger. There was a man asleep on the carpet in the upper landing, his head resting on a day pack.

Justin found Finn's room with one of the few original doors and knocked. A minute passed with no answer so he knocked again, louder.

"Who is it?"

"It's Justin Collins."

"Who?"

"Justin Collins. Remember me from St Crispins?"

"Justin Collins?"

"Yes. Remember me?"

Justin felt awkward having to explain himself like this from the other side of a door, and tried again remembering that they had once lived in the same street.

"Justin, from Murray Street Hawthorn."

"From Murray Street."

Footsteps approached the other side of the door then after some fumbling at a lock, the door opened. Finn stood there, a shadow silhouetted by the dim light of the room which had its blinds closed. Justin smelt unwashed clothes and old plumbing.

"Hi Finn. Do you remember me."

"Yeah. Justin from Murray Street."

Finn smiled showing gaps in his dentition. It was a warm smile of recognition and Justin shook his hand. Finn looked older than his late fifties with a pinched face and long, oily hair. As his vision adapted to the dark of the room behind him, Justin noticed its features; it was cluttered with old furniture and the floor was covered with papers and empty take-away food containers. The squalor was shocking and he felt an urge to enter the room to find out for himself just how bad it was.

"What brings you to my humble abode Justin?"

The edge in his voice was disturbingly ambiguous and it was only later that Justin was able to recognise this as an innocent expression. Finn made no indication that he was going to move from his place in the doorway.

"I wanted to see you to talk about a reunion. Would you like to go somewhere for coffee?"

"Yeah. Coffee."

Finn left the room and laboriously locked the door behind him then walked along the corridor to the stairs. Justin followed. Once outside, Finn asked Justin if he had any smokes then looked at his pockets suspiciously as if he was lying when he said no.

"Where do you want to go for coffee Finn?"

"Ruby's."

They walked along Fitzroy Street to a coffee shop with plastic tables and chairs on the footpath in front. Finn sat there and Justin asked how he would like his coffee.

"Cappuccino, two sugars."

Justin went into the shop to order and pay for the coffees but kept an eye on Finn through the window. There was so little connection so far that he wondered if Finn would just wander off. Back at the table Justin worked hard at making conversation. He found that Finn's attention fluctuated; at times he was detached and monosyllabic but then he would show some emotion and put a few sentences together. He was at his best with memories of their games in the under 16 A football team during Finn's last year at St Crispins. Justin asked,

"Did you hear that Kevin died?"

"Nuh. What happened to him?"

"He hanged himself. They tell me he was upset by all the reporting about the Royal Commission into child sexual abuse."

"The poor guy."

At that point Finn drifted off, his hand frozen on his half full cup of coffee.

"Do you remember Father Stephen, Finn?"

"Of course I remember the fuckin' arse hole. I hope he rots in jail."

"He had a terrible effect on us didn't he."

"Well I've fuckin come down in the world, haven't I?"

They finished their coffee in silence and Justin had just about decided not to invite Finn to his meeting, or even mention that he was planning it but then Finn started asking Justin about his life and more about Kevin, so he changed his mind.

"I'm arranging a meeting for the gang from the drama class Finn just to talk about how our lives have gone. Would you like to come?"

"Yeah."

Justin walked with Finn back to the Gatwick and left him at the stairs. As he watched him walk away, he wondered if he would remember any of their conversation. He saw Mary watching him from her office. She called him over and asked,

"How did you go?"

"I don't know really. What's wrong with him?"

"He's an ABI."

Justin looked confused and she continued,

"Acquired Brain Injury. Drugs, alcohol and too many hits in the head from fights and falls. He's OK and never causes any trouble here. His room's a pig sty; we send him off and clean it out every now and then. Is he going to your school reunion?"

"I asked him. Who knows?"

"What school did yous go to?"

"St Crispins."

"Ah. Was it sexual abuse from that priest?"

Justin nodded.

"We've got lots of them here."

A week before the meeting, Michael and Frank emailed Justin to confirm that they would be attending. Then Justin received an email from Moira Dowling, the mother of Kevin Dowling whose suicide had first prompted Justin to arrange the meeting. She wrote,

Hello Justin. I would have preferred to phone you but Peter tells me that you don't use a phone and kindly gave me your email address. Peter told me about the meeting you are arranging and I was moved to hear that you are doing it in response to the death of my dear Kevin. As you can imagine I was shattered by his death and have been reflecting on his life and the sad pathway it followed.

I have an unusual request and I will quite understand, and accept, if you refuse. Could I please attend your meeting to

represent Kevin and tell you about his life. I understand that you have probably conceived your meeting as a very personal one for men only, but my idea is to attend at the beginning of the meeting, say my piece then leave.

Bless you Justin

Moira Dowling

Justin remembered Moira as a tall, rather stern woman who loved football and always watched Kevin's matches. Kevin was big and usually played on the back line, sometimes as ruck. His mother would shout at him if he didn't play to her satisfaction. The email made Justin uncomfortable but he knew immediately that he had to let her attend. The meeting wasn't about him even if he was the organiser and seemed to be in control; it was something bigger than him and any of the individuals who would be attending. Most of all Justin was alarmed by the power Moira was conferring on him by giving him the choice of accepting or rejecting her.

6

On the morning of the meeting, Justin phoned the Gatwick and was pleased to find Mary was in the reception office. She remembered Justin and they had a surprisingly warm and rambling conversation. She judged it best not to warn Finn that Justin was coming but she would keep an eye out for him. He rarely left his room before midday anyway.

Justin walked to St Kilda buying a Myki card for Finn on the way. At the Gatwick, Mary greeted him and wished him good luck, she was involved and Justin appreciated her support. At Finn's door, the scene was similar to when Justin first visited, with Finn slowly emerging from his strange inner world to engage. Justin was not sure if Finn had remembered the plan to go with him to Peter's place but at least Finn left the Gatwick with him without any fuss. He stank of cigarettes and unwashed clothes and Justin winced at the thought of him in Peter's tidy living room but he rationalised that seeing each other and hearing each other's stories was what the meeting was all about. They had coffee at Ruby's and Justin bought him a pack of cigarettes.

They caught a tram to the city and sat together on a double seat. In the confined space, Finn's unwashed smell was even stronger and Justin couldn't help but look away, not wanting to be associated with him. Finn started rocking gently back and forwards and Justin wondered if he always did it or was it something he did to reassure himself while travelling on a tram. Finn was one of those strange people whom you see if you travel enough on public transport. The tram filled and Justin felt like offering his seat to one of the standing women, but he knew no one would want to sit next to Finn so he remained seated and gazed out of the window.

Finn followed him passively from the tram stop, through Flinders Street Station and onto the Hurstbridge Line train. When the train went underground after Southern Cross Station, Finn became agitated, muttering and turning his head from side to side. Other passengers looked concerned and Justin worried that he might do something disruptive. He put a hand on his arm and said,

"It's OK Finn. We'll be out of the tunnel soon."

Finn settled down and remained relaxed for the rest of the journey, enough for Justin to enjoy the trip. He liked looking over the mixed urban landscapes from Richmond to Clifton Hill where industry had given over to gentrified housing, then the leafier suburbs to the hills around Ivanhoe. At Eaglemont, he enjoyed once more the embrace of the quaint shopping centre but Finn retained his closed look and seemed oblivious to his surroundings.

As planned, Justin and Finn arrived early. Finn rallied and showed some basic social skills with Peter. He wanted to smoke so the three men stood outside in the wintry cold of Peter's backyard for a while then Justin took Finn with him to the local pub, the Eagle Bar, to get some wine and beer. The beers and wines were mostly different from the ones he knew from the last time he had entered a bottle shop but he found some familiar Penfolds and Finn helped him with the beer.

The others arrived within minutes of the appointed time. Most of them had not seen each other for over twenty years and were amused by the physical changes; Frank in particular was almost unrecognisable as the athletic school boy because he was now obese and had the red face and swollen nose of a heavy drinker. He greeted everyone in an exaggerated, bossy manner. There was much hand-shaking and a few hugs from Pat who seemed good at judging who to hug and whose hand to shake. Finn stood smiling, saying 'Yeah' and 'How are ya mate' frequently but Justin, who was watching him anxiously, wondered how well he remembered the others. After a spattering of conversational topics which ended quickly, they came to stand in a rough circle in front of the chairs then sat. The mood was light, manic even with the unsettling distraction of accommodating Finn into their circle and accepting his smell. Frank dominated the conversation and set a tone something like that of a sporting social function referring to the others as 'you buggers'. Glen was holding back and Justin wanted to help him into the conversation. Pat irritated him with the way he spoke, the echo of some forgotten conflict. Justin was annoyed with himself for feeling that way and willed himself to be compassionate. Gerard spoke little but generated a core of self-confidence which was immune to Frank's bluster.

Moira had arranged to come at 3.30 and at precisely 3.30 the doorbell rang. Justin guessed that she had been waiting in her car outside in order to arrive on time. Peter brought her into the living room and her presence transformed the gathering. She was tall and straight, holding herself with the type of dignified poise which is no longer taught. She was dressed in a tailored dress and jacket with the subtlety and elegance that spoke of a lifetime of wealthy living. In any situation, she would have been a commanding figure but here, in addition, she bore the gravitas of being a deceased friend's mother. The men were humbled and respectful; schoolboys again. They stood and shook her hand as she passed around their circle then she sat in the chair Peter offered her. The men sat, trying to look as straight-backed and receptive as was possible in the lumpy lounge chairs. Moira spoke,

"Thank you for letting me join you today. I promised Justin that I would say my piece then leave so I won't keep you long."

She reached into her handbag and took out a framed portrait. It was a professional photograph in an old-fashioned metal frame of a boy who looked about eleven or twelve years old, her son Kevin. She carefully stood the frame on the coffee table next to her facing into the circle. The gesture was theatrical but sincere and the men all stared at the portrait.

"There he is, just before he started at St Crispins. He was a lovely child with a beautiful, sunny disposition. He was relaxed and easy-going, always smiling, always around wanting to chat. I had four children and they were all different; Geraldine would disappear to read books, Des restless and wanting to play sports, Gary always looking for mischief. Kevin was a pleasure to be around.

We felt honoured when Father Stephen asked to have him in his second form drama class. It was later that year, soon after he turned thirteen that he started to change. It upset me that he withdrew and didn't want hugs any more. My husband Reg laughed and said that it was normal, that boys become monsters when they enter adolescence and I accepted that.

We knew Danny well and when he ..."

At that point, Moira paused. All the men knew what she was trying to say and that she was wanting to put it as delicately as possible.

"... committed suicide we were devastated. As the truth came out about Father Stephen's behaviour, we went into a state of shock, we couldn't believe that such a sophisticated man, and a priest, could do that. I'm from a very sheltered and devoutly Catholic background, I'd heard about homosexuality but I didn't know that there were some men who preyed on children. And a priest!"

In the silence that followed all of the men relived in different ways their treatment at the hands of Father Stephen, the emotional manipulation and the progressive physical coercion. And then there was the crisis of Danny's death and the devastation of their families. It was a time when their security and certainties collapsed around them, a time when they saw their parents in new lights. Pat took out a handkerchief and tried to strangle some sobs.

"Reg was furious. I think he would have killed Father Stephen but the school spirited him away quickly. We saw the headmaster several times and believed he was sincere in trying to deal with Father Stephen. We didn't know what to do; I tried all sorts of approaches to get Kevin to talk about his pain but he didn't want to discuss it. We talked about taking him to doctors, psychologists, psychiatrists but that just upset him and he refused anyway. We didn't know anything about the potential long-term effects. We worked hard at being kind and giving him more time. Reg talked about the resilience of youth but I never quite believed that. We kept the whole business secret from the other children but it was like a blight on what was once a happy household. And we kept going to mass as we always had!

Our sunny child had changed but he kept doing his homework and he still loved football. The teachers at St Crispins seemed to be on-side and gave special attention to all the boys who had been abused, in your year and the years ahead of you. The headmaster told us that there were legal reasons why he couldn't tell us where Father Stephen had gone.

In form five, Kevin started using marijuana, something else I knew nothing about. On several occasions, I commented on his eyes being red and he said that was from the chlorine in the swimming pool. I found cigarette rolling papers in his trouser pockets and told him off for smoking, what I thought was tobacco. When I asked him about the sweet smell on his clothes he said it was the deodorant he was using and I accepted this thinking I had embarrassed him for talking about his personal hygiene. He would come home late with all manner of excuses. That was a dreadful time, when we discovered how dishonest he was being with us. Reg was furious with him and saw it as an issue of personal morality. I handled it badly, when he lied to my face I couldn't bare it.

His marks dropped, he became like a stranger in our home. Reg worried about him being a bad influence on the other children. He only just passed his HSC but he could have done much better. We had been hoping he would do law and he did have the intelligence to get in. He started doing an Arts degree and he would drift off to Uni but I don't know how many lectures he attended. Then money started disappearing. I did a thorough search of his room and that was when I found the needles and syringes.

I know countless numbers of parents have gone through the horror of finding that their children are drug addicts but we felt so alone. Reg ordered him out of the house, men seem capable of making hard decisions like that but I never could have. He found a place to live in Carlton, a horrible, dirty place and I made a point of visiting him regularly. I had to brace myself before those visits; I didn't ask him about his drug use, I gave him home-prepared meals and tried to just let him know that I loved him and he behaved well on those occasions. Reg thought I shouldn't visit him so I kept my visits secret. Dealing with Kevin caused a terrible strain on our marriage, but I'm not here to talk about that.

The following years were what they call an emotional roller coaster for me. Kevin would go into rehab, stop using drugs and get a job, then he would use drugs and the lies would start again. He would steal things from our house and sell them to buy drugs, Reg lost the most valuable old books from his collection. I always kept in contact with him and managed to separate in my mind the drug behaviour from the beautiful boy I once knew. He was helped by psychologists and came to have a better understanding of himself and the effect the abuse had had on him, the terrible sense of deep shame. I was learning too and as more came out in the nineteen nineties I was appalled by the extent of abuse that had been happening at the hands of priests and how the church had protected them. I discussed it with our parish priest whom I had known for ages and he arranged for me to see Archbishop Scuttle. That was a revelation for me, the day I changed my mind about the Catholic Church.

I wanted to describe to him the impact Father Stephen's abuse had had on Kevin, what had become of him and how it had affected me, my marriage and my whole family. I was composed and courteous. I'm not sure what I was expecting, I think I wanted him to show understanding then tell me what changes the Church was making to prevent it from ever happening again. He listened but then he gave me a lecture on the importance of the Church and its ancient history; that a rotten apple like Father

Stephen mustn't blind us to the majesty of the Church and the nobility and authority of its priesthood. That we mustn't lose sight of our roles as Christians to serve God and respect and support the traditions of the true Church. He droned on and on with that theme and I could feel myself growing more and more angry. Then I told him, 'No you are wrong. The Church is not about its grand tradition it's about the people who are part of it; the parishioners who go to mass and the weddings and funerals and confirmations. It's about the people who support the church financially. People such as my beautiful little boy Kevin and his family who put its faith in the Church ..."'

Moira was furious now, she wasn't looking at the men but was reliving the conversation she had with Archbishop Scuttle. She ran out of words then shrank back in her chair and spoke in a quieter tone,

"I stopped going to mass after that and the Church sickens me now. Leaving the Church has come at great personal cost for me; I have lost friends and even some of my family shun me now. I am bitter and blame myself for having had such a narrow and accepting view of the Church for most of my life. The evidence of the fallibility of the priests was always there if you cared to look for it. I now think of the Catholic Church as an organised crime network that commits unspeakable crimes then uses its wealth and power to cover them up."

There was absolute silence, then eventually Moira stood, her tall figure a picture of resolution and strength. Not once during her speech had she been tearful.

"Thank you for listening. I've said my piece and will go now. I want to thank you all for your friendship with Kevin during his school days and early adulthood. Special thanks to you Peter for getting him back on track in recent years."

She took the photo from the coffee table and put it back in her bag, an action that seemed more final than the descent of a coffin into a grave, then started walking from the room. The men moved, all standing at once and Peter escorted her to the front door. When Peter returned, Frank said,

"I feel gutted. Let's have a drink."

They looked to the fridge and the clatter of glasses for relief, Finn walked outside to smoke.

They served themselves drinks and shuffled around uncomfortably, all deeply affected by Moira's speech and unwilling to make small-talk. Justin felt the pressure of them looking to him to show some leadership and spoke,

"Thanks for all of you coming today. I'm still recovering from Moira's speech. As you know, it was Kevin's death that prompted me to get you together and then Moira asked if she could speak for him. She's certainly set a tone. Perhaps we should start by making a toast to the four of us who aren't here; Danny, Colin, Jasper and Kevin."

The men raised their glasses and in soft but fairly coordinated voices toasted the four friends who had committed suicide. Justin continued,

"I've been thinking a lot about how Father Stephen affected me. I suppose you all have. I'll go first.

You'll probably remember how he worked on Danny and I, how he picked on us in front of you all for failing to be good team members. That was because I resisted him for a while, refused the alcohol, and I suppose Danny did the same. I was devastated by that, the drama class was so important to me. It shows how clever he was in manipulating us and I'll never forget that sense of letting down the team.

After Danny hanged himself and it all blew up I didn't want to talk about it. In retrospect, I can see that my parents did the best they possibly could but I was so ashamed that they knew about the pornography we'd been watching that I clammed up. They kept letting me know that they loved me."

He paused; Pat, Glen and Frank lowered their heads as if to hide their feelings. Finn was standing rigidly, a fixed, glazed expression on his face.

"I think I recovered fairly well at the time. I loved sport and studied hard. I had my first girlfriend in Year 12. I didn't get far with her but I did with my next girlfriend at Uni."

Some quiet laughs.

"I did well at Uni, enjoyed a joyous heterosexual sex life then worked my way up at Baxter's to make a lot of money in my twenties. And I loved the life of being young with money. I drank expensive wines and went to Melbourne's best restaurants. By twenty-eight, I was driving a red Alpha Romeo. By thirty, I had 2 investment properties and a decent share portfolio. Then I became dissatisfied; at the time, I saw it as a philosophical or spiritual thing and resigned my job to go travelling. I think it was at that time that I started having dreams about a church burning, it became a recurring dream and I still have it occasionally. I had nothing to do with the church after school, but I didn't have any strong feelings of resentment about it or anything. I had good memoires of St Crispins and enjoyed meeting up with old school friends.

I travelled for years, mainly in Asia. In Nepal, I had a satisfying job working as a volunteer in an orphanage. I had some great girlfriends but the relationships lasted one to two years and I can see now that it was my fault that they failed. I was faithful but didn't meet their emotional needs, I wasn't giving enough of myself.

I became more spiritual, wanting to spend more time alone. I did several pilgrimage walks in Europe; I did the Camino de Compostella the long way, starting at Paris. I still love the peace and solitude of walking. I eventually got tired of moving around and quite disgusted with my self-indulgent lifestyle, living off my investments while my friends seemed to be getting on with their lives. So I decided to stop somewhere and try being a hermit. I ended up on a beautiful island in the Outer Hebrides, South Uist, and rented a little cottage. I was enjoying being a hermit but within a month I got involved with a woman who lived on the island, Morag her name was. She had been married to an alcoholic who had treated her badly and they were separated. I tried to manage a part-time relationship with her so that I could spend a lot of time on my own but she gradually drew me into her life. I went to more and more social functions and got involved with the seasonal activities on the island such as cutting turf and all sorts of things that you had to do with the sheep. I was quite enjoying island life and could see myself settling down with Morag but then the same thing happened, I couldn't satisfy Morag as a partner. The sex was great but she said I was too vague and didn't care about anything. She got sick of me and went back to her brutal husband.

So, I left South Uist and was ready to return to Melbourne to try being a hermit there. I went to Broadmeadows first where there wouldn't be anyone who knew me but that failed because my wonderful Iraqi neighbours wouldn't let me be alone. I finally settled in Toorak which is probably the best place in Melbourne to be a hermit because your neighbours put up high fences and don't want to know you. And that's where I've been for the last fifteen years, reading, meditating, playing my viola, shopping once each week. No relationships.

I often wonder who I am and what makes me the way I am. I usually conclude that I'm just a vague, solitary sort of person."

He finished his story leaving them with a sense of reluctance and sadness about describing himself as such. When he thought about this afterwards, he thought he had given them the wrong impression because it didn't really reflect his satisfaction with the way he lived. Gerard said,

"Tell us about your dream Justin."

"It's brief. There is a black wooden church which suddenly bursts into flame and I stand watching it in a state of paralysis. What amazes me is the power of the dream and it's not just a visual image. I often hear the crackling of the flames and smell the smoke."

He could have said more, he could have explained to them his technique of interpreting dreams but that was a long conversation which he didn't feel like having with them at that time.

7

"Kevin's story is like mine, so I'd better go next," said Glen.

"I treated my mother like Kevin treated Moira. The drugs, the lies, I even stole from my grandmother. I did it all, one thing led to another. When I was on drugs I didn't care and when I wasn't using I felt so ashamed that I went back to drugs. When two of my mates OD-ed I got off the drugs, that was when I was twenty-two and stayed off of for the next eight years. That was long enough for me to get a degree, a good job, a wife and son. During that time, whenever I was depressed or anxious or angry. I saw it as my own weakness, I had an addictive personality and life was a battle to stay off drugs. I eventually stuffed up and lost everything. My ex-wife and my son don't want to know me and I don't blame them. I've wasted my life."

Glen closed his eyes and started sobbing. Justin was sitting next to him and put a hand on his shoulder. They thought he had finished speaking but he took a deep breath and continued.

"So, what am I like now? I live in a shit apartment in a high rise surrounded by drug pushers and crazies who scream in the night. The only decent people around me are the refugees and they get out of the place as soon as they have sorted themselves out. I've been there for over twenty years and will probably be there until I die. I'm on the methadone program. Every now and then I think I'm OK and start to reduce but then I use heroin and have to go up again. I use a lot of Valium which I get on the street so my doctor doesn't know about it. I've got hepatitis C which will probably kill me. They tell me it causes liver cancer which usually gets you in your fifties. I've been offered the eradication treatment but I don't think I deserve it so I haven't asked for it. I've got a record, in jail three times, unemployable. I've only got one sister in my family who will talk to me and I've lost all my good friends, the ones I have now would steal from me if I didn't hide my money. And I have blackouts. I end up in places such as stations not knowing what day it is and how I got there. It's got much worse since the Royal Commission started and now I don't listen to the news or read the newspapers. The psychologists tell me my blackouts are dissociations, caused by my brain blocking out Father Stephen's sexual abuse. I can't remember what he did to me, I only know what he did because I was told later. I have nightmares and flashbacks in which I feel Father Stephen's beard against my skin. The police wanted me to talk to the Royal Commission and I said I would but then I had to pull the plug when I got worse."

He paused, gathering energy for something more to say.

"I used to think it was me, that I was just a fuck-up and I blamed the drugs for a long time. Now I think this shouldn't have happened; I come from a good family, my brothers and sisters have all had good lives and I was OK until I was thirteen."

Frank broke the gloom that had descended on the group by standing and announcing,

"I'm having another drink."

He walked over to the table and poured himself a glass of red wine, some of the others followed then returned to their chairs. Frank spoke again,

"I'm glad I've come today but this is not the sort of thing I would usually do. Justin caught me with his invitation at a time in my life when I have been uncharacteristically 'reflective.'

He held up two pairs of fingers for quotation marks, as if to mock the idea of being reflective.

"I had a heart attack six months ago followed by bypass surgery then rehab. I should have, 'changed my lifestyle,' but I've decided nope, full steam ahead. I'll continue to smoke, drink heavily and work my guts out. I'm not going to become a vegetarian or a philanthropist or write a book about how I saw the light. I'll die prematurely but so be it.

So, what am I like? I own a mining company and I'm on my way to becoming a billionaire. I'm a workaholic micro-manager, I start work at 6am and often work until 11pm. As a business man, I'm a hard-nosed bastard. Many people have accused me of being a bully which probably means that I am. My entertainments are deep sea fishing and driving expensive sports cars. I pay for escorts when I want sex. I was married for four years and had a daughter and another daughter by a later relationship but I didn't know about her until years later. I treated my wife badly and don't have any contact with her or my legitimate daughter. I have a sort a relationship with the other daughter. She's tough like me and is probably cultivating me for an inheritance.

So, I'm probably the classic, driven, type A personality. Until recently I thought it was just me; my father was a hard-working business man and I'm like him on steroids. I now wonder if my life has been an exercise in avoiding intimacy. Anyway, I've compensated with a lifestyle that suits me.

With regards to the Catholic Church, I hate it. Whenever I see a Catholic priest I feel like smashing his face in. I moved to Perth when I was nineteen because I wanted to get away from all memories and connections with my schooling and Catholic childhood."

He turned to Glen and said.

"It's been devastating to hear your story Glen, and Moira's story about Kevin's life. I didn't realise it could be so bad. I've got more to learn and think through."

Peter cleared his throat suggesting he was about to speak and they all turned to look to him.

"Like Frank, the avoidance of intimacy is a theme that has pervaded my life."

He spoke in a slow, considered manner as if he was striving for clarity. Justin could picture him giving a lecture in a similar way, holding the attention of his students.

"This difficulty with intimacy has been very painful for me. I go over and over in my mind conversations I had with my wife Margaret and conversations I should have had but didn't. I let her down badly as a husband and as a human being. I'm not going to change and have disqualified myself from ever having a serious relationship, I don't deserve it. I've been divorced for fifteen years but have retained a decent sort of friendship with my ex-wife.

Anyway, back to the start. My parents were emotionally limited and were unable to give me the love and warmth that might have made a difference. My father was a traditional breadwinner sort of man who worked long hours and had little to do with the raising of his children. My mother left me feeling that I was somehow to blame for Father Stephen's abuse and didn't miss a beat in her devotion to the Catholic Church in general and priests in particular."

Peter paused, looking up at the ceiling.

"About a year before she died, my mother broke out of her gruff, blunt persona and told me, without making any eye contact, that she neglected me when I needed her and that she was very, very sorry that she hadn't done a better job as a mother. It was an embarrassing experience for both of us but I'm glad it happened.

At school and then university I put my energy into study and I was ambitious. I've had a good career as a historian, in terms of publications, the conferences at which I speak and the popularity of my teaching but I've always been aware that I was diverting energy and avoiding emotional responsibilities. Until recent years I thought it was just me and didn't understand the psychological process that started with Father Stephen.

Margaret and I were deeply in love and the early years of our marriage were happy. She had poor health and was eventually diagnosed with endometriosis which caused her to be infertile. I said it didn't matter to me but she was bewildered and instead of showing kindness I behaved like my mother, treating her with silence and staying late at the university to avoid her neediness. The divorce was very polite; I instructed my solicitor to be generous in our settlement. My meetings with her now are the high-light of my life, she's very kind to me. I'm still in love with her."

He spoke with such detachment that it took a few moments for the others to grasp the emotional impact of his story. Justin thought of himself as a student taking notes in a lecture dispassionately jotting down, 'I'm still in love with her'. Peter smiled then continued in a lighter tone, returning to more comfortable territory.

"If you'll permit me to be the historian for a while, would you cast an eye over these books here?"

He walked over to a bookshelf where a group of books was isolated from other books on the shelf by a pair of mulga wood book ends. There were about fifteen old books with a variety of coloured bindings.

"These are the novels of Ethel Stonehouse who wrote most of her books under the pen-name of Lindsay Russell. It took me over twenty years to track them all down and collect. She is a forgotten early twentieth century Australian writer and understandably so because her novels have little literary merit, they are out-of-date Mills and Boon type romances. What interests me about her novels is that most of them are variations on the same theme, stories of innocent young women who are seduced by Catholic priests, then abandoned. This theme is so repetitious that it seems autobiographical and indeed in 1910, Ethel took a priest by the name of Michael Francis Quinn to court for breach of promise; a shocking scandal at the time. Three of her novels are published under the pen-name of Quinn as if to rub his nose in it, that she should have been Mrs Quinn."

Peter removed from the bookshelf a blue-bound novel.

"This novel, *Love letters of a Priest,* contains a series of wheedling, manipulative letters from a lusty priest. They are so different stylistically from the writings of Ethel that I think they really are the letters that Michael Francis Quinn wrote to her. In this book, the girl dobs in the priest to the local bishop. And what does he do? He moves the naughty priest to another parish. And that seems to be a large part of the work of bishops, and has been for the last thousand years, dealing with the sexuality of priests who are meant to be celibate. The people who study this estimate that about fifty percent of priests have sexual relationships; mostly with consenting adults but about six percent are paedophiles. The celibacy rule creates a climate of shame and secrecy which in fact encourages priests to have sex with children because they are easier to coerce to remain silent, boys in particular.

The celibacy rule has never had anything to do with Christianity, it is all about the wealth and prestige of the church.

For the first thousand years of the Church's history priests could marry. In the eleventh century Pope Benedict the Eighth prohibited the children of priests from inheriting property. Thirty years later Pope Gregory the Seventh issued a decree that priests could not marry and later councils entrenched that rule. Now, the upper echelons of the church hierarchy are the most conservative and don't want to admit that for the last thousand years the church has been dehumanising priests and causing the abuse of countless numbers of children."

Peter sat down. These were concepts that Justin already partly knew but no one had ever put them so succinctly for him before. He thanked Peter and several others also muttered their thanks. Frank walked over to the book shelf to look at the Lindsay Russell novels and the others took this as a signal to rise for another interval; some walked outside and others poured themselves a drink. Finn smoked a cigarette but maintained an unfocussed stare which discouraged the others from trying to communicate with him. They drifted back to their chairs. Justin noticed Gerard's look of concentration, as if he was rehearsing what he wanted to say.

"My turn now," said Gerard and the others braced themselves for another sad story.

"Anger was the big issue with me. It took a long time for me to understand its various manifestations. From the age of sixteen I was doing stupid things, dangerous things, pushing the limits of risk taking. I wrote off two cars and committed some pointless acts of vandalism. By twenty I was drinking heavily and it was only the discipline of playing football for St Crispins Old Boys and my job that made me look after myself. I married a wonderful woman, Nancy, and had two sons. I realised that I was a lucky man and struggled with my anger but then started directing it towards Nancy. In my thirties, I would have alcohol-fueled periods of rage followed by remorse and reconciliation but Nancy eventually left with the boys. I don't blame her, she should have done it earlier. It was only then that I joined AA and I haven't had a drink now for eighteen years and nine months. Nancy remarried and I have good relationships with my two sons.

I didn't understand the anger and I thought my alcoholism was genetic; there's been a fair sprinkling of alcoholics in my family. Through AA's twelve step program and some counselling that I had, I came to understand the link between my anger and what Father Stephen did to us. As media reports emerged about the behaviour of the rapist priests I'd flare up and have fantasies about doing destructive things but I've learnt all sorts of things to do to manage my anger. About nine years ago I joined *Broken Rites*, I'm a director now. It's an organisation founded by people who have been abused by priests that researches and documents the priests and church cover-ups and helps the victims to get the best outcomes in terms of counselling and legal redress. I've learnt just how immoral and cynical the Catholic Church is when it comes to protecting its property. The Church set up an in-house complaints system called *Towards Healing*, ostensibly to help victims of priest-abuse but in reality, to dissuade them from going to the police and to minimise compensation pay-outs.

It also tips off the priests that someone has lodged a complaint about them. *Towards Healing* is actually funded by the church's insurance company, Catholic Church Insurance Limited!

So now I divert my anger into exposing the church and getting the best deals for its victims. The legal system is far too generous in its punishment of the rapist priests, they usually only get a few years in jail. But at *Broken Rites* we gather the evidence and as more victims speak out, these priests know that their lives are going to be dominated by criminal charges. That bastard Father Stephen only got nine years but ..."

At that moment, Pat interrupted with,

"He's out. I saw him a month ago."

There was a stunned silence. Pat looked down and closed his eyes, then took a deep breath, looked up again and continued.

"I saw him in Westgarth. I'd been to an afternoon film and when I left the theatre, I saw what looked like him in the distance. I followed him but I was feeling sick and not wanting him to see me. He walked up a driveway at number 17 Bolton Road, there's an old house at the front and a newer unit built at the back and I saw him go into the unit. I looked in the letter box for unit 2 and there was a magazine with his name on it. I can't bear to go anywhere near Westgarth now."

Another long silence. Gerard's talk had made Justin feel angry about the Catholic Church and now he felt himself becoming furious with Father Stephen. Gerard broke the silence.

"So, he's out after only six years. That's typical."

They were all expecting Gerard to say more, either about Father Stephen or to continue his own story but he turned to Pat and said,

"Would you like to tell us your story now Pat?"

Pat, feeling the pressure of expectation to speak suddenly slumped forward and sobbed. Pat choked through a few sobs to say,

"I can't do this. I shouldn't have come."

Then he blew his nose and started to speak,

"I'm a paedophile. I'm successfully suppressed now but my life has been shit."

The others sat rigidly in silence, not sure if Pat would say more or whether they should respond. Justin later recognised that the mood was more of sympathy than horror. In the context of that meeting it was a time and place for listening and accepting.

"For years I lived with the shame of my interest in children, spying on them. I didn't do anything, just lived a wasteful, self-destructive life, in and out of studies and low-paid jobs. In my late thirties, I came under the influence of some like-minded men and started looking at child pornography. I accepted my nature and took on the attitudes that go with manipulating and abusing children. I even convinced myself that it had been me who attracted Father Stephen with my tendencies in the first place. I used the grooming techniques I had learnt from him."

He paused, blew his nose again and took a few deep breaths.

"I served time at Ararat. There I saw a psychologist who explained how when children are abused, they have a survival mechanism of turning pain into pleasure and that's why so many men who are abused become abusers themselves. They reset their sexual pleasure instincts. I still have the tendency but keep away from children and will never abuse again. I think the theory is right and now I wonder what I would be like and what sort of life I would have had if Father Stephen hadn't fucked me."

He bent forwards and rested his face in his hands then spoke again,

"I'm sorry. Please don't tell anyone."

Michael broke the oppressive mood that followed and the others relaxed under his soothing barrister tones.

"You're right Pat. I've followed the cases of several men on paedophilia charges. They get a bad press but they often have stories like yours.

I'd better tell you my story now. It's different from yours and in fact I hesitated about coming today. I thought I might be striking a discordant note or feel uncomfortable amongst you. I'm distressed to learn about the impact that Father Stephen has had, but I'm glad I've come.

First of all, I'll tell you what happened eighteen years ago. It was a busy time in my life, a time when I was working long hours doing back to back trials and earning a bit of a reputation as a go-to barrister. I was invited to be on the Council of St Crispins and although I was really too busy for the extra work this was a prestigious position and I accepted it. During my first few months on the Council I kept a low profile, learning the personalities of the headmaster and the other Council members.

It became apparent that the Council members had a role in practical matters about the running of the school but when it came to policy and image, the power lay with the Church. Bishop Clapper attended the meetings as an ex officio but the spectre of Archbishop Drumm always loomed large in the background. I was conscious that there was division within Victoria's clerical hierarchy between the majority of progressive priests and bishops on one side and Drumm's circle of conservatives who held the real power and who had the ear of the Pope. Clapper was very much a Drumm mouth piece and I learned that the same sort of conservative representation exists on the councils of most of the Catholic schools.

I had been on the Council for about six months when there appeared in the correspondence of the agenda a report that Drumm's Melbourne Response had successfully settled a complaint from a student about abuse at the hands of one Father James McPhalan in 1990. I was shocked, I had the idea that after Father Stephen, St Crispins would never again suffer the depredations of a paedophile priest. I commented on the correspondence and asked how many students had alleged abuse by Father McPhalan. Immediately a chill went around the board room, then Bishop Clapper put on an oily smile and said words to the effect that I was relatively new to Council and was probably unaware that it had long ago been agreed that Council would refer all accusations against priests to the archbishop and what a great job he was doing with the Melbourne Response. The chairman quickly moved on to the agenda.

I don't think I've ever felt so angry. I have always prided myself for showing a dignified calm in all my relationships and my work but I could barely contain my rage for the rest of that meeting."

Justin was moved by Michael's story but couldn't help being amused by the image of Michael being angry. He remembered him from school where he had the reputation of being a swot, boring the class with his long-winded answers to questions in History and Latin classes.

"I quite lost my composure and couldn't contain my outrage over the next few days. I thought of all sorts of aggressive things I could do but eventually focussed on the question of governance. The Council has a moral and legal duty to provide good governance for St Crispins and has responsibility for any matters involving legal process. I considered phoning all Council members but followed due process and phoned Joe Politti, the Chair of Council, who is also a barrister. I expressed my concerns in no uncertain terms but was disappointed with his response; he echoed Clapper's thoughts and in defending the stance of the Church pointed out that, and I quote, 'this comes from Rome'.

My wife Anne commented on my state of agitation. At first, I didn't feel inclined to discuss it with her but then decided that I would tell her the whole story including how I had been abused by Father Stephen, something which I had never mentioned to anyone before. Anticipating this confession filled me with shame but my anger was such that I was committed, regardless of her response. Anne's a strong and unemotional sort of woman. She can be quite formidable and I felt humbled as I told my story and watched her expressions of surprise. She handled it well, she said, 'I suppose that explains the dreams.'

I apparently have nightmares every now and then during which I cry out in my sleep, 'No, no, no.' I don't wake up and I never remember the dreams.

As the next Council meeting approached I steeled myself to present the legal imperative of Council to assert its governance role. Shortly beforehand, I was summoned to an interview with Clapper, Joe must have spoken to him. He asked me my views about governance and didn't try to defend the Church or put up any counter arguments. In retrospect, I can see that he was assessing if I was clubbable as a Council member, and I failed. Late in the interview he spoke sympathetically about my mistreatment at the hands of Father Stephen, something he had only recently learned about, and said it hadn't come up when I was being considered for a position on Council. They had been insensitive in exposing me to the issue of paedophilia amongst the priesthood. He put on a great performance of being kindly, I left feeling confused and uneasy

Two days before the next Council meeting Joe phoned and explained, with studied gentleness, that I was sacked. He apologised for his lack of knowledge of my personal experience of sexual abuse and was sending a letter which he hoped would counter any embarrassment. The letter was full of praise for my services to the Council and expressed the regret of all councillors that I was unable to continue serving. That dismissal could have been very embarrassing for me, but fortunately had no impact on my reputation; they have been very discrete. Since then my opinion of the Church has changed.

Forgive me for taking up so much time, I have come prepared to discuss my personal life. I have always thought of myself as unaffected by Father Stephen's abuse. At the time, he made me feel special, privileged, loved. When he was exposed my mother explained how priests love us but sometimes they go too far and that Father Stephen was very wrong in the way he treated me. I accepted this and my memory of the feelings of my thirteen-year-old self was one of sadness that the relationship was over.

I have always been strictly heterosexual and have a wonderful, loving relationship with Anne. I remained, like the rest of my family a devout Catholic and have brought up my children the same way; three of the four of them are still church-going. My two boys went to St Crispins. I have seen myself as a person who attempts to promote progressive changes from within the church and express my views within the Parish Council of which I am a member. I was initially supportive of Drumm's Melbourne Response but now see it as merely a cost-saving exercise which denies the victims of abuse their legal rights to appropriate compensation. I've been following closely the proceedings of the Royal Commission into the institutional responses to child sexual abuse and been horrified by what I've learnt. On a personal level, I see how exceptional I am, that sexual abuse has dreadful consequence for the victims and everyone close to them. I've also learnt what a hard line the Church has taken in court, that its primary motive is the protection of Church assets and care of the victims is secondary."

"Tell us about the Ellis Defence Michael," Gerard interjected

"Ah Yes," Michael replied. "John Ellis, a lawyer, suffered abuse at the hands of Father Aidan Duggan in the nineteen seventies when he was a choir boy. In 2006 the NSW Supreme Court allowed Ellis to sue the trustees of the Church for the archdiocese of Sydney. The Church took the case to the NSW Court of Appeal arguing that priests are not employees and hence the Church cannot be sued for crimes committed by priests. The Church won. Ellis appealed to the High Court and lost. So, in Australia, you can't sue the Catholic Church for any crime a priest commits."

"You can sue the Catholic Church anywhere else in the world and the Church has paid out hundreds of millions in the USA but because of the Ellis Defence the Church has saved millions in Australia," said Gerard.

"Yes," nodded Michael. "In Australia, you can sue the Anglican Church or the Salvation Army, or any other church but not the Catholic Church."

This legalistic conversation between two of the men was not the direction Justin had anticipated but it gave him a sense of relief. It was rational and therefore less traumatic than the personal stories. Those stories had left Justin paralysed and exhausted with rage but listening to Michael and Gerard converse gave some focus to his anger. Michael continued,

"I'm conscious that I'm talking too much but there's something else I want to tell you about. I read with interest Myron Downy's testimony at the Royal Commission. He is the current headmaster at St Crispins; I know him, he's a good man. He was involved with the compensation of victims of McPhalan. Under Archbishop Drumm's instruction, the school contracted the solicitors Duffy and McCord who have been doing work for the Church since the nineteen twenties. Rachael Zydrid from Duffy and McCord met with the victims in their homes, ostensibly to arrange compensation and counselling. In practice, she was gauging how they would stand up in court as witnesses and intimidating them by threatening them with the consequences of not accepting the Church's deals. Downy got wind of this and stuck his neck out by sacking Duffy and McCord. I see this as an example of the difference between the laity and the Church hierarchy when it comes to dealing with the matter of priest child abuse."

He paused and Peter took the opportunity to ask what probably all the others were thinking.

"What do you think now Michael about how Father Stephen affected you?"

"I'm exceptional and very fortunate because I wasn't damaged in the way that most victims are. I ask myself, was it my nature to cope with the abuse the way I did? Were my parents particularly successful in how they supported me? Was I attached to the Church enough to counteract the harm that Father Stephen did? I now struggle with my commitment to the Church. For most of my life it has been my rock, the centre of my spirituality but now I realise I have been duped. It's like finding out that your dearly loved father is a monster. In the past, I accepted the view that

Father Stephen was a rotten apple, someone whom we should pray for. Anne still thinks of the paedophile priests that way and that is the attitude that has been promoted by the Church. But no, the church hierarchy is the problem, not individual priests."

He turned to Peter,

"Thank you for your information about the impact of celibacy Peter, that's something I didn't understand before. My creeping disillusionment has been about the misdirection of the authority of the Church, I now believe that the Church, and by that I mean the Pope, has to declare that crimes committed by priests will be dealt with by the police. Perhaps he should also declare an end to celibacy."

There was a sense of 'rounding up' of the afternoon's conversations in Michael's last statement. It was a pleasant fantasy that the Pope might change things, even if they didn't believe it. Justin noticed Finn sitting opposite, still rigid and glaze-eyed as he had been for most of the afternoon. He asked him,

"Do you want to say something Finn?"

Silence, as if he had not heard Justin. He tried again,

"Finn. Do you want to tell us about your life?"

Finn surfaced from some deep place and said,

"Nuh."

At that moment, Justin remembered another image from his school days. He was good at blotting out memories of Father Stephen but the incident he remembered was the look of delight on the face of thirteen-year-old Finn when Father Stephen surprised him with a birthday cake in the class room at the end of a drama class. The memory brought tears to his eyes. He suspected that all the others, like him, had no need to hear Finn's story, that they had already filled in with their imagination the gaps between their school days and now.

Peter offered tea and coffee but the offer provided the excuse for all the men to do what they wanted to do, and that was to leave. They all thanked Justin for arranging the meeting, except for Finn, and Frank in particular was effusive in his thanks. Frank said the meeting had given him some ideas to work on. Justin helped Peter to clean up then left, taking Finn with him.

During the train and tram journeys back to St Kilda, Justin agonised over the meeting; he couldn't help thinking that it had been a pointless exercise in stirring up issues which would have better been left at rest. They had all been damaged, to different extents, and now forty-five years later none of them was going to make any significant change to the patterns of his life. Would any of them feel better on a personal level as a result of the meeting? Probably not. Justin himself was experiencing anger like he had never felt before; his stomach muscles were tight, he kept clenching and unclenching his fists and he felt like punching through the train window. He could not look at Finn because his passivity worsened this rage and he was afraid that he would say something hurtful. When they got off the tram at St Kilda, Justin walked all the way back to the Gatwick with Finn. This was an unnecessary gesture but Justin needed a clear end point to his task, his responsibility in delivering Finn back to his home, so that he could then indulge fully in his own disturbed feelings.

He walked briskly back to his flat, oblivious of the human energy pumped out by the youth culture of Chapel Street and the glamour of Toorak Road. His flat offered no comfort; he could not sit or eat and his most calming music seemed to mock him. He eventually went for a run around the cold, dark streets of Toorak, pushing himself to a state of physical exhaustion then showered and sat in an arm chair. He sat there for a long time, willing his mind to be calm and it dawned upon him that his rage was more than just a response to the information about the crimes of the Catholic Church, this was an inner rage, something personal and deeper. What had upset him most that afternoon was Glen's description of feeling Father Stephen's beard against his skin. That horrified Justin; the memory of a touch must be as powerfully subliminal as the memory of a smell. As he sat there he found himself placing his hands on his hips, pressing on them, an automatic action triggered by Glen's memory. From that gesture emerged a memory that Justin had felt that hand pressure like that on his hips before.

He took a deep gasp, audible in the silence of his flat, followed the by a sense of revelation. Was that it, was he remembering Father Stephen grasping his hips from behind?

Justin stilled his mind, permitting himself to remember. Following the crisis of Danny's death, he had told his parents, and himself, that he was not badly affected by Father Stephen, the alcohol had blurred any unpleasant memories. That narrative made him feel proud, superior to the others but the remembered feeling of hands grasping his hips was real. That night Justin had his recurring dream of the burning church; he wasn't surprised.

8

During the next few days, Justin re-established his routines of music, reading and meditation and immersed himself in simple domestic chores such as working in his vegetable garden. By concentrating on each minute of each task he achieved the relaxation he was seeking. As he walked to the Dandenong Market on a bitterly cold morning he reflected on his life in a new light, thinking of himself as a person who had adapted to deep trauma rather than someone who had merely accepted eccentricity. Did it change the person he was? At his age was any change possible? If he had failed at intimate relationships as a result of psychological damage, so much time had passed and so much energy had gone into accepting himself, was he not a success as an individual? Was there any point in exposing himself to the probings of a psychologist?

A week after the meeting, Justin phoned Peter, Frank, Glen, Gerard, Pat and Michael. For himself Justin, thought that the meeting had been a negative experience but the six men were all grateful that he had arranged it. They wanted to meet again but not talk about Father Stephen next time. Their conversations touched on a variety of topics; Frank wanted Justin to visit him in Perth, Peter wondered if there was anything they could do for Finn and Pat gushed about his gratitude that the meeting had taken place. Michael spoke at length about the Royal Commission into institutional responses to child sexual abuse and was hoping that it would recommend a legislated cancelling of the Ellis Defence. Gerard praised Justin for arranging the meeting and spoke with great insight about its usefulness for each one of the men who attended. When Justin said that they were all too old to make any significant changes in their lives he agreed but spoke of the value they could derive from obtaining peace and acceptance about themselves. Then he added,

"Justin, I have been thinking that I should say something to you about the way you were affected by Father Stephen. Do you think you might have repressed memories?"

In the moment before he answered Gerard, Justin passed through phases of shock, then denial, then relief that there was someone with whom he could talk about it.

"Yes Gerard, I felt dreadful after the meeting then I had a memory, something I can't talk about yet. Since then I have been re-thinking my life and how it has evolved, which is possibly a consequence of repressing memories."

"Good on you Justin," Gerard replied.

"There are counsellors who can help with that sort of stuff. Let me know if you want to see someone."

The conversation with Gerard left Justin feeling comfortable with himself for the first time since the meeting. That night Justin had a dream, a significant dream, the sort that he recorded and analysed. In the dream, he was part of a landscape, an Australian landscape with long views over gentle valleys filled with eucalypts. There was a strong sense of movement, as if he was flying though the landscape at a low level. In the distance, he saw the solitary figure of a man with a domed, balding head wearing an old-fashioned uniform. The feeling associated with this dream was one of sheer joy at moving through the welcoming landscape and the feeling persisted when he woke from the dream. He recognised the dream as a message from his subconscious, that he should go walking in an Australian landscape, but he didn't know where. He could not understand the role of the distant figure in his dream but speculated that it was an older version of himself calling him forward. He dressed and put on the scarf he wore prior to performing an active imagination ritual to interpret a dream.

When he was ready, Justin lit a candle and sat in his reading chair. He closed his eyes for a while to immerse himself in the silence of the room, then opened his eyes and reached for his Icelandic scarf, ready on the table beside him. As he changed scarves he said out loud,

"I am now removing the scarf I associate with my conscious self and putting on my beautiful Icelandic scarf to enter my subconscious world."

He replaced the tartan scarf he had been wearing with a thick, woollen scarf of several natural colours which he had bought as a young man when he had travelled in Iceland, drawn there because of his love of the Icelandic sagas. He then described his dream in detail and asked,

"Is there someone there to help interpret this dream?"

As always, he heard a voice as soon as he finished his question.

"Yes Justin. I'm here."

It was a deep, educated, female voice which Justin recognised immediately.

"Briony! Lovely to hear from you again. But I'm surprised that you have come, you're the historian. Why you?"

The voice of Briony replied,

"There is an historic context to the dream and that's why I'm here. What do you make of the dream?'

"My subconscious is telling me to go for a walk in an Australian bushland setting, but I don't know where. And who is the man?"

"Can you recognise him Justin?"

"No. Is he an older version of me?"

"No; he is an historic character. That's why I'm here."

"Of course, but I can't recognise him."

"Come on Justin. Who is a historic character you associate with a long walk in Australia?"

Justin struggled to think of the person. Burke and Wills, Giles and Leichardt came to mind, but they explored desserts, this landscape was different.

"Help me Briony; I can't get it."

"Remember the book you bought yourself, over twenty years ago, about a long walk in Victoria."

"Yes. I've got it. The Major Mitchell Trail. The figure in the dream was Major Mitchell. Thanks Briony."

"A pleasure Justin."

"I love the idea of doing the Major Mitchell Trail; I'll do it as soon as I can."

After resting with his eyes closed for a while Justin changed scarves, blew out the candle, wrote up the dream and its interpretation then went to his book shelf to find the book that he had almost forgotten. It described the route Major Mitchell had taken and how one could retrace the route today by car or on foot in Victoria. It told the story of Major Mitchell's trek, how he had travelled down the Darling River, then up the Murray Valley to near the modern-day site of Cohuna. From there he travelled south-west through the Grampians to Portland and then north-west back to the Murray near Wangaratta. On his journey, he found rich grazing lands and was so delighted with what he saw that he called the land Australia Felix, 'Happy Australia'. Once he reported his discoveries there was a rush by pioneers to take up the valuable lands he had described.

The Major Mitchell Trail was 2,100 kilometres in length. Justin estimated that it would take him two to three months to walk it but he was energised by the thought of the walk. He already had the boots, the backpack and the cold-weather sleeping bag necessary. He bought a light-weight tent and tested it by sleeping in it for one night in his courtyard. He told Maureen his plan and agreed to phone her occasionally. Because he would be away for so long, he told Mrs Weissmann and gave her Maureen's phone number in case there were any problems with his flat while he was away. Mrs Weissmann was baffled by the thought of going for a long walk in the country during winter and surprised Justin by telling him that she would miss him. Four days after the dream Justin caught a train to Mildura to start the walk.

9

With the television going in the background, Gerard finished washing the dishes and tidying up the kitchen after his lunch. He had eaten a meat pie with sauce, a tradition he associated with football, especially on Grand Final day. If he was with others, they probably would be eating party pies at half time but today he was alone. On the television the pre-match broadcasting was coming to its end and the footballers were lining up for the national anthem when Gerard settled in his chair in front of the screen.

As Kate Ceberano, belted out Advance Australia Fair, Gerard could feel the restlessness of the capacity crowd at the M.C.G. It was not a respectful silence for the national anthem, but a barely contained desperation for the game to begin. When the siren blasted, Gerard felt tingles down his spine; his team, Hawthorn, having won the last two Grand Finals, was competing in its third Grand Final in a row. The possibility of winning another Grand Final was almost too exciting to imagine.

The ball was bounced and the players threw themselves into the game. As always at the start of a final, there was some initial scrappiness with the players so revved-up with adrenaline that they were fast but uncoordinated. It wasn't long however before Hawthorn settled down and started scoring goals, then to dominate the game. His heroes, Roughead and Rioli, were firing and Gerard completely lost himself in the game. At quarter time Hawthorn was leading the West Coast Eagles 30 to 11 having kicked five goals straight and the magic was with the Hawks. Some people would speak of football matches being 'good matches' meaning that the scores remained close throughout the match but dedicated fans like Gerard thought that was meaningless, he would rather see his team massacre the opposition. As Gerard stood at the toilet during the break, he smiled as he reflected how he could be totally consumed by a football match on today of all days.

Hawthorn started well in the second quarter but about half-way through the quarter, the West Coast Eagles pulled their way back in one of those changes that can happen in finals, when the gods seem to be on one teams side and they can do no wrong. Gerard's jubilation changed into an urge to make his team perform better, to be in front, to grasp the ball and control the Eagles. The Hawks won the quarter again and had a handy lead at half time but Gerard was relieved when the siren sounded to put an end to the Eagle's recovery, which felt stronger than the score suggested. The start of the third quarter was going to be important.

However, Gerard would not be there to see it. He collected his keys, locked the flat and walked the short distance up his street to Heidelberg Road and around the corner to the milk bar. He nodded to Ron, the store's owner, when he entered the shop and selected a small container of milk from the large fridge. Ron served two customers before Gerard, who commented that he supposed people were out to get things during the half time break. Ron said that he hadn't anyone in the shop until now, since the Grand Final started.

Gerard started walking back towards his street but instead, when he saw a gap in the traffic, crossed the main road and walked down a side street. He had gone over this walk many times in his mind and thought of the walk as a series of vulnerabilities. Crossing Heidelberg Road was one of those vulnerabilities and he was glad that the usually-busy road was so quiet; less chance that someone who knew him would recognise him. It was quiet because, of course, most of Melbourne was watching the Grand Final.

There were no people or cars moving in the side street and Gerard turned into the driveway of a house with a 'For Sale' sign in front, a house which he had determined on an earlier reconnaissance, was unoccupied. He walked down the driveway around to the back of the house and retrieved a black back pack which he had hidden behind some bushes the night before. The backpack was larger than the usual day-pack and had two separate compartments. He removed from the backpack an Akubra hat, dark sunglasses, a long-sleeved grey shirt, a black tracksuit bottom and a pair of shoes. He had bought the clothes and sunglasses from Op shops but the shoes, an inconspicuous pair of black runners, from a shopping strip in a distant suburb where he was sure there were no CCTV cameras. Until now those shoes had been kept upside down in a cupboard at his flat; their soles had never touched the ground.

He was wearing jeans, a short-sleeved checked shirt and brown shoes and he changed from these into the Op shop clothes and the new shoes, then carefully put his other clothes into the smaller section of the back pack. Finally, he put the back pack on his back, which was heavy and uncomfortable from the thick metal pipe it contained and walked to the front of the house. After determining that there were no cars or people about, he walked out into the side street and continued his journey away from Heidelberg Road.

With the Akubra hat pulled down firmly on his head, Gerard walked north towards the railway line. He was unaccustomed to wearing sunglasses and the world looked different. He enjoyed the subtle differences between the suburban landscapes on the two sides of Heidelberg Road. In his part of Alphington, the emphasis was on trees and architecture but here there was a more domestic feel. The houses were older but renovated and the front yards spoke of young families, with cubbies and tree houses. Some people had made fish ponds or planted veggie gardens in their front yards; they probably voted Greens.

At the end of the street, Gerard turned west along the walking track beside the railway line. There was a woman working in the community garden and he tilted his head slightly so that the brim of his hat hid his face. He walked through an underpass to the quieter side of the railway line as he approached the Fairfield shopping centre. This was another point of vulnerability. Here, someone who knew him, could drive past and recognise him, or even worse, a pedestrian could come up and speak to him. If that happened, he would have to abandon his plan and return home. Even with his face obscured someone might recognise him by his posture or his gait. As he crossed Station Street, he concentrated on holding himself more erect than usual and took longer strides, deliberately slowing his walk. He reassured himself that he was just a daggy old man out for a walk and that no one was interested in him anyway.

He continued his walk north of the railway line beyond the Fairfield Station. The street scape changed again; now there were Tibetan prayer flags, the balustrades favoured by Italian immigrants and un-mowed nature strips. It was down-market but more eclectic that Alphington. He crossed back south of the railway line at the Dennis Station through an underpass. Some of the underpasses had CCTV cameras but Gerard had made sure that this one didn't. A little further along he turned into the northern end of Bolton Road.

He looked at his watch; the walk had taken him thirty-two minutes. On the previous three occasions he had walked this route it had taken him thirty-four minutes to reach this point, but it was understandable that today he had walked slightly faster. The timing was good, he would be at 17 Bolton Road early during the third quarter of the Grand Final. Bolton Road was very quiet with no moving cars or people anywhere. In front of number 17, there were more cars than usual. The old house at the front of the block was occupied by several young men who neglected the garden, possibly students. They probably had their mates around today to watch the Grand Final. As Gerard walked down the long driveway beside the house, he heard a collective cheer coming from inside the house, confirming this idea. Gerard observed that, as usual, the blinds of all the windows on the driveway side of the house were drawn but he kept his hat tilted to that side anyway.

When he reached the granny flat at the rear of the block, Gerard avoided its front and slipped down the narrow space beside the flat and into its backyard. He peeped through the kitchen window and could see Father Stephen seated with his back to him, watching television. The volume was turned up loud and Gerard could hear the roar of a football crowd and the excited voice of a football commentator. He walked past the window into the small gap behind a garden shed near the back door. There he removed the backpack, put on a pair of rubber gloves and took the metal pipe out of the back pack. He rehearsed in his mind what he would do during the next few minutes.

He walked over to the power box near the back door, opened its door, turned the main power switch off and closed the door. Then he quickly moved back to his hiding place behind the shed. He could imagine Father Stephen's consternation as the television went dead. When Gerard had known him as a boy Father Stephen had been a mad, keen Hawthorn supporter and probably still was. He would be as excited about Hawthorn's third Grand Final as Gerard was. Once Father Stephen noticed that all the power was out in the house, Gerard anticipated that he would do one of two things, he would walk out of his flat and go out to the street to see if the whole neighbourhood was suffering a power outage, or he would go to the power box. After what seemed to Gerard a long time, but was probably less than a minute, Father Stephen came out through the back door and went straight to the power box.

This was the moment Gerard had thought about dozens of times and knew that he had to move fast. It would not take Father Stephen long to scan the dials and switches in the power box, notice that the main switch was turned off and turn it on again, then probably look around before he returned inside. As Father Stephen opened the power box door Gerard walked quickly and as silently as possible towards him, raised the pipe with both hands and just as Father Stephen was turning on the switch brought the pipe down as hard as he could on the back of his head. Father Stephen dropped with a thud onto the ground and lay motionless.

At that point, Gerard had an overwhelming urge to drop the pipe and run away. He said quietly to himself,

"Calm down. Take a few breaths and think."

He had felt a crack when he struck the head and there was a large, bruised swelling at the site but he couldn't be sure Father Stephen was dead. He placed the pipe against the side of Father Stephen's head to measure the distance, raised the pipe and struck again, this time connecting with the rough edge of the pipe, which sank several centimetres into the skull. There was a splash of blood followed by a continuous ooze but the spray was away from Gerard and had not gone onto his clothes.

Feeling calmer now, Gerard wiped the blood from the pipe on Father Stephen's trousers, walked over to his back pack and put the pipe into the large section of the back pack. He took a short, sharp knife from the backpack, returned to the body and rolled it onto its back. Next, he pulled up the jumper and shirt to expose the pale expanse of Father Stephen's abdomen. Gerard place his gloved, left hand on the soft skin and cut a line about five centimetres long into the flesh. He had practised this cutting several times already on the skin of legs of pork and knew how large to make the letters he planned to cut and, as he had also anticipated, the warm human skin was softer and more movable than the pork skin so he had to keep the skin tight with his left hand. There was less oozing of blood than he expected but by the time he had finished his work his gloved left hand was covered with blood.

When Gerard had finished, he put the knife and the soiled gloves into the back pack and put on another clean pair of gloves. He put the back pack on and walked over to the body. This was a time that, during his planning, he had judged as critical; a time to carefully take stock before he left. He had not left anything behind and there was no blood on his clothing. The back door and the power box doors were still open, that was something he had not thought of. He was a tidy person and felt the urge to close both but reasoned that there was no need to do that, there was no purpose in misleading the police about how he had committed his crime. During the weeks after the murder he often thought of that decision with a feeling of pride, he had not given the police that clue that he was a tidy person.

Gerard walked back out along the driveway, another moment of vulnerability in case someone walking along the street saw him but that did not happen. He could hear the football on the television in the house and walked quietly past the drawn blinds of the front room to the front door. He listened for a moment to make sure that there was no one in the hall behind the door then took from his pocket with his gloved hand a folded piece of paper and slipped it under the door. He walked away from the door and out into the street, removing his gloves and putting them into his pocket. He walked north along Bolton Road, the way he had come with his hat tilted towards the houses he passed, reminding himself to walk slowly and calmly. Once again, there were no moving cars or people in the street. At the end of Bolton Road, he walked around the block and down a parallel road to Heidelberg Road. He stood behind a pole for a while, waiting until the road was clear of cars then crossed to the park lands beside the Merri Creek on the other side.

He did not want to be seen south of Heidelberg Road in his murder garb. A young man rode quickly past him on a bicycle but no one else saw him before he made it to a cluster of trees and changed from his grey shirt into a blue T-shirt. It was inevitable that he would be seen by a few people in this park but only passed a woman walking a dog and a mother pre-occupied with her small child as he walked towards the Yarra River. He walked east along a track beside the Yarra, under the Pipe Bridge to a bushy area out of view of the bridge. After pausing to make sure that there was no one on the track who could see him he climbed through the bushes to a hidden space near the water's edge.

Gerard removed his hat, sunglasses and his outer clothes and put them in the small section of his back pack, then dressed with his original clothes. He removed the container of milk and put it aside. The back pack was heavy with the pipe inside but he cut holes in it to make sure it sank easily. After carefully watching and listening for movements on the track, he tossed the backpack and was pleased to watch it sink rapidly from view. From his pocket he took out his old transistor radio with an attached ear plug and turned it on; the Grand Final was twenty minutes into the last quarter. Gerard drank the milk he had bought and settled in to listen to the rest of the match. With Hawthorn so far in front at that stage they were just coasting, the final scores were 107 to 61.

When the siren sounded Gerard crushed the empty milk container and put it in his pocket and put the transistor in his other pocket. He crept back through the scrub and onto the track back under the Pipe Bridge. Hoping that none of his neighbours were about, he walked along paths skirting the Fairfield Boathouse and up to the road at the top of the hill. From there he walked down a road back towards the river, around a block and into his own street. He was nearly at his flat when a car emerged from the driveway with Dave, his neighbour from the flat next door, looking out of the window while he reversed. Gerard had anticipated meeting a neighbour and had a story ready about going for a walk after the big game. He smiled at Dave then raved about Hawthorn's straight kicking and command of the game. He was acting but it wasn't difficult because he was so excited anyway about Hawthorn's victory. Back inside his flat he dropped the empty milk container into the bin and his mission was complete; stage one anyway. Shortly afterwards, he drove to his son's home for dinner.

10

Justin did not enjoy the first few days of the Major Mitchell Trail. After leaving Mildura much of the early part was along the Sturt Highway, which was monotonous and intimidating, with trucks regularly passing at high speeds. Someone threw an empty beer can at him from a passing car, striking him on the back of the head. His legs were accustomed to long periods of walking but his shoulders ached from the back pack for the first week. For the first few nights he slept poorly until he became used to his thin sleeping mat. It was however the psychological, rather than the physical discomfort which disturbed him most. At a time when he wanted to empty his mind, he could not help returning to the question of what sort of a person he was. The comfort and stability of his slowly-built self-image had been shattered by the meeting.

He sought distraction in the small towns along the route. He would linger in the coffee shops listening to the local people talking at length about the small issues of their lives. He enjoyed the accents and listened for the plural 'yous' which he decided was better than the urban plural 'you' because it added meaning to the language. People would ask him what he was doing and he found, to his surprise, that no one had heard of the Major Mitchell Trail. He rarely took up friendly invitations to engage in conversation and he was left in peace. He usually found a place out of view to camp overnight but would occasionally stay in a hotel or a cheap motel and eat pub meals, which he found were too large for him.

After ten days he reached Cohuna, an important landmark where he turned away from the Murray River and started the long walk across Victoria's heartland towards Portland. By then, he was used to his back pack and felt that he could walk forever. The landscape became more interesting and he looked forward to interactions with people he met, their conversations and kindness, and would occasionally accept their offers of transport to the next town just to enjoy the conversations they could share in the vehicle.

His anguished existential ponderings eventually petered out but then he found himself thinking about Father Stephen. He imagined visiting him at his home in Westgarth and talking with him. He rehearsed in his mind the different approaches he would take and the way the conversations could turn on themes of damaged lives. At times, he spoke out aloud in the silence of the bush, listing victim impacts and at other times dwelt on forgiveness, picturing a repentant Father Stephen crying, on his knees, begging for forgiveness. On another day, Justin barely noticed the forty kilometres of landscape he crossed as he thought through anger-filled confrontations and saw himself physically attacking Father Stephen. He came to hate the way Father Stephen was taking up so much space in his mind but at the same time sensed that it was inevitable, something he had to go through.

Near Stawell, he changed a flat tyre for three women who had been looking for native orchids in the forest. They showed him some of the spectacular sun orchids and spider orchids they had found. Justin found something magical in the generosity of that shared experience and the feeling remained with him, breaking the cycle of his obsessive thinking about Father Stephen. He took Major Mitchell's side route from the trail to climb Mt William and was delighted to find orchids all along the route.

He enjoyed the solitude of the trail as he passed through the forests to the west of the Grampians. The wattles were in flower and he loved the bands of yellow they created in the under-story amongst the smoky greens of the bush. He felt privileged to see the rare red-tailed black cockatoos shrieking in the River Red Gums near Harrow. Cars passed him but he went a week without speaking to anyone.

He spent one day thinking about friendship. From having no friends at all for years and by his own choice, he now wanted to re-establish friendships with Peter and Gerard and, if possible with Frank. Why was this? It was because he had enjoyed the feelings of warmth and acceptance when he was with them. Despite the years that had passed, they knew and accepted him, and liked him and he liked them. It was his fault that their friendships had lapsed but they did not blame him or judge him, they welcomed him back.

So why had he separated himself from his friends in the past? There was a pattern which came from him; he would gradually withdraw by ceasing to communicate and if they communicated, be brief and unresponsive. There were no dramas, no arguments or crises, just gradual withdrawals. Some friends had expressed the hurt they felt at his withdrawal, others just disappeared from his life. This pattern went back all the way to his teens and he did it regularly in his twenties, that was a socially busy time with University then the fast living of his working life. At that time, his cutting off of friends was easy and became habitual. Part of the pattern was to identify a fault in a friend, something to focus on when the time came to end the friendship. He remembered examples of these faults, trivial things such as failing to reciprocate shouts of beer, self-centredness, lack of punctuality. They were all common human failings, the sorts of characteristics that friends accepted in each other, but for Justin they were his justifications for withdrawing. It was the same with Rebecca, Heather and Morag, the three women with whom he had his longest relationships. Rebecca, he judged to be superficial, Heather class-conscious and Morag controlling. Even with his sister Maureen he clung to a nugget of disapproval that she was materialistic. He was the problem, he stored up these judgements to allow himself to feel better when he withdrew.

These friends and lovers, they were all good people. They were the sorts of people who could still be close friends if he let them. He made himself miserable as he thought of what might have been. Particularly painful were the memories of incidents when he had let down his girlfriends, the times when they, in various ways, had appealed to him for emotional support and he had blocked them. He owed them apologies.

So why did he sabotage his relationships? He couldn't 'think' that through, no one has a rational reason for wrecking friendships. To take the process further would mean speculating about his psychological processes. The simple answer was that he couldn't trust people as a result of his abuse by Father Stephen and perhaps that simple answer was the best answer. Since his adolescence he had built up layers of self-image and consequently ways of dealing with the world, but perhaps it was all self-deception. If he peeled away the layers, he might find at the core a frightened little boy trying to protect himself.

He had come to this point of speculating many times before. He had read books on psychology, spirituality and philosophy and attempted to see the wold in different ways. Modern novels and films were full of stories of catharses, stories which finished on the theme of 'now I understand, I will change my life and live happily ever after', but that doesn't happen. He was angry to have arrived at this point once again. In a few years, he would be sixty. Whoever made any significant changes at that age? And who cared?

These speculations left him emotionally exhausted and nauseated to the point that he couldn't eat that night. The next morning however, he woke with a different outlook which went something like this, 'forget the psychology, you want to have friends so just be more open with yourself and don't look for faults in others'.

The Trail continued through a softer and greener landscape and as he approached the coast near the Glenelg River, he felt like an explorer himself. On the last day of September, he walked into Portland, feeling uncomfortable to be back in such an urban environment. He was keen to be back on the open road so he left Portland early the next morning. He was now on the last leg of his journey, the long strip running north and east across central Victoria back to the Murray River. There was an end in sight now but he regretted it, he wanted the journey to continue for longer than the estimated month he would take from Portland.

Two nights out of Portland, while camping near Heywood, his tent was flooded in a torrential downpour, soaking his sleeping bag and most of his clothes. He started walking to warm up and soon found a bed and breakfast place to stay. There he was spoiled by the elderly couple who ran the place, who insisted that they wash and dry his wet things for him. After that Justin slowed his walking pace and spent more time lingering in cafes, willing to tell strangers more about himself and what he was doing than he usually did. He found himself thinking about his time on South Uist, and in particular, Morag. He recalled, in great detail, conversations they had had and the moods that passed between them. He was surprised by the detail of these memories and attributed them to the experience of walking alone for so long. He enjoyed this process of recalling, even the bad memoires.

11

Detective Inspector Brian Hannay and his partner Craig Theophanous looked over the scene at the back of Father Stephen's flat, then stepped under the blue police tape and walked over to stand beside the body.

"So, what do you reckon?" Brian asked Craig.

Craig anticipated the question, looked forward to it, and took a few more seconds to gaze around. They had been working together for nearly a year now and had settled into the sort of relationship Craig had always hoped for with a senior partner; something like the relationships he had seen in crime films during his youth and which had made him want to be a detective. Brian was old-school and initially showed his contempt for the university-educated younger generation. He found reasons to make digs at Craig about his Greek ancestry, even though he was third generation Australian. Craig had handled this well and gained Brian's respect with his insights when they investigated the Merri Creek murder. Now they worked well together, as a twenty first century variation on the theme of good cop/bad cop. Craig replied, his eyes tracking the places he described,

"He's inside, probably watching the Grand Final, when the power goes off. He checks a few switches and works out that it is not just the television, but the power to the flat. He walks out the back door to the power box, opens it and looks for a blown fuse. The murderer had turned off the power switch. Look. It's still turned off."

The power box's door was open and Craig pointed to the switch.

"The murderer hits him on the back of the head and the priest drops, no signs of a fight, no blood spattered around. He was probably hiding behind that shed and came over quickly as soon as the priest turned his back to him. So, he drops to the ground."

Craig bent over the body.

"Several blows to the head, making sure he's dead. A blunt object, possibly round, like a metal pipe. You can see a scalloped indentation on the side of his head there. Then he's rolled him over onto his back, pulled up his shirt and done his handy work with a knife."

Craig looked closely at the letters carved across Father Stephen's abdomen spelling out, in capital letters, PEDOPHILE. He continued,

"Jeez he's a cool one. The letters are all the same size, evenly spaced. He took his time and did it carefully. Does this priest have form?"

"Yes. He's done time for abusing boys at one of the Catholic Schools. I think it was St Crispins. What do you think of the spelling?"

"Well, he's left out the 'A' so he's not all that clever. But I suppose there are lots of people who can't spell paedophile."

At that moment, Senior Constable Janet Mulheron from the local branch returned. She had taken the call, spoken with the boys and sealed off the area before calling Homicide. She was feeling confident because she had something important to report and wasn't going to be intimidated or give the impression of being over-helpful.

"Found anything Senior Constable?" Brian asked

"There's a Mrs Verrell, three doors down, who saw a man worth investigating. She saw this man, who she's never seen before, walk past the front of her house. She's not sure of the time but it was late in the third quarter. He had a small backpack on his back."

"Good description?"

"He was wearing a light-grey, long-sleeved shirt, an Akubra-style hat, black track-suit pants. Didn't see much of his face because of the hat and he was wearing sun glasses but he looked middle aged. She was curious about him because you wouldn't expect anyone to be walking around during the Grand Final."

"Which way was he walking?"

"North. Away for here."

Brian paused, then surprised Craig by saying,

"Well done Senior Constable. Did the boys leave the path here at all?"

"No, they stayed on the path and kept well back from the body. One of them took a photo with his mobile phone."

"The dickhead. Did he put it on Facebook?"

Janet smiled

"No, I've checked his phone and deleted the photo. They're a nice bunch, they've been freaked out by finding the body."

"And they found the note just after the Grand Final?"

"Yes. One of them had been busting to go to the toilet and went just after the siren and saw the note under the door when he came out of the toilet."

Brian looked at the note through the clear plastic bag in which Janet had placed it. Spelt out in capital letters was 'YOUR NEIGHBOUR AT THE BACK HAS BEEN MURDERED'. He turned to Craig and said,

"So, he wanted us to know straight away. It was important to him that we got his message."

Craig said,

"Perhaps he's got some clever alibi worked out and wanted the body found quickly."

Brian grunted, a sign of approval.

The forensic team arrived and Brian and Craig left. They spoke with Mrs Verrell, who was a shy and anxious woman but a good observer. Brian let Craig ask the questions.

*****

Forensics added little to what Brian and Craig had already figured out. Father Stephen had been struck twice on the head, each blow producing skull fractures and major brain injuries. There were rust fragments in his hair confirming that the murder weapon was metal. There were no recent finger prints on the power box switches, the note or the body. There was evidence of someone standing behind the shed but no foreign soil particles from shoes. All this confirmed the impression of careful planning. They decided to suppress any mention that a word that was cut into Father Stephen after his death. The Press reported that Father Stephen had spent time in jail as a paedophile. When the suspect's appearance was reported, a reliable witness came forward to report that she had seen the same man walking near the Fairfield Station on the afternoon of the murder.

When they looked at a list of the boys whom Father Stephen was known to have assaulted, Brian recognised the name of Pat Gilroy. He had had dealings with him in the past. Brian and Craig visited Pat at his home where he very quickly became a sobbing mess. He described seeing Father Stephen and following him to his home, then went on to describe the meeting with the other men at Peter McBride's place and that he had told them about finding Father Stephen's home. They regarded the eight men who attended the meeting as prime suspects and set about checking where they were at the time of the murder. Pat, Michael, Glen and Peter had alibis; they were watching the Grand Final with other people. Frank was in Perth. It took them a few days to find Finn. He confessed to murdering Father Stephen by stabbing him but by that stage in the interview, Brian and Craig had already realised that he was brain-damaged. He had vague memories of the meeting at Peter's place but couldn't recall who attended.

That left Gerard Connolly and Justin Collins. Their investigations had made them interested in this pair and Brian had made up names for them before he met them; the Broken Rites zealot, and the crackpot hermit. They planned their visits carefully, with search warrants ready should they be necessary.

Gerard looked surprised when they arrived at his door, but he invited them in and offered them coffee, instant coffee, which they refused.

"I thought you might want to talk to me," he said. "Is it about the murder of the priest?"

Craig registered the impersonality of his question. Brian rapidly assessed the ambience of the flat; neat and clean, sparsely decorated, cooking smells. The home of a well- organised, single man.

Gerard's question was an opening for Brian to put him off balance with something like, 'and why do you say that' but Gerard's lack of defenciveness prompted another approach. Brian said,

"Yes, we are making enquiries. We understand you are on the Council of Broken Rites?"

"Yes I am. Father Stephen's name came up at one of our meetings recently. I suppose you know Father Stephen was a rapist priest?"

"Yes, we do," Craig said, noting the easy way that Gerard dropped the expression 'rapist priest', such a horrible description but more accurate than the softer sounding 'paedophile priest' which rolled so gently off the tongue. Brian was pleased Craig took the initiative; his instinct was that Craig's softly softly approach was appropriate here. Craig continued,

"How did his name come up?"

"Father Stephen went to jail for raping boys at the schools where he taught. I was one of the ones he raped at St Crispins. Two men have recently come forward whom he raped when he was teaching in Adelaide. We are doing some counselling with them and, if the men want it, we will assist them in taking legal action against him. We thought he was still in jail but I recently found out that he was out, and living in Westgarth. I would have preferred to see the bastard back in jail."

"How did you find out he was out of jail?"

"I met a former school friend who saw him going into a flat where, presumably, he lives. Lived."

Gerard corrected himself, not with the sense of respect that people often show when they put the deceased in the present tense, but with a look of disappointment. Both Craig and Brian were surprised by how forthcoming Gerard was, so early in the interview. Brian couldn't resist asking the question,

"Do you remember the address?"

"It's Bolton Road, I can't remember the number but I've got it written down, it's in the minutes of a Broken Rites meeting."

"Are you sure that's where he lived?"

"Pretty sure. My friend who saw him go in checked the letter box and there was mail addressed to him. I actually drove over to have a look at the place, it's a granny flat down the back. I shouldn't have done that, we record their addresses but we never approach the rapist priests. I didn't see him."

By this stage, Brain had concluded that Gerard was innocent or very, very clever. He wondered what Craig was thinking. He asked Gerard,

"Have you ever been back to Bolton Road since then?"

Gerard looked him in the eye and said,

"No. I only went there the once."

There was a brief silence. Brian felt uncomfortable, the feeling he got when the person he was interviewing gained control of the process. Craig gently insinuated another question.

"The friend who told you he saw Father Stephen going in to flat. Could you

tell us about him?"

"Pat Gilroy. He's a nice guy, works as a bar tender in Collingwood. I think he's gay.

If you interview him, go easy on him. He's flakey. He suffered badly from the abuse."

"Yeah, we met him," Craig said. "We could see the whole business is pretty traumatic for him. He told us about the meeting you had. How many of you were there?"

"There were eight of us from St Crispins, and Mrs Dowling. She's the mother of Kevin, another one us from St Crispins, who recently killed himself. It was one of the saddest meetings I've ever been to. I'm dealing with this stuff all the time through

Broken Rites but it is still devastating to hear people speak of how their lives have been affected by being raped in their childhoods."

"What was the reaction when Pat said that he had seen Father Stephen?" Craig asked.

Gerard thought for a moment, then said,

"Everyone was a bit stunned. I think they were having memories of how he treated us."

"Did anyone say anything in particular about him, or about going to his flat?"

"No. There was just this sense of resignation that the bastard was free. Then we got on with it."

Gerard looked at both Brian and Craig and said,

"And I'm guessing that all eight of us are suspects because we found out where he lives."

The pause was brief, but in that gap Brian remembered past dealings with suspects who had been "helpful". Most people are very helpful with the police, a helpfulness born of fear regardless of how innocent they are. In two cases, he had been tricked by people who had been very helpful and were in fact very clever. They both got away with murder, one from lack of evidence and one that didn't even go to court. If there was any pattern in their behaviour, it was that they were very chatty, keen to win you over to their personal views. That wasn't the feeling he was getting with Gerard but, as a mentor for Craig, he was going to be very careful with this character. Craig filled the gap with a smile and a gentle reining in of the issue.

"Yes. We will be making routine enquiries about anyone who knew where Father Stephen lived. Can you tell us what you were doing on the afternoon of the Grand Final?"

They asked Gerard about his movements on the Saturday and looked through his wardrobe. All his shirts were bluish with either check or stripe patterns. They were arranged with the short-sleaved shirts separated from the long-sleaved shirts and all facing the same way. He had two hats, a white terry towelling one and a natural coloured straw hat. As they moved around the house Craig asked most of the questions,

"Do you remember if Father Stephen was keen on football?"

Gerard winced at the mention of his name.

"When he was our teacher, he was a mad keen Hawthorn supporter. He would make a fuss about Hawthorn on the Monday mornings if they won on the weekend. Most of us lived in Hawthorn and barracked for Hawthorn too."

In the kitchen, Brian picked up a container of pills and said to Gerard,

"I take these. Have you got arthritis?"

"Yeah. I played a lot of football in my youth, my knees are bad."

Brian continued,

"How long have you been involved with Broken Rites?"

"Fifteen years now."

"What prompted you to join them?"

"I'm an alcoholic and joined AA eighteen years ago. I haven't had a drink since then, but through AA, I became a mentor and learned a bit about the psychological aspects of childhood abuse.

That lead me to Broken Rites, I've been on their Council for nine years."

Brian nodded and seemed to lose interest. Craig took this as a signal to get back to their planned approach,

"Could you do some writing for us?"

Gerard looked surprised.

"OK. What do you want me to write?"

Craig handed him a notebook and pen and Gerard sat at a table.

"Just write out the letters of the alphabet in capital letters."

Gerard took the pen and wrote out the letters. He put the letters, evenly spaced in five rows on the notebook and handed it back to Craig.

"Thank you. Now could you have a look at these photos. They're a bit gruesome, they're photos of Father Stephen taken at the mortuary."

Craig took three enlarged photos from an envelope and handed them to Gerard. The first two photos were of Father Stephen's face and Gerard showed no expression when he looked at them. The next photo showed Father Stephen's abdomen with the letters cut into it. They were watching Gerard closely when he looked at the photo. It was slight, only a small contraction of the muscles of his forehead, but he definitely flinched. Then he pushed the photos away and said,

"That's horrible."

Brian and Craig left shortly afterwards. They took with them Gerard's computer hard drive and his mobile phone to be checked by their IT specialists. Gerard was reluctant to hand over his phone but conceded without them needing to produce their search warrant. They promised him it would be returned to him in a few days. He had been very quiet since seeing the photo.

They checked with Gerard's neighbour David, who confirmed that Gerard had spoken to him as he was driving out of the flats soon after the end of the football match. He told them he had never seen Gerard so excited and that it was hard to get away from him because he wanted to talk about Hawthorn's victory. David also told them he was certain that Gerard's car had been in its allocated parking place for the whole afternoon because David could see the space from his front window and would have noticed, and been surprised, if it wasn't there during the Grand Final.

They checked with the milk bar owner, who remembered Gerard being one of the locals who came to the shop during half time. He couldn't remember what Gerard was wearing but he could tell them that it was the same sort of stuff that he usually wears and he wasn't wearing a back pack.

Next, they drove along Heidelberg Road and turned into Bolton Road. They parked the car outside number 17. Craig spoke,

"Mrs Verrell lives three houses to the north, so if Connolly did it, he didn't go home the shortest way."

"No," said Brian. "But he wouldn't have come along Heidelberg Road. He's more likely to be seen that way, and the other witness had him approaching Bolton Road from near the Fairfield station. The Grand Final is a great time to commit a murder, there's hardly anyone about.

Now let's go and see how close he lives to the Yarra. That's where he'd dispose of a murder weapon."

They drove back to Alphington and down a side street near Gerard's place to the bottom of the hill where they could see the strip of forest beside the Yarra. It wasn't far. They parked the car. Craig said,

"That's a long way to walk, between half time when he was at the milk bar and the end of the match when he spoke with his neighbour. Do you think he could do it?"

Brian answered.

"Four kilometres. He could do it, if his arthritis isn't too bad. I gave him the opportunity to carry on about his arthritis, do a bit of limping for us, but he didn't. How did he go with his spelling test?"

Craig took out the notebook and a copy of the murderer's note.

"I noticed as he was writing that he did his As in the more conventional way, with a pointed top instead of a round top."

Craig looked carefully at the two pieces of writing.

"And Connolly does his Rs with the diagonal stick coming off the vertical stick, whereas our murderer has the diagonal coming out of the bulge."

Craig put away the notebook and paper.

"Another little piece of evidence in favour of him being innocent, or very clever."

Brian said,

"I thought his reaction to the belly photo was genuine."

"So did I," said Craig. "His thoughtful mood afterwards was more convincing. I think he was trying to work out who did it."

"Yeah. We should have let him keep his mobile phone for a bit longer. He might have made some interesting calls. He didn't comment on the spelling of paedophile."

"No. I think he was so shocked by the photo that he didn't notice. So what do you think?"

Brian paused. He thought Connolly was innocent but wanted to challenge Craig.

"If he is the murderer, he didn't have to tell us that he went to Bolton Road. He didn't have to tell us that Father Stephen is a keen Hawthorn supporter and therefore most probably watching the Grand Final."

"Unless he's very clever and knows that we will probably get that information by

interviewing the others.

"What about his visit to Bolton Road?"

"He's thought that the forensic team might find Bolton Road soil samples at his place, so he has an explanation."

"So, he has motive and opportunity. Let's find out more about him. Our most important suspects are those who knew where Father Stephen lived; we'll have to include the other Broken Rites Council members who found out. I've got a bad feeling about this. Everyone we talk to will suspect someone they know and because they are all secretly delighted that Father Stephen has been murdered, they won't want to incriminate anyone.

I don't think we'll get anywhere with Connolly. He reminds me of my father; he's a dry alcoholic. Alcoholics Anonymous becomes like a religion for them, makes them very straight and rigid."

– – –

After they left, Gerard made himself a cup of tea and sat, thinking about the interview. They had been gentler on him than he expected. They hadn't wanted to go over the flat forensically looking for blood, perhaps that would follow. The young one struck him as intelligent but cunning. The older one made him nervous; he would have ways of assessing suspects beyond Gerard's imagination. He spoke less but seemed to take in more. They would be skilled in picking up little clues of intonation and body language which he couldn't hide.

They would speak with the other men who attended the meeting and find out as much as they could about him. That didn't worry him; that would just confirm that he was, how he presented himself, an honest person.

They would probably want to talk to him again. If they suspected him they would have some strategy for tricking him into exposing himself. He would have to think very carefully about all possible scenarios. More likely, they would think, because of his experience with Broken Rites, that he suspected someone and was trying not to expose them. That was the image he would try to present as a way of confirming his innocence. Frank or Justin would be the best candidates. It wouldn't matter if he embarrassed them on the short term because the whole charade was going to end on Christmas Day anyway.

Overall, he thought his performance had been fairly good, but he probably talked too much. Something to avoid next time.

12

The next day, Brian and Craig went to Justin's home. He wasn't home and as they were leaving they met Mrs Weissman standing near her front door. She asked,

"Are you looking for Mr Collins?"

They introduced themselves as police officers and said they were making some routine inquiries. She looked at them suspiciously but was forthcoming,

"He has gone away for a long walk in the country."

"Did he say when he would be back?"

"No, but not for several months." Then she added,

"He gave me his sister's phone number. She might know."

She went inside and returned with a piece of paper with Maureen's phone number. They wrote it down. As they were leaving Mrs Weissman said,

"You don't want Mr Collins. He is a very good man."

Maureen was surprised to receive their call and explained that he was walking the Major Mitchell Trail. She had phone calls from him occasionally and had heard from him the previous week when he had phoned from Portland. She didn't know when he would phone again but would get him to phone them when he did.

Neither Brian nor Craig had heard of the Major Mitchell Trail. They looked up the route and estimated that he must be somewhere in Central Victoria with several weeks of walking to go. They had already learned from Peter McBride that Justin didn't have a land line or a mobile phone and left an email message but had little faith in getting a quick response. They decided to give him a few days and if they didn't hear from him, they would get a warrant and a locksmith and go over his flat.

Brian and Craig interviewed the seven other members of the Broken Rites Council, of which Gerard was a member, five men and two women. They were all polite and helpful and had Gerard's dignified and patient demeanour. They all had alibis for the Grand Final afternoon. None of them had shown to anyone else the minutes of the meeting in which Gerard reported Father Stephen's address. They spoke with admiration of Gerard and emphasised how hard he worked for Broken Rites. They impressed Brian and Craig as people with the depth and kindness that comes from deep spiritual conviction. As Brian said,

"They're the true Christians."

There was nothing of interest for them in Gerard's hard drive or his mobile phone; no suspicious deletions, no cryptic communications. By looking through the previous minutes of Broken Rites meetings they found that it was a normal routine for the Council to record reports of any paedophile priests going to, or being released from jail and, if known, where they lived. So, Gerard wasn't doing anything unusual in reporting Father Stephen's address.

They were sickened by what they learned by researching Father Stephen's career as a paedophile. He was known to have abused boys in schools in three states where he taught. He liked boys aged twelve or thirteen and was charismatic and extremely skilled at grooming them. When his predations were exposed, during the nineteen-seventies and eighties, the church moved him from a school in Sydney to St Crispins in Melbourne and then to a school in Adelaide. When some of his victims from St Crispins tried to take legal action, about fifteen years earlier, the church's lawyers intimidated them into accepting payouts on the condition of remaining silent.

In Adelaide, six former students took Father Stephen to court. The magistrate accepted the defence's proposition that the six might have conspired and held six separate trials. So, six separate juries heard the testimony of one man against Father Stephen, who denied all charges. Many of the men had mental health problems as a result of their abuse and were easily rattled by the aggressive cross examinations of the defence barristers. The result was, Father Stephen was found not guilty in all six cases.

In a later case, in 2008, he was convicted on the charges of three other pupils who came forward later and were allowed to make their cases in the same trial. He was sentenced to nine years in jail but was released after six. The church had spent millions of dollars on his defence and provided the flat in Westgarth for him rent-free.

Craig spent many hours researching Father Stephen's life. The legal records only scratched the surface, his best source of information was the research published by Broken Rites. He was known to have abused at least eighty boys at the schools. He had probably abused other children in his earlier life as a parish priest because of the way the church had moved him frequently. He left untold damage, in terms of mental health problems, drug addiction and suicides. From every class of boys that he taught there were suicides and these were continuing forty years later. Craig did the maths; an average of two suicides per year for twenty-four years; forty-eight deaths. Father Stephen could be indirectly Australia's worst mass murderer.

Craig phoned Gerard when they had finished with his phone and hard drive. He told him that someone would bring them to his house "in the next few days" but invited him to come and collect them from him at the St Kilda Road headquarters if he wanted. As he had hoped, Gerard agreed to collect them and arrived at Craig's office a few hours later.

Craig rearranged the furniture as best he could in the small space, to create an informal atmosphere. He greeted Gerard apologetically for the inconvenience they had caused by taking the phone and hard drive which, he reported, had nothing of any interest to them. He said,

"I've learned a lot about Father Stephen during the last week. What a monster he was. I've been reading all the stuff that has been coming out through the Royal Commission but reading Father Stephen's history really brings it home. It's appalling; his crimes have caused so much suffering. Our best source of information is the research published by Broken Rites. You lot have been doing a great job; your research needs to be more widely published."

Gerard listened impassively. Flattery was one of the tactics he had anticipated. He told himself to look relaxed but be on guard. Craig continued,

"You are probably the best person we could find to help us understand Father Stephen. Have you got a bit of time? Can I ask you some questions?"

Gerard agreed to stay and wriggled into a comfortable position on the leather chair. Craig asked,

"This might be difficult for you, but could you tell me how Father Stephen went about grooming the boys at your school?"

Gerard gave an ironic laugh and answered.

"I used to think grooming was something you did to a horse. I'll tell you about it. I have long ago managed to separate myself from the emotional context of the raping.

At St Crispins, it was an honour to be part of Father Stephen's drama classes. He actually was a good drama teacher and the productions his drama classes put on were always exciting. He picked radical and controversial plays that were quite exhilarating for middle class Catholic boys in the seventies. We all held him in awe for years before we got to form two, hoping we would be picked for his class. There was the idea that only the elite kids got into his class and then there was the mystery and thrill about the weekend sleep-overs at his house where there were sex education films.

In his class, he made us feel special, that there were rules that applied to the rest of the school but we were superior and had our own rules. He emphasised team work and he had all sorts of subtle ways of rebuking us if we didn't behave as part of the team, which came down to cooperating with him and keeping secrets. He had a big house with a pool. We'd go there for rehearsals on Saturdays then swim in his pool, eat all the good food he prepared for us and have alcohol. He showed us his sex education films. At first it was tasteful soft porn stuff and he'd tell us it was normal and OK to masturbate; that was at a time when we probably were all doing it and were filled with religious guilt. Then he showed us these low-budget films of sex acts; different positions, oral sex, anal sex. All heterosexual stuff with the context that by seeing it we would make better lovers.

The next stage was individual drama lessons at his house. He would give us whisky, massage us, wank us, and finally get us to submit to anal sex. So that we would have better understanding of how to satisfy a woman."

Gerard looked up, disgusted by the memory.

"Deep down we all knew that it was wrong. It all came to an end at St Crispins when Danny Muldoon, one of the boys in the class, hanged himself. He left a letter describing to his parents what happened at Father Stephen's place, then the shit hit the fan."

Craig screwed up his face,

"I'm sorry Gerard. I shouldn't have asked."

"It's OK."

Craig stood up, walked around his office and looked out of the window.

"And now it's our job to find out who executed the bastard. Have you got any idea?"

Gerard was surprised he asked the question so directly. He expected a more subtle approach. Perhaps Craig thought getting him to talk about Father Stephen would put him in a mood for dobbing possible suspects. This gave him a sense of superiority, that he was in control.

"There are probably hundreds of people who wanted to see Father Stephen dead. If I'd come across him thirty years ago I could have murdered him. But in answer to your question, I don't know. He made us all internalise our anger, to hate ourselves, to destroy ourselves."

Craig said,

"From our point of view, the most likely suspects are those who knew where he lived. Could any of your class mates have done it?"

"I've thought about that and the reality is I don't know any of them well enough, I haven't had much contact with any of them during the last thirty years. I saw them a bit with Old Boys sports in the eighties but not much since. As a group, we're the wrong age, we're at a stage of acceptance. The damage has been done, nothing is going to change the direction of our lives now, we just want what peace we can get. Killing him wouldn't make any difference."

Craig was going to ask a question but Gerard got in first.

"There's something I've been wondering about."

"What's that?"

"The word that was cut into Father Stephen's chest. I was shocked when I saw it, but later I thought, had paedophile been spelt wrongly. Did the murderer leave out the 'A'?"

"Yeah. There was no 'A'."

"I thought that was the case and it's been bothering me. At first, I thought, he can't spell, it's a difficult word. But then I thought, victims of paedophiles never spell it wrongly, they read all the newspaper articles about paedophiles. They know the word."

"So what do you think.?"

"The murderer wants you to believe that he killed Father Stephen because he was a paedophile. But what if that was a distraction? What if there was some other reason for murdering him, nothing to do with the paedophilia, hence his ignorance of the spelling of the word."

Craig didn't know what to make of that. Was that the insight they had been looking for or was Gerard throwing up a distraction? And if so, why? He stumbled out with,

"I see your point. That's something for us to look into."

Uneasy now, Craig chose to get back to the questions he had been wanting to ask, about the other men at the meeting.

"Can you tell me about Frank Rowe? What did he think of Father Stephen?"

He's a big business man in Western Australia. He put St Crispins, the Catholic Church and Melbourne behind him when he left school. He's managed his anger by indulging himself in material interests. He's probably a cut-throat businessman. I was surprised he came actually. He's had a heart attack and that's made him think about his life, but I don't think he's interested in Father Stephen."

"What about the others?"

I've thought about that. You can forget about Finn Magee. He's brain damaged and probably can't remember what day it is, let alone Father Stephen's address. That was horrible to see. Michael Crawley is a comfortable conservative and a devout Catholic. Even if he is nursing some secret anger I doubt he would have the imagination to do anything about it. Peter is a gentle, sad man who has intellectualised his damage. He only wants to be a historian and spend time with his ex-wife. Glen and Pat strike me as fairly chaotic. If either of them murdered Father Stephen I think it would be something spontaneous and they wouldn't have been clever about it, you would have caught them straight away. I can't see either of them cutting into Father Stephen's belly like that. By the way, I know you can't tell me much, but did the murderer cut 'pedophile' into his belly after he was dead? I only know what the paper's say, that he was bludgeoned to death."

Gerard's look of concerned sincerity prompted Craig to respond without hesitation,

"Yeah, that happened after he was dead. It wasn't torture. What about Justin Collins?"

"He's a strange one. He was lovely in his teens, good at everything, kind and great to be with, a golden child. Now he lives the life of a hermit. A sensitive soul who was badly damaged and who has coped as best he can by withdrawing from the world."

Gerard stopped there. Craig thanked him, escorted him to the lift and gave him a card with his phone number.

In the meeting with Brian that followed he put his view that Gerard was in fact the honest man he appeared to be. He suspected someone he knew of murdering Father Stephen and had made the decision to protect him. As Craig explained,

"He was horrified by the word cut into the abdomen and it was important to him to know if it was torture or not, before he committed to keeping his suspicions secret. So who does he suspect? I reckon it's Collins. He's given us plenty of accurate information about the meeting, more so than any of the others but he didn't say much about Collins. Most of the others mentioned how Collins talked about a recurring dream, but Connolly left that out. He's got a good grasp of psychology, he would have known that was important."

Brian said.

"It's time we had a look at Collins' flat."

13

When the locksmith had the door open, Brian and Craig put on their disposable overshoes and latex gloves and slipped into Justin's flat. The first thing they noticed was the closed smell of the flat, then its sense of space. It wasn't a large flat but it was unusually bare, with fewer furnishings than you would expect and no pictures on the walls.

One of the forensics started examining the mat inside the front door while another went into the bathroom to swab the band basin and the shower recess. Brian and Craig looked around the living room, there was a desk with a computer on top. It was an old one with a bulky hard drive box, the sort that you rarely saw now. There was a small couch with a single, matching lounge chair of an old-fashioned design with floral-patterned fabric. In the corner of the room was a wooden pedestal with a stuffed animal on it.

"A rabbit," said Craig, surprised by the sight.

"That's not a rabbit. That's a hare," said Brian.

There was no television, no record player or radio. In the kitchen, there was a small fridge which was turned off and had the door propped open. The fridge did not have a freezer compartment. There was a whiteboard and marker pen on top of the fridge. On this there was written, in neat block letters, some items for a shopping list. Brian read out some of the items.

"BASIL SEEDLINGS. TOILET PAPER. He does his 'A's with round tops."

"Yes," said Craig,

"But he does his 'R's with the diagonal coming out of the stick."

The master bedroom was also bare of any sort of decoration and the only furniture was a futon. They opened the built-in robe, which contained fewer items of clothing than most men have in their wardrobe. There were two long sleeved shirts of different shades of grey which Brian removed on their hangers and hung them on the door handle for the forensics to look at.

What would have been a second bedroom was filled with books. High bookshelves filled three walls of the room which had the rich and musty smell of old books. Craig looked at the titles and rattled off the types of books.

"Psychology, philosophy, history, lots of history. architecture, religion, literature, good literature. He's quite the intellectual and very widely read."

There was a simple chair with its back to the window and facing an empty music stand. On an otherwise empty shelf of the adjacent bookshelf, was the closed case of a musical instrument. Brian tried to remember the name of the instrument bigger than a violin but couldn't. Craig opened the case, looked at the instrument and said,

"He plays the viola."

Next, they unlocked the back door and went out into the small backyard. It was completely given over to neat beds of herbs and vegetables. Craig walked along a small path between the rows and listed the plants.

"Leek, onions, rhubarb, carrots, sage, thyme, marjoram. That's salad burnett, I haven't seen that for a while. And that's French sorrel."

"O.K.," said Brian,

"I've got the picture. He likes his veggie garden. Is there anything important out here?"

They returned inside where one of the forensics was putting the computer hard drive into a large, sealable plastic bag. Brian summarised,

"So, he's a hermit who reads a lot, plays the viola and works in his garden. He doesn't watch TV or listen to the radio, although he might do that through his computer. Is there any alcohol in this place?"

There was no wine or spirits on display anywhere and they found no alcohol when they looked through his kitchen cupboards. They looked in the desk drawer where there were receipts and bank statements in neatly ordered piles. Brian said,

"We'lltakethesetolookat.Anythinginterestinginthebathroom? The cupboard in the bathroom had common bathroom items such as shaving equipment, bandaids and soap, but fewer objects than you would expect in a bathroom cupboard. There were no medications, not even Panadol and no condoms.

"This guy gives me the creeps," said Brian,

"Let's see if his neighbour has anything to tell us."

They walked up the driveway to the front flat where Mrs Weissman was standing at her open front door.

"Hello Mrs Weissman," said Craig who was good at remembering names.

"How are you today?"

"I'm well. Why are you looking in Mr Collins' flat?"

"It's all routine work. We had to do it because he is still away and no one knows where he is. But there is nothing of interest to us in the flat. It is very neat and tidy."

"Ah yes, he is very neat and tidy. He sits in there all day, reading and playing his viola. He plays beautifully, I can hear him from my back room. But no records, no television."

"Does he have many visitors?"

"He never has any visitors," she said with her eyes bulging.

"No women ever visit him. Such a waste."

She paused and added with significance.

"No men visit either."

Craig took the lead that she was in the mood for talking,

"Do you see much of him?"

"Not much. He is very good to me, very helpful. Whenever I have a problem I ask him and he helps. I am alone since my poor Herman died. I have arthritis in my knees, my hips and my hands.

He climbed that tree there and rescued my cat Hennie when she couldn't get down."

"Does he go out much?"

"No. He goes shopping once per week. He leaves early and I see him coming home. He is a vegetarian."

Mrs Weissman screwed up her face at that, then continued,

"He has hardly any rubbish to put in his bin. Hardly any mail, only bills and things. He is a very strange man."

When they left Justin's place to drive back to St Kilda Road, Craig was frustrated. He was driving and Brian could tell by the way he held the steering wheel that he was annoyed. As they were about to turn right into Toorak Road, a Mercedes, coming in the other direction, accelerated to get through the lights and prevented Craig from making his turn.

"Did you see that? The bastard. They drive like that around here; rich, entitled bastards. They don't indicate and they stop you turning right. They're the rudest drivers in Melbourne."

He didn't want an answer and Brian didn't give him one. It was true, Brian had often noticed inconsiderate driving in the arc that took in the wealthy suburbs of Toorak, Hawksburn and Malvern. But he was quietly amused by the class-consciousness of Craig's outburst. He would have to tease him about it sometime, call him a socialist.

The IT specialist didn't keep Justin's hard drive for long and said that it was boring. It had hardly any deletions and they were old. There were no passwords and no unusual codings. Craig spent hours going through Justin's writings, emails and internet connections.

"He's incredible," he explained to Brian,

"He goes on the internet once per week, always on Sunday. He then reads stuff, like the stuff on his book shelves; philosophy, history, spirituality, psychology."

"What's his taste in porn?" Brian asked

"There isn't any, but a few years ago he looked at some websites for asexuals, they're the ones who aren't interested in sex. He didn't communicate with any of them. They have social functions where they can go without worrying about being propositioned. He's got lots of money; in shares and investment properties but he only spends about $40.00 per week after paying his utilities and rates. He's definitely been on the Major Mitchell Trail; he withdraws a few hundred dollars from banks every now and then and occasionally pays for motel accommodation with his debit card. You can trace his route through his bank account statement. He withdrew $200.00 when he was in Portland two days before the Grand Final and $200.00 dollars when he was in Hamilton four days later."

"So he could have caught a train to Melbourne, killed the priest and returned to his walk during that time," said Brian.

"Yes," replied Craig,

"But his whole walk has those gaps, he must camp a lot. What's really interesting is the file he keeps about his dreams."

At that point, Brian rolled his eyes.

"Did he dream that the devil told him to kill Father Stephen?"

Craig laughed.

"No, but listen. He has been recording dreams for about fifteen years, there are over a hundred of them. With every dream, he records a conversation with someone who answers his questions about the interpretation of the dream. There are lots of names for these informants and they are obviously supernatural, his father appears frequently and we know that he died eight years ago. Most of the people he doesn't know and he asks them when they entered his subconscious. They give answers such as, when you were in primary school or when you were sick in India."

"So, he's a nut case, a schizophrenic or something," said Brian.

"Possibly. In the last dream, he recorded he met someone who told him to go and do the Major Mitchell trail, so he did! What's interesting, is that he has a recurring dream about a church burning. I've printed out the latest, which he had three months ago. I'll read it out to you,

Burning church dream 17/7/15

I am alone at the door of an old church. I fiddle with the door handle, not sure how to use it and the door opens. I enter the church which is very dark. I can see the altar, a vague series of lights behind it where you would expect to see stained-glass windows and sculptured images of the stations of the cross around the walls. I hear a quiet cracking sound which becomes steadily louder. I smell smoke and realise that the church is on fire. I don't feel heat or see flames but there is a red glow around me. I close my eyes. There is no fear or desire to leave the church. I wake up and the feeling is, "Not again, I'm sick of this dream".

I went to my subconscious and Dad came, his voice was quite clear. I said it was good to hear his voice and he said it's good to be back. Then I said, "You've come as a symbol of authority again, haven't you." And he said "Yes" with a quiet chuckle.

He explained

The door represents an obstacle which I can overcome if I choose

The church is dark and uninviting, an unpleasant place, representing the Catholic Church

The fire is damaging the church, not me. I want the fire to burn the church

As usual, my subconscious is telling me that I am angry with the church. It is a recurring dream because I am not resolving the anger.

I thanked Dad and said goodbye.

Brian was irritated by Craig's enthusiasm for the dream. He said,

"So, a man who was raped as a child by a priest has recurring dreams of anger towards the church. They probably all do. Psychologists would like it but we need a lot more than that to link him to Father Stephen's murder."

The next day they received the report from forensics about the examination of Justin's house and clothing. It went for several pages but, in summary, they found nothing that could link Justin to the murder, no blood, no particles, no metal objects buried in the garden.

Justin finally made contact with the police that afternoon. Craig took the call. Because they had nothing concrete to link him to the murder, he decided to make it an informal interview, and Justin agreed to meet with them. They would drive to where he was on the Major Mitchell Trail.

14

After he left Portland, Justin walked through a gentler, more humanised landscape. It was flat with few patches of forest and dotted with small towns. At first, he missed the forests but then he came to enjoy the openness and the stately charm of the rows of sugar gums and cypress pines that fringed the farms. He was still inclined to camp in isolated places, looking for dense clusters of trees where he could camp overnight unseen. He had enjoyed the experience of staying with the family at the Heywood B&B so much that he now looked for the small B&Bs that he sometimes found on the edge of towns, hoping for some conversation.

He could easily walk forty kilometres per day if he wanted, but now the end of his journey was in sight and he wanted to slow his progress because he was enjoying the experience so much. Justin carried with him a book about the Trail and up until now, he had been sticking to the trail route shown, but now he was varying the route to take in more small towns. He would linger in these towns having long conversations with people in shops, the barber who cut his hair, even people who were gardening in their front yards. One day, he sat on a park bench just to listen to the distant sound of children playing at the nearby school in their lunch break.

One morning, when he was camped amongst some trees near a small reedy creek, he was wakened by some unfamiliar bird calls. He crept out of his tent and found some brolgas dancing on the swampy land beside the creek. In the early morning sunlight, this was a rapturous sight, something he had read about but never witnessed. The feeling of delight stayed with him all day and the need to tell someone was so strong that he phoned Maureen when he came to the next town, the small town of Willaura. It was then that he heard that Father Stephen had been murdered and that the police wanted to speak with him. The news was so unreal, so detached from the spirit of his walk that it took some time for its significance to sink in. He wondered what the police would want with him and eventually realised that the eight men who attended the meeting would be suspects because of Pat's revelation of Father Stephen's address.

Craig took the call. Justin spoke with a courteous, humble tone and he responded similarly, trying to suppress the urgency he felt about interviewing him. Justin thought that the police would only have a few questions for him over the phone and was surprised that they wanted to see him. Craig had never heard of Willaura. Justin offered to catch a train to Melbourne for the interview but Craig arranged to meet him at the Ararat police station nearby the following afternoon.

It took time for Justin to register the impact of the news about the death. Father Stephen didn't exist as a real person for him but as a symbol, a symbol of a monstrous system. Over time that symbol had declined in significance for him as Justin walked his many philosophical and spiritual pathways. Did the death have any meaning for him at all? He must have been in his eighties anyway. Justin wondered if Father Stephen's death would put an end to his recurring dreams of the burning church but suspected it wouldn't, the dreams were not about the priest.

As he walked to Ararat the following morning, he became concerned that the murder had been committed by someone he knew. Someone who had been abused by Father Stephen might have taken their revenge but would now have their life damaged for the second time by being sent to jail. It saddened him that there might be someone who carried so much anger that they would commit the murder.

He wished he had asked Maureen when Father Stephen had been murdered. As a suspect, the police would want to know his movements. He had kept a detailed diary of his time on the walk but there were periods of several days when he had no contact with anyone. He was feeling quite nervous when he walked into the Ararat police station.

*****

The clouds put on a show of showers and dazzling sunlight as Craig and Brian drove along the Western Highway towards Ararat. There were newborn lambs in the paddocks, some wriggling their tails as they suckled from their mothers, something Brian hadn't seen for many years but he didn't want to comment on such a sentimental sight to Craig. The expression 'gambolling lambs' came to mind: what a weird word.

There was the very real possibility that this strange Collins character wouldn't turn up for his interview, but they enjoyed the excuse to get out of Melbourne. If he didn't show, they'd get the locals to arrest him and bring him down to St Kilda Road.

Craig was in a good mood but Brian was more circumspect. He said,

"Let's get the alibi stuff in quickly. If he's got one, we'll concentrate on his knowledge of the others. We'll have to bring in Connolly and give him the treatment because he's the only one with an incomplete alibi, but I don't think we'll get anything new from him. What if one of the fifteen people, the ones at the meeting and all the Broken Rites directors who knew the priests address, was lying and told someone else? What if the postie did it? What if the accountant who pays his rent hates his guts and did it?

"And what if the paedophile angle is a distraction, as Connolly thinks?" said Craig.

Between Beaufort and Ararat, they had a call from the Ararat Police Station to tell them that Justin had arrived. As they drove into Ararat, Craig said,

"Notice how Ararat's main street zig-zags up a hill? Can you think of any other country towns that have that?"

"No," Brian answered, amused by the question. He knew that Craig would have some quirky explanation.

"Omeo. Why do you think that Ararat and Omeo have the same, crooked main streets?"

"I dunno. Did they employ alcoholic town planners?"

"Close. What's similar about Omeo and Ararat?"

"Nothing! Different parts of the state, Omeo's much smaller."

"No. They are similar historically. They were both gold rush towns. They didn't have any planning, they just sprang up where the carts went and where people chose to put up buildings."

"Well, you live and learn," said Brain with mock sarcasm.

When they arrived, Justin was sitting in the waiting room drinking a cup of coffee that the duty police officer had given him. He had a dirty backpack beside him. Brian and Craig had a conversation with the local then took Justin to the interview room. They exchanged some pleasantries about their journeys to Ararat. Justin was brown from his months on the road which made his blue eyes even more intense than usual. His demeanour generated so much warmth and cooperation that it wasn't easy for Brian and Craig to slip into their no-nonsense interview personas. Brian started the process,

"We are grateful for your attendance here today Mr Collins. As Detective Inspector Theophanous explained, we are making enquiries into the murder of Father Stephen O'Dwyer. We understand that you knew him?"

"Yes, but only from my school days. I haven't seen him since I was thirteen."

Brian continued.

"You attended a meeting with seven other men a few months ago at which Father Stephen was mentioned and his address was disclosed."

"Yes. Pat Gilroy saw him and followed him to his house. He said the address, but I can't remember it."

"Can you tell us where you were on October the third?"

"I can't remember off hand, I've been walking for months and the dates blur, but I have been keeping a diary. I've got it with me."

He reached for his backpack but Craig said,

"October third was a Saturday, Grand Final Day."

Justin beamed.

"That's easy to remember. I spent the day with a wonderful couple at Heywood. I watched the match on TV with them. I don't follow football now but I used to barrack for Hawthorn. It was a great match."

Craig and Brian remained stony-faced. Brian asked,

"Who were the people you were with?"

"Don and Charlotte Smith. They run a B and B and I stayed with them overnight. They were very good to me, the night before there was a heavy downpour and all my clothes and sleeping bag got soaked. They washed and dried everything for me while we watched the match."

"Do you have their contact details?"

"Their B and B is called 'Doo-Us'. It's just outside Heywood, on the southern side. I didn't keep their phone number. I wrote in their guest book. Was the murder on Grand Final Day?"

Brian left the interview room, googled the bed and breakfast place and phoned the number. There was no answer but he left a message asking them to phone him urgently. Justin was relieved that he had an alibi. Craig had established that Justin knew nothing about the murder but was not giving him any details. Justin said,

"I'm guessing that the eight of us are suspects because we were abused by Father Stephen at school, and it was at our meeting we learned that he was out of jail and where he lived."

"Yes," said Craig. "That's why we need to speak to you all. It's taken us a long time to track you down."

Justin smiled at that. Craig continued,

"In the course of our investigations we have examined your flat."

Justin was surprised but didn't express any annoyance.

"I suppose my flat was a bit musty after being closed up for so long. My veggie garden must be a bit of a mess by now."

They asked him detailed questions about the seven other men at the meeting; how well he knew them, what they said at the meeting and if he thought that any of them could have murdered Father Stephen. Justin gave thoughtful replies, he was less verbose than Michael Crawley and more sympathetic than Gerard Connolly but his recollections were similar to all of the others. When they asked him about Gerard, his thinking was interrupted by a memory, a powerful image of an incident on the football field during their school days. St Crispins was playing in the finals in a tough match against the big, outer suburban boys from Haileybury College. It was halfway through the final quarter and the scores were close when Justin saw Gerard go down after being sandwiched between two opposition players. For a moment he lay still on the ground then, to Justin's surprise, he got up and played hard for the rest of the match. After the match, Gerard had to go to hospital with three broken ribs.

This image filled Justin with a sense of Gerard's toughness and determination. The police were waiting for his answers and he continued without a noticeable pause. It was only later that he had time to reflect on that flash-back, he often had these flash-backs. There was a time in his life when he saw them as clairvoyance, something which anyone could have, but you became better at receiving 'messages' if you permitted yourself to be open to them. He put these insights in the spiritual dimension. In recent years, he had come to see the flash-backs as subconscious phenomena, a normal process of memories being triggered but in his case, because of the reflective life he lived, these experiences could be very intense. What meaning did this memory have for him? Was it that he recognised the possibility of Gerard being the murderer? That he had the determination to do it? Justin didn't believe, didn't want to believe that any of the men at his meeting could have killed Father Stephen. The image was however powerful enough that Justin decided to visit Gerard in the near future.

Justin had no new information for Brian and Craig. In the absence of confirmation of Justin's alibi, Craig decided to ask about his psychological state by raising the issue of his recurring dream. He told Justin that he had looked at the contents of his computer Justin said,

"If I was concerned about my privacy I'd be most upset, but I'm not like that."

Craig continued.

"You keep records of your dreams and you have conversations about their interpretation."

"You read the records of my dreams?"

"Yes."

Craig was expecting some resistance from Justin, something different from his mildness and cooperation. But no, he smiled and said,

"That must have been confusing for you. I'd better give you a long answer. Have you heard of Karl Jung? He was a pioneering psychiatrist, a contemporary of Freud."

Craig answered that he had. Justin continued,

"He taught that our minds have conscious and subconscious states and that the subconscious is very important, it influences everything that goes on in our conscious mind, He compared our minds to an iceberg with the bigger part, the underwater part, like the subconscious. His concept of dreams is that they are messages from our subconscious, alerting our conscious mind to things that would be useful for us to know. The trouble is we can't dream in language, we can only dream in symbols, and that's why it is so difficult for people to interpret dreams. Some of these symbols are common to most people, for example dogs usually symbolise companionship or guidance. On the basis of these common symbols people have written dictionaries on dream interpretation. Each individual, however, has his or her own system of symbols so it takes a lot of insight to interpret your own dreams.

Some Jungian analysts teach a method of communicating with our subconscious. It involves some ritualistic practices and calling to your subconscious for help, and you actually get answers, you hear voices that explain your dreams. I use the technique and it works for me. I hear voices, not as distinct as on the telephone but real, recognisable voices. When these voices explain the dream, it always seems obvious and I wonder why I couldn't have worked it out consciously. That makes sense because I'm only talking to myself anyway."

Brian and Craig looked unconvinced. Justin continued,

"I'm not schizophrenic, I only hear the voices when I ask for them. And I must admit that I got a bit of a fright when I first started using the technique. I don't have any illusions that the voices are external, spiritual beings or anything, they come from inside my head."

Craig asked,

"I read that you have a recurring dream about a church burning. What do you make of that?"

"Recurring dreams are important, they mean that you are not dealing with the message that your subconscious wants you to know. I have put a lot of time and energy trying to deal with that dream. You see I don't feel anger towards the Catholic Church in my conscious mind. I don't think about it much, I don't get anxious or angry when I see a Catholic Church. I hadn't thought of Father Stephen for years until recently. Because of the dream, I accept that I have repressed anger, but nothing is happening with that anger. I know I live an unusual life but I am content with my life. I'm not bothering anyone."

Craig was interested now and asked what was the point of understanding these dreams. Brian was annoyed that the interview had taken this pathway and considered Craig's indulgence of Justin to be unprofessional. His phone rang, a return call from the Smiths of Heywood. He was relieved to leave the interview room to take the call.

Mrs Smith was phoning. She was alarmed to receive an urgent phone call from the police. She confirmed that Justin had spent the whole of October the third at their Bed and Breakfast home and accurately described him, even his backpack. When Brian returned to the interview room Justin and Craig were discussing the value of self-knowledge. Brian broke them up,

"That was Mrs Smith conforming your alibi Mr Collins."

"That's a relief. She's a lovely person."

"She described you well, she liked your blue eyes."

The three of them laughed.

Brian and Craig managed to complete the interview in a more professional tone, asking Justin about why he arranged the meeting with the seven men. When they finished, Craig asked Justin if he needed transport anywhere. He didn't, he wanted to explore Ararat and stay there overnight.

As they drove back to Melbourne, Brian teased Craig about his fascination with Justin, calling him "your boyfriend" but he couldn't help admiring Justin himself. He said,

"Guess who Mrs Smith said Justin reminds her of?"

"Who?"

"Jesus!"

They brought in Gerard for a formal interview at headquarters and cautioned him. He refused his right to have a lawyer present because, he said, it wasn't necessary. He remained calm and courteous despite some fairly aggressive questioning from Brian. Gerard didn't change his story and they learned nothing new.

15

Justin loved walking through the Goldfields region of Central Victoria. It was Spring and the wattles were in bloom. Mica and quartz glinted from exposed patches in the shallow soil and native peas and tiny bush orchids were in flower. He kept coming across signs of long-past human activity in surprising places; he found mullock heaps, collapsed mines, piles of bricks, rusted iron and the occasional chimney. In some places he found gnarled fruit trees where gardens had once been. The small towns were dotted with the history of their unplanned eruptions; abandoned buildings, purposeless fences and earthworks and the remains of engines. Justin would linger in these places and try to imagine the bustle of one hundred and fifty years earlier. He found metal objects and old bottles which he would hold for a while, a long-dormant instinct for possession, but then the objects would lose their context for him and he would return them to where he found them. He came across modern homes with shiny vehicles and wondered what dreams motivated the owners to add another layer to the complexity of human settlement. Did they find their place here and feel a part of the landscape, or did they fret about water supply and bushfires?

He was swooped by a magpie, which cut the back of his scalp. It gave him a shock but he wasn't angry with the magpie, he felt it was a suitable reminder that it was all very well to enjoy passing through this landscape, but there were custodians that had importance here, such as a magpie defending its territory. He could feel that the edges of the scalp wound were separated and it bled profusely so, with a handkerchief pressed firmly against his scalp, he walked ten kilometres to Clunes to find a doctor. He told himself that he was lucky because this was the first injury he had suffered for the whole walk.

Getting his scalp laceration repaired was a good experience. The doctor who did it came from Zimbabwe and, while he was stitching the wound, described to Justin the activities of the witch doctor in the village where he had spent his childhood.

North of Euroa, the landscape became flatter and lost the weight of history that clung to the goldfields. It was now early December and a few days of hot weather prompted Justin to quicken his pace, it felt like the journey was approaching its natural end. The long days of walking created a mind-numbing, meditative rhythm for him but in the quiet of the evenings, Justin thought about what would happen when he returned to Melbourne. It was time for a change. He battled the thought; he had long ago discarded the concept that life had meaning, he was free to live life as he chose, and yet there was the inevitability of change. He felt an over-riding importance to speak with the seven men he had met with at Peter McBride's home. He had set something in motion with that meeting and he had a responsibility to, at least witness its aftermath. Who knows, one of the seven might have murdered Father Stephen. Some of them, he thought of Pat and Glen in particular, might have been traumatised by police interviews. The thought of visiting them reminded Justin of his reason for separating himself from people in the first place; the heaviness and weariness he felt when people told him their stories which were mostly of petty interpersonal conflicts and desperate material neediness.

Behind his sense of impending change was the question, recurring despite his decades of psychological self-care, of what damage he had suffered at the hands of Father Stephen and what, if anything he should do about it. An image came to him, a memory of a balloon found weeks after a childhood birthday party, it had slowly leaked and lay three-quarters deflated, distorted and forgotten in a corner. He felt like that balloon.

On the last night of his journey he checked in to a hotel in the heart of Albury. He wanted to do something celebratory, or at least go through the motions of doing so. He walked the streets of central Albury with a heightened sense of awareness because he had reached a destination after months of walking. But in this state, he was confronted only with unattractive scenes; a drunken argument, a blast of smell and television noise with the opening of the door of a grotty hotel, a road rage incident at a traffic intersection. He ate a meal at a Vietnamese restaurant but was saddened by the gloomy expression on the face of the young woman who served him. He couldn't talk himself out of his concern for her, it almost brought him to tears. He phoned Maureen, enjoyed their long conversation and accepted her invitation to join her for a family Christmas.

The next morning, at the Albury Station, there was no one to meet Justin. There were no photos taken and no local newspaper to report the end of his unusual walk. The woman who sold him his ticket to Melbourne barely noticed the scruffily dressed man because she was preoccupied with the argument she had had with her husband that morning.

*****

When he arrived at the Southern Cross Station in Melbourne, Justin decided to walk to his home in Toorak, the distance seemed trivial after his recent walking routine. It felt strange to be in a crowd of people again and he had lost his sense of spatial awareness when walking amongst people. He needed to concentrate as he walked to coordinate his movements with the people around him. As he walked along Flinders Street, he was amazed to find that the long strip of pavement beside the Flinders Street Station was occupied by homeless people. He had never seen them there before. He noticed that they were very well equipped; instead of strips of cardboard they had sleeping bags, pillows and suitcases. In most cases their baggage was clean and new-looking. He offended one of these homeless people by gazing for too long and was told to "fuck off".

As he approached his flat, he wondered if he would be able to slip past Mrs Weissman unseen. Surely, she would have got out of the habit of lying in wait for him? But no, she appeared at her front door when Justin walked down the driveway. To his surprise. she gave him a hug.

During the next few weeks Justin visited most of the men from the meeting and in each case, was very welcome. He apologised about the way the meeting had made them all suspects for a murder but none of them blamed him. He felt very relaxed with Peter who told him that he made people feel comfortable and urged him to do some sort of counselling work, perhaps Gerard could arrange something with him. Michael was ponderous but expressed some excitement at his indirect involvement in the drama of the investigation. Pat had had a nervous breakdown and wasn't working but blamed himself because it was he who had described where Father Stephen lived. Glen, like Pat, was glad that Father Stephen had been murdered. He was so pleased to hear about the murder that he had become motivated to speak with the Royal Commissioner and had made an appointment to do so. Justin found Finn having lunch at the Sacred Heart Mission. He greeted Justin warmly but couldn't remember either the meeting or the police. Justin took him for coffee at Ruby's where he spent most of the time talking about a rumour that the Gatwick was going to be sold and he would have nowhere to live.

Justin had a long phone conversation with Frank in Perth who was surprisingly reflective. He told Justin that the meeting had been very important for him and he was now thinking about how he could use his wealth to support the victims of paedophile priests. He would visit Justin in the new year to discuss this further.

It wasn't until Christmas morning that Justin phoned Gerard to arrange a meeting. They had a long conversation about the police and Justin learned that Gerard had been a prime suspect and seen the detectives several times. They spoke with amusement about Brian and Craig as a bad cop and good cop combination. Gerard wouldn't arrange a date to meet, something which surprised Justin because, he said, "my life is about to get very complicated", but he agreed to communicate with him in the near future.

16

On Christmas Day, Justin caught a train to the Williams Landing Station then walked to the home of his niece Siobhan at Point Cook. He hadn't seen Siobhan and her husband Chris since he attended their wedding eleven years earlier. It was to be a small gathering, just Siobhan, Chris, their two children Byron and Chandler, Maureen and Chris' parents Harold and Wilma. Because of the animosity that still existed between Maureen and her ex-husband Fraser, he was having dinner with Siobhan and family that night. Justin had been an absent uncle and he felt nervous about attending the family dinner. He had no idea what sort of presents to bring; Maureen told him, "Just bring things they can eat". She warned him that he would find the family to be very materialistic.

He had never been to Point Cook before. He had read that the relatively new suburb had the advantage of proximity to Melbourne but the disadvantage of poorly planned access to the Melbourne Road so that morning commuters spent ages queueing at a bottle-neck on their way towards the city. Justin wanted to arrive after Maureen so he zig-zagged his way through the suburb enjoying the novel streetscape. The suburb was filled with large homes on small blocks giving the streets a crowded feeling. Most houses had two stories, mock Georgian and Italianate designs were the most popular. Most homes had two or more cars which spilled onto the driveways and streets. Large, shiny, four-wheel drive vehicles and tradies' vans were common. There were lots of wrought iron fences revealing symmetrical displays of white rose bushes. Many of the houses had elaborate Christmas light displays which were probably spectacular at night but which looked untidy and tacky in the bright December sunlight. Justin found himself looking for humanising features, such as basketball rings upsetting the symmetry of stark facades or bicycles left lying on lawns or in driveways. Very few people were visible but, disappointingly, there were some men busy with noisy gardening equipment, such as lawnmowers and leaf blowers, shattering the peace of the holiday noon.

Siobhan and Chris' place was a grey neo-Georgian cube and its blocky immensity brought to Justin's mind a mausoleum. The double garage was incorporated into the design, matched on the other side of a columned, central door by shaded windows. There was no front fence. The immaculately trimmed front lawn was disrupted by a hole in its centre.

Justin was greeted warmly at the front door by Maureen, Siobhan and Chris. In the front hall was an electric Santa Claus that jiggled and made Christmas carol noises. They led him into a large living room where he was introduced to Harold and Wilma, whom he could remember meeting at the wedding. They still had the strong Liverpudlian accents they had brought to Australia with them forty years earlier. The room was dominated by an enormous television screen which Byron and Chandler were watching. They were both obese and reluctantly responded to Chris' "Say hello to your Uncle Justin".

His hosts were very attentive and Justin realised that he must have a mysterious image within his extended family. He wondered if Maureen had misled them with the myth about him being a traumatised ex-soldier, and if so, should he correct it. He felt the need to be reassuring, that he could converse and behave normally and forced himself to be charmingly conversational. Chris, an electrician by trade, was proud of his home and it was easy to encourage him to elaborate on its technological features.

They nibbled at finger foods on platters which Justin felt compelled to eat because they were offered so frequently. Harold and Wilma sat next to each other in the middle of a large couch. There was a jarring rigidity about them, Wilma especially, as if they were trying to maintain a certain stature within the informality of the family gathering. Siobhan drifted off to the kitchen and Justin ended up in the small back yard where Chris was cooking a turkey buff in his Webber. Harold and Wilma stayed on the couch.

Justin enjoyed drinking beer with Chris and in the men-around-the-barbecue ambience Chris visibly relaxed and talked about his life. In that context, it was a beautiful narrative; the non-academic only child of English immigrants does well in his chosen trade, falls in love and marries and he and his wife work hard to own their dream home. It was in the spirit of congratulating Chris on his success that Justin asked him what he thought of Point Cook, thinking he would describe it positively, as the dream suburb of like-minded people, but at the question, Chris' face clouded. At first, he had liked the suburb but he had had a succession of disappointments with his neighbours. In particular, he described a recent upset,

"Did you notice the hole in my front yard?"

"Yes," Justin answered.

"Ten days ago, I planted a Japanese weeping cherry there. It's something I've always wanted and since we bought the block, I've planned to plant one, as a special feature in the middle of the front yard. I loved it. I spent ages just looking at it, the way the branches came out so evenly around the trunk. Then four days after I planted it, someone stole it. They came and dug it up in the night. I've heard of that happening around here and I went walking around the local streets and found it! It was planted in the front yard of a bastard who lives around the corner! I confronted him and he just laughed and told me to go to the police. I did, but they were useless because they said I wouldn't be able to prove it. I had photos to prove it was mine but they just said those trees all look the same. I can't steal it back because he has a high fence and Rottweilers. I want to kill the bastard."

At that moment, Siobhan appeared and Chris looked sheepish.

"Come on Chris," she said. "Don't talk about your tree today. Will the turkey be ready soon?"

The food was well-prepared and the mood around the table relaxed. They had seafood cocktails, roast turkey and vegetables then a traditional plum pudding with brandy butter that Wilma always made. Justin was the centre of attention and within that small group felt comfortable describing his recent walk and past adventures overseas. He surprised himself by saying, "I want to be less of a hermit now" when he described how he had re-met some old school friends and wanted to spend more time with them. He didn't mention his reason for re-meeting them. Byron and Chandler were uncomfortable at the table and their handling of the cutlery seemed clumsier that he would have expected for their ages. It dawned upon Justin that it was probably rare for the family to sit together for a meal. Siobhan and Chris both worked long hours and the children spent time in after -school care each day. They grizzled for permission to leave the table and rushed off to the television when Chris relented.

The family's Christmas routine was to open presents after the dinner so they all moved to the Christmas tree and sat nearby. Byron and Chandler showed some excitement for the first time and Siobhan asked them to pick up the presents and read their labels. As people unwrapped presents and dropped the wrapping paper to the floor, Wilma would swoop over, grab the wrappings, fold them and put them in a cardboard box. No one commented, this was obviously something that always happened. Justin recalled some legendary stories Maureen had told him about

Wilma's meticulous neatness. During Chris' childhood the family had gone to Lakes Entrance for their first Australian holiday. Wilma found the cleanliness of the holiday accommodation not up to her standards, so they drove home. They never attempted a holiday again. Her cleanliness was spoken of with awe, pride even. No one, apart from Maureen, saw it as a psychological problem.

Chris suggested a walk and Justin was the only one who felt like joining him. Chris took Justin a short distance around the corner then stopped in front of a house with a high wrought iron fence. There in the front yard was the tree which he believed was his stolen tree. Chris stood staring at the tree in silence and showed no indication of continuing the walk. Justin felt uncomfortable. Chris eventually broke the silence,

"I often come here, just to look at my tree. I hope the bastard sees me and it reminds him what a crook he is."

They continued the walk but the mood had soured and Justin was relieved to return to the house.

Maureen drove him back to his flat, she didn't need to but she and Justin were pleased to spend some time alone together. The family Christmas had given Justin a sense of goodwill and he wanted to emphasise that the experience had been a good one, irrespective of the dynamics and background issues. He laughed at the memory of Wilma and the wrapping paper. Maureen asked questions about the effect on Justin of Father Stephen's death.

The next morning Justin went to his computer to check emails. There was one from Gerard, not a personal message for him, but a blank email with an attachment. Justin was amazed by the enormous list of recipients heading the email, there were hundreds of them, including Australian and international media outlets. He opened the attachment which was a video recording of Gerard, seated, speaking to the camera. Justin watched the whole recording which lasted about eight minutes. He was appalled.

17

Gerard couldn't help but feel anxious after the aggressive interview at police headquarters. He was confident that he hadn't altered his story but kept going over the questions, and his responses, wondering if the police could have gleaned something he hadn't anticipated. For weeks after the interview he expected another visit from the police. He wanted to hear news about the investigation. He read newspapers and watched the news. He felt like phoning the other men who attended the meeting but decided that might be a sign of guilt and the police might be monitoring his phone calls. He even wanted to walk along the Yarra near the Fairfield Boathouse to see if any of the clothing he had discarded had washed up on the banks. That amused him, he recalled the phrase, "The criminal returns to the scene of the crime". He was thinking like a common criminal.

By late November, with no further news or interest from the police, the murder was feeling anti-climactic. He spent time reflecting on the years of planning and how he would carry out the next stage. He knew he could bail out now and probably get away with the murder, but his commitment and conviction that he had chosen the best course never weakened. There was so little that a single person could do to draw attention to the monstrous crimes of the Catholic Church. The public even seemed to be anaesthetised to the regular reports coming from the Royal Commission. He was taking a personal stand, making a symbolic gesture. He had no control over what happened next, his gesture might be ignored or dismissed as the criminal outburst of a disturbed individual. He imagined newspapers describing his behaviour as revenge, or in terms of psychological illness or his past alcoholism. On the other hand, people might take up his cause, take a fresh look at the rotten core of the Catholic Church and its legal mercenaries. Gerard had come to regard his planned attack on the legal profession to be even more important than his symbolic attack on the personnel and property of the Church. There would be no real change in attitude or policy from the Vatican but if it was possible to shame the legal profession out of its complicity with the Church's abuse of power if magistrates could become more compassionate with the victims of rapist priests, if the barristers were ashamed to take on their cases, there might be some hope, in Australia at least.

It bothered Gerard that he would be misunderstood but in the years of planning he had been reconciled to these feelings. He had made many drafts of the speech that he would record, all on paper and destroyed so that the police had nothing to find. He might get another opportunity to explain himself in court, but he couldn't depend on that. He would write personal letters of explanation to his sons.

On December 24, Gerard posted large envelopes to his two sons. They contained power of attorney documentation and his letter of explanation. He also included information about where to find his house and car keys and his suggestion that they rent out his flat and use the income as they chose.

On Christmas morning Gerard was delighted to get the phone call from Justin because he had been wanting to talk to him. He had thought a lot about Justin since the meeting and had tried to visit him recently, only to learn that he was away on a walk and uncontactable. They were opposites in many ways. At school, he was the tough guy while Justin was gentle. On the football field, Justin was graceful and dodged while Gerard barged through. In a way, he had loved him when they were at school together, in an innocent way and something he couldn't possibly have acknowledged to himself at the time. He felt for justin now, he shouldn't have withdrawn from the world the way he did. They were both damaged; Gerard was doing something in character, something tough and self-sacrificing, he wanted Justin to do something too.

Gerard's family's Christmas dinner was everything he wanted it to be. Present were his two sons, their wives, his three grandchildren and his ex-wife. Just watching the joy of the three small children with their presents and all the Christmas fuss, was sheer delight for the adults. At one stage during the meal, Gerard compared his relaxed immersion with the pleasure he felt watching the first half of the Grand Final. He wondered if anticipating committing a crime enhanced everyone's pleasure, or was it just him.

Back at his flat, as darkness was falling, Gerard packed his car with a ladder, his lap top computer and backpacks containing petrol. On this occasion, he had no need to hide the traces of his equipment, he had nothing to hide from the police after this evening. He drove to a suburban street behind St Crispins and parked his car. He sat in the car for a while to make sure there was no one in the street, then took a backpack from the back of the car and climbed over the low fence that ran around the back of the school. He walked around the oval then in amongst the school buildings. There were lights attached to the buildings and the grounds were patrolled at irregular intervals so he looked and listened carefully as he moved. He came to the school's old chapel which was unlocked, the legacy of an attitude of having it available "for quiet contemplation" at all times for the boarders. It was a glorious old building with elaborate stonework, beautifully carved wooden features and nineteenth century stained-glass windows. It was too small for weddings but popular with former pupils for Christenings. Gerard resisted an impulse to cross himself, amused by the reflex, as he walked in front of the altar.

He took a can of petrol from the backpack and moved quickly, dousing the carpet and the curtains around the sides of the chapel. The fire took hold quickly with only one lighted match and as he left the building smoke detectors blared. He returned to his car quickly, seeing no one on the way.

Next, he drove to Kew and parked his car in a bluestone alley behind a row of commercial buildings. He sat patiently in his car for a while, his next move would be one of his most vulnerable. He took the ladder and a backpack from the back of his car, put the ladder against a fence and climbed up and over, then pulled the ladder after him. He walked over to the back door of what was the offices of Sullivan, Brown and McCarthy, barristers and solicitors, a firm he had chosen because it often represented the Catholic Church in trials of paedophile priests. The building was securely locked and had bars on the windows but in his reconnaissance, Gerard had found that there was a one-centimetre gap under the back door. On the inside of the door there was attached a rolling wind-stopper but he had found that this could be pushed up from the outside and he had fashioned a flattened hose to poke under the door. He pushed the hose through for several metres then connected the hose to his petrol can and poured in the petrol. It made a loud gurgling sound in the still of the night but Gerard waited until all the all petrol was inside. Next, he stepped away from the door and set up his laptop computer on the ground. He turned it on. It took an unbearably long time to start up, then he opened emails and pressed the send button to distribute the video recording of his speech. He then returned to the door and ignited the petrol with a match under the door. The petrol exploded and smoke alarms went off.

Gerard wasn't sure how long it would take for all his emails to be sent but he felt he was in the clear now. He carefully packed his laptop into the backpack, climbed the fence and lifted the ladder down the other side to descend to his car. No one had seen him. He left the ladder against the fence and drove down to the other end of the alley then home thinking about the fires. The St Crispins chapel was made of stone but had timber ceilings, "gutted" was the word he expected to be in newspaper reports of the fire next morning. The Sullivan and McCarthy building was built of wood, he hoped it would be completely destroyed.

When he arrived at his driveway, Gerard checked the laptop and was pleased to find that all emails had been sent, his task was complete. It was close to midnight and he didn't know how long he would have to wait for the police. As a matter of courtesy, he sent a text message to Craig Theophanous, he liked him, using the phone number on the card Craig had given him. In the message, he confessed to the murder and the two acts of arson and 'regretted' that he had needed to mislead him.

Ten minutes passed and Gerard couldn't bear the waiting so he drove back to Kew, parked his car and joined a crowd of on-lookers who were watching the fire brigade putting out the last flames of the destroyed building. When the show was over, he had an urge to hand himself in to the police who were at the scene directing traffic, but decided that it would be better manners to return home and wait for Craig Theophanous to come and get him.

18

The period between Christmas Day and New Year is the time when news rooms run on skeleton staffs. There is plenty of sport to fill air time and reserve news readers have time to rehearse their lines. When Gerard Connolly's video arrived on Christmas night, the late-night news crews recognised that something important had happened. Everyone who watched Gerard's speech was impressed by his calm and dispassionate monologue. He first confessed to the murder and the arson, then gave a concise summary of the extent of clerical abuse in Australia, the power of the Catholic Church in preventing change and the culpability of the justice system, emphasising the Ellis Defence, something unique to Australia and the Catholic Church alone of all the churches. Finally, there was Gerard's chilling conclusion and call to arms, that the only way to bring about meaningful change was to kill rapist priests, destroy church property and shame the legal profession out of perpetuating the abuse in the court rooms.

The newsrooms' legal advisers ruled out reporting the advocacy of violence and cautioned against showing the video. By midday on 26 December the line for the story had solidified to the vengeful criminality of a disturbed victim. The story, with small variations between the different channels, showed a brief segment of the video with no volume and interviews of shocked people who had loved the St Crispins chapel or who had worked at the offices of Sullivan, Brown and McCarthy. Most finished with a few sentences about Father Stephen O'Dwyers' criminal record. There was much more air time given to the Sydney To Hobart Yacht Race.

By the night of 26 December, enquiries were coming in from all over the world and the foreign news agencies were running sections of Gerard's video including the controversial section advocating violence against the Church. The foreign news became the news and late that night there was a report about a man in Spain, murdering a priest who had abused him as a child then confessing and announcing that, "The Australian is right. We must kill the rapist priests." The line of the television newscasts was confused that night and lapsed into appeasement with a description of the work of the Royal Commission into the institutional responses to child sexual abuse.

On the night of 27 December five Catholic Churches were set on fire in Australia, two of them in Melbourne. A church incinerated in New South Wales was another church where Father O'Dwyer had worked. The arsonist had been abused by him and, like Gerard, released a video confession advocating the destruction of church property. These attacks were described as "copy-cat" crimes but the news crews were researching and reporting clerical abuse in Australia. There were international calls for the Vatican to comment.

On the night of 28 December, three solicitors' offices and another fifteen Catholic Churches were set on fire, in all states and territories of Australia. Two paedophile priests serving time in jail were attacked by fellow prisoners; one died and the other was left unconscious. In Tasmania, a man murdered a priest then took his own life. From overseas, there were reports of two priests murdered in Italy, one in New Zealand and a Bishop in Canada.

This rapid escalation left the nation shocked. Politicians returned to Canberra from their holidays and announced emergency measures. The police were taking special measures to protect church property and priests. All priests in jail were being separated from the other prisoners. Journalists were arriving from overseas and filming their reports in front of incinerated churches.

The following Sunday there was a widely reported, ugly incident at Melbourne's St Patrick's Cathedral. During the mass, a man stood in the aisle and started shouting at the priest. It was reported that he accused the priesthood of being part of the systematic cover-up of rape by priests. There was a scuffle as some of the parishioners tried to remove him and an elderly man collapsed with a heart attack and died.

The politicians' call for calm was undermined by controversialist and Independent Federal Senator, Terry Lynch. In a tearful press interview, he revealed that he had been abused by a priest in his childhood. He was sickened by the lack of progress in dealing with the damage done by paedophile priests and warned that Australia was full of thousands of traumatised men who were, "an army which is finding a focus for its anguish". He echoed what had become a common pattern for people who spoke to the press, that is, starting by condemning violence but moving on to a more nuanced statement or even support for the violence. The press took up Lynch's concept of a revolution taking place with a sense of pride that it had started in Melbourne. They became more confident and assertive in their questioning. There was a memorable press interview with Melbourne's Catholic Archbishop who was patiently explaining the process of compensating the victims of abuse. A journalist challenged him that the vow of chastity was the problem and asked had he ever broken his vow of chastity? At that point the Archbishop became embarrassed, muttered something about disrespect and ended the interview. Anyone watching the interview would have concluded that he had in fact breached his vow.

On the talk-back radio programs the conversations changed from shock and the personal sense of loss from destroyed churches to urgent calls for reform, with most of those calling for reform describing themselves as devout Catholics. The Church commissioned a public relations company to speak for them and, for a short period a dignified middle-aged woman was facing journalists. This however backfired because the journalists kept asking her why the Church was spending money on her company rather than adequately compensating victims.

It was then that Frank Rowe became a public figure in the on-going trauma. He took out a full page add in a Perth newspaper in which was listed the names of all the Australian legal firms that had defended paedophile priests. There was a swift reaction from the lawyers and the newspaper didn't repeat it but the add and its withdrawal became a news item. Frank was interviewed on television and presented himself very well as he argued his case. He said that he wasn't advocating any violence to the solicitors or their property, and the firms were on the public record anyway, he wanted to educate the public and bring about change in the way that court cases are conducted. He said,

"We all want good defence lawyers, they are an essential part of the good functioning of our legal system. But when these guys go into court to 'defend' (he emphasised the word defend) the priests, that's not what they're doing, they are out to destroy the victims. What they smugly describe as challenging the witness is a process of humiliating and abusing people who have possibly spent their lives dealing with deep emotional trauma. To put it bluntly, they rape the victims for a second time, and to their shame the judges let it happen. It's not just the victims of paedophile priest who go through this. How many women feel that they have been raped for a second time when they go to court? This is a serious fault of our justice system and it needs to be changed."

He then shocked the reporter by saying that he too had been raped by Father O'Dwyer when he was twelve. This left the reporter speechless while Frank went on to describe the six court cases of the Adelaide students, how in each, Father O'Dwyer lied and the lawyers knew he was lying. He then described the damage caused by sexual abuse in childhood which went unacknowledged in the courts; the mental health problems, the damage to families, the drug addictions and suicides. He said,

"In my class of twelve boys who were raped by Father O'Dwyer, four have committed suicide. When he finally went to jail, he only served six years. Is anyone counting the suicides amongst the thousands of children who have been raped by priests?"

The shocked reporter shook her head. Frank continued,

"I am going to do whatever I can to change the way in which the courts treat the victims of rapist priests. I will also try to match the millions of dollars that the Catholic Church spends defending them, so that the victims can have good quality legal support."

Shortly after the interview, the Federal Government announced a review of the way witnesses are treated in court.

Frank gave the reporter the contact details of Moira, Kevin's mother, and she too was interviewed on television. Her interview had even more impact on the public than Frank's. She told the story of Kevin's life, holding his photograph as she spoke. The reporter asked her what changes she would like to see the Catholic Church make, and she said,

"First of all, they need a policy of reporting to the police any accusation of misbehaviour by the priests rather than dealing with it themselves, which has been a catastrophe. And then they need to abandon their rule of chastity so that priests can live normal lives, rather than express their sexuality in a shameful and secretive manner, abusing vulnerable children and manipulating them into keeping secrets."

Following this interview, the chatter on talk-back radio was all about the role of chastity. This drew out many traditional Catholics who regarded it as a core doctrine of their faith, others challenged its role, criticising it on theological grounds and putting it in its historical context. Many, like Moira, regarded it as a significant pre-condition for the abuse of children and called for legislation to ban individuals who had taken vows of chastity from working with children.

Three weeks after Gerard launched himself in the nation's consciousness, the issue seemed to be settling down. There had been no church burnings for a week and the regular, calming announcements by the police had stilled the sense of panic. The public regarded Cardinal Drumm, then serving at the Vatican, as Australia's representative of the Catholic Church and there were frequent calls for him to make statements and return to Australia, but he disregarded these calls. The urgency for change had softened but there were political processes underway and the public was primed for accepting the recommendations of the Royal Commission.

But then there was another murder which once again rivetted the nation by the sheer power of its symbolism. In a country town in Victoria, a man in his seventies visited a nursing home and while there, went into the room of a ninety-two year old, former Catholic priest who had suffered severe dementia for many years. The priest had sexually assaulted the man as a child but this had never been reported. While in the room with the priest, the man used a small length of rope to strangle him, then he reported his action to the nurses on duty and asked them to call the police. He was widely reported as saying,

"It was something I just had to do for my self-respect."

*****

For Craig and Brian, all leads dried up during the second month of their investigation into Father O'Dwyer's death. They had put the time in but by late November, the investigation was wide open. Craig was despondent but Brian reassured him, reminding him it was always going to be an uphill job because no one wants to dob in someone who has murdered a paedophile. If it was a one-off, the murder might never be solved, but if there was another priest-killing there would be more clues, some pattern to work on. But it wasn't just their failure that was bothering Craig, it was his realisation that there was a system, a power structure that was embedded in society which tolerated unspeakable crimes. He wasn't religious but his parents were and he respected the calendar of Greek Orthodox rituals which they observed. He now suspected that all religions had this dark underbelly because religious leaders were held in such high regard that they could get away with crimes against children.

Craig was asleep when Gerard sent his text message of confession but Brian phoned Criag in the early hours of the next morning after watching Gerard's video, which had been sent to the police. They drove around to his home in Alphington where he greeted them with,

"What took you so long?"

He was courteous and completely cooperative. Later that day, he walked them along the route he took on the day of the murder and showed them where he had thrown the murder weapon and bag of clothes. A police diver retrieved them. He clarified for them all the things they didn't understand. Why Grand Final Day? He explained that he wanted to commit all three crimes on Christmas Day, the Catholic Church's big day. He had, in fact, tried to on Christmas Day of the previous year but the rapist priest he had chosen wasn't home. He decided to commit the murder on Grand Final Day because he thought that Father Stephen would be home and besides, during the Grand Final,

"It's a great time for a murder. There aren't many people about."

Craig asked him how he had managed to space the cut letters on Father Stephen's belly so accurately and wished he hadn't when Gerard gave his answer, that he had practiced repeatedly on legs of pork. Craig suspected that he would think of that for the rest of his life whenever he ate pork. Gerard wanted the police to understand that Father Stephen was murdered because he was a convicted rapist priest. From Gerard's point of view, any priest would do. The incorrect spelling was a distraction to help him stay out of jail until he had finished his job with the arson on Christmas Day.

Craig and Brian were embarrassed by their failure to solve the murder but they were satisfied they had been thorough in their investigations of Gerard. They hadn't gone over his flat forensically but Gerard confirmed their belief that they wouldn't have found anything and besides, they never had enough on him to justify the search warrant. Never-the-less, they copped some flack amongst their peers.

As the crisis and panic followed the circulation of Gerard's video, the police force was energised. The increased profile lifted their morale and they were proud of the Police Commissioner who found himself in the spotlight and responded well. There was actually less police work necessary than the public realised because most of the arsonists were confessing. Individually, most of the police had some sympathy for Gerard's campaign but, with some of their colleagues grieving for the loss of the churches where they were married, this was rarely expressed.

The impact on the men who had been abused by paedophile priests was enormous. Many of them were already going through their own personal crises as they emerged from decades of suppression with the news from the Royal Commission. Some had been influenced by the likes of Terry Lynch and were battling urges to commit acts of violence. The police were casting a broad net in their search for unconvicted arsonists and although their instructions were to be "sensitive" in their enquiries they were leaving many men feeling traumatised by interviews.

Craig was only directly involved with the nursing home murder, but his experience of interviewing Gerard and the other men from Justin's meeting had made him interested and sympathetic for the men who were being brought to the St Kilda

Road headquarters for interviews. He joined the team that was making follow-up calls to some of these interviewees and spoke with them about having counselling or contacting Broken Rites. He phoned Justin, explaining that he thought that some of the men he was seeing wouldn't take to professional counselling easily. Would Justin see them? Justin was surprised by the request but agreed to do so.

Craig's involvement with Gerard and Justin affected him more than he realised at the time. He admired Gerard and the personal stand he had made at great personal cost. Other members of the police force felt the same way, that was OK, it was possible to have views like that and remain completely professional in all aspects of their work. What disturbed Craig was the way that powerful people, and institutions such as the Catholic Church, had advantages over the less powerful within the criminal justice system. This was something which had bothered him at other times since he joined the police force.

Craig had come a long way since his student days. Much to the alarm of his parents, he had become involved with left wing politics at university. They were relieved when he started police training, something he wanted to do because he was sure he could make a difference as a compassionate cop. He did well and earned the respect of his peers for his intelligence and hard work. He enjoyed the work and discovered that he was ambitious, however, four years after the murder of Father Stephen O'Dwyer, he left the police force and entered federal politics. He could relate his change of heart back to his meetings with Gerard and Justin.

Through this work, Craig met John Holian, a social worker and ex-priest. John left the priesthood to marry and now, he and his wife had three children. John explained that, in leaving the priesthood, he was one of the rare ones. Many priests took up with women or visited prostitutes, it was something the bishops managed all the time. It was accepted as long as it didn't disturb the public image of the church. He had left the priesthood because he didn't want his love to be a sordid secret. He found it ironic that he was actually contributing to maintaining the celibate image of priests because he was the public face of what a priest must do if he wants to have a relationship with a woman. He still had friends in the priesthood and estimated that more than half of them were having sexual relationships with consenting adults. Of ones that remained celibate, there were many conservative priests, or as he put it, the psychologically disturbed conservatives and it was this subgroup that generated the paedophiles. The feeling among the most of the priesthood was that the secrecy caused by the celibacy rules was harming the church and needed to end, but in the meantime, vocations were drying up and the good works being done by the priests was being clouded.

Despite being an ex-priest, or perhaps because of it, John had the respect of the men who were receiving counselling for sexual abuse. Craig put him in touch with Justin, who was now very busy and had earned a reputation for kindness and support for men who "had been through the ringer" of psychological care. John found Justin to be enthusiastic and keen to learn how to better manage groups of men.

19

Justin watched Gerard's video several times. After his initial shock, he wanted to find some understanding of Gerard's behaviour. Somehow it all made sense; Gerard explained himself in an even, logical manner as if his life had led up to his acts, and in a way, it had. He was a strong, determined man who had personal experience of abuse by a priest and years of involvement with the processes of what happened to victims. Justin regretted that he hadn't visited Gerard before Christmas, even though he realised there was nothing he could have done to alter Gerard's behaviour. Still, he felt sad that Gerard would probably now spend the rest of his life in jail.

As Australia dealt with the aftermath of Gerard's attacks, Justin felt the need to be involved, if only as a witness. He looked at news on the internet daily or twice daily. He spent time in coffee shops reading newspapers and found reasons to engage strangers in conversation. As public opinion lurched and swirled he swam with its tides. At times, he was horrified by the violence but then he found himself feeling proud about the "success" of Gerard's campaign.

When Frank emailed him, asking him to attend a meeting at Peter McBrides's home, he was keen to attend.

Frank had also invited Michael, so there were four of them at the meeting. They couldn't help recalling their previous meeting and talked about Gerard, wishing he was there. Frank was bursting with enthusiasm, a man who had found a role which he loved. He had called the meeting because he was setting up a committee to supervise the distribution of money he was donating, to support in court the victims of paedophile priests. This would involve choosing appropriate cases, hiring the legal teams and supporting the victims throughout the process. He wanted Michael, Peter and Justin to be on the committee. He also wanted a representative from Broken Rites. He smiled as he said that Gerard was his first choice but that he was unavailable. Michael explained that, because of conflicts of interest, he could not be a member of the committee but that he would find a suitable representative from the legal profession. Frank said nothing but looked annoyed as he listened to Michael's long-winded explanation. Justin thought that some role such as this was meant for him, it was as if the last piece of a jigsaw puzzle was falling into place and he had no hesitation in accepting, but he asked Frank,

"Why do you want me on the committee?"

"You're good with people Justin. You make them feel good. The victims are going to have months of trauma with these court cases, regardless of the quality of our legal teams. I can see you meeting with them regularly, supporting them through the whole horrible business."

Frank rushed off as soon as he said what he wanted to say and Michael left soon afterwards. Peter asked Justin to stay awhile because he had something to discuss with him. He had spent a few hours with an old friend named Darryl. Darryl had been a year ahead of them at St Crispins and had also been abused by Father Stephen. Darryl had an overwhelming urge to burn down a church and Peter had tried to convince him not to. Daryl had eventually burst into tears and Peter had left feeling that he had made a hash of speaking with him. Would Justin talk to him?

The next day Justin went through the process of getting a mobile phone. A young woman helped him, explaining how the phone worked but still he was very confused by the whole business and it took him some time to understand what a 'bundle' was. He then phoned Darryl and arranged to meet him.

Justin caught a train to the Ivanhoe station then walked across to Darryl's home in North Balwyn. He found some lovely examples of Art Deco houses but most of the housing looked post war. He speculated that North Balwyn was a 'fill-in' suburb. In the early twentieth century, housing would have developed around Melbourne's radial train lines then, as motor transport became more widely available, the patches of farmland between the railway corridors would have been developed for housing. It was a hot day and he appreciated the shade of the established deciduous trees. As he approached Darryl's home, the blocks became larger and there were many modern homes and the mess that goes with housing construction. It had become an area where the people purchasing real estate demolished and then built their own houses, so the area looked like it was evolving into another Point Cook.

It was a Saturday afternoon. Darryl greeted Justin then took him through to a spacious, air-conditioned room at the back of the house over-looking a neat garden. Darryl lived with his wife and he had arranged the meeting for a time when she was out. It was a large house, there had been three children but they had grown up and left home.

Darryl, who was an accountant, was wearing shorts and a T-shirt. He was grey, nearly bald and overweight, looking like a man at ease in his environment. He offered Justin beer and spoke in a welcoming but mildly forced manner. He spoke of his friendship with Peter McBride. Justin was reluctant to direct the conversation in any particular direction and Darryl eventually ran out of steam, put his beer down and directed his gaze outside. Then he said,

"Thanks for coming Justin. There aren't many people I can talk about this with. Peter would have explained to you that I have this total pre-occupation with burning a church down. I know it's irrational and I know a psychologist would say that I'm having obsessional thoughts. The feeling started when I kept hearing and reading reports from the Royal Commissions investigations, then it got focussed when Gerard did his bit. I knew Gerard, used to play football with him with the St Crispins

Old Boys. He's someone I've always admired, and that's probably one of the reasons I want to burn down a church."

He paused and drank some of his beer, then turned to Justin,

"That's the trigger, but in reality, I've been suppressing my abuse stuff all my life. I can look back now on patterns of behaviour that show how damaged I was; the focus on work, the need for control and occasional breakouts of bad behaviour, doing stuff I'm deeply ashamed of. I've managed, until now anyway. I love my wife, I think I've been a good father, I've earned plenty of money."

He stopped talking. Justin waited for him to continue but when he didn't, said,

"Do you have a particular church in mind?"

"Yes, a local one, St Brigid's. I've been there several times at night, just to look at it and plan how I could do it. It's locked except for Sunday services and they've installed all sorts of security things now. It's not even one of the churches where a paedophile priest worked. I like Gerard's idea of destroying their churches. It's just a church that I know and it must have built up in my subconscious as a symbol for everything that's wrong with me."

"You know yourself well, don't you?" said Justin

"Yes, I do."

"I can imagine the terrible inner turmoil this must be causing for you. Your feelings about burning the church and your rational side of knowing the consequences."

"In a nut shell," Darryl replied, then continued

"I'd probably go to jail, and the reputational damage would be disastrous. I'd lose my job, my wife Melanie would probably leave me."

"Have you told your wife?"

"No. I can't tell her. I've never told her about being abused by Father Stephen."

Justin thought for a moment. He had never had any training as a counseller and he had only his instincts and his own personal insights to be guided by. He had strong sense of the importance of getting it right with Darryl. He said,

"Can I go and have a look at the church with you?"

Darryl looked surprised but pleased by the suggestion.

"Yes. It's not far. Would you like to walk or will I drive?"

They walked the kilometre to the church, which was in a suburban street set amongst houses. It was a brick building of a traditional nineteenth century design with a large central door and high, narrow stained-glass windows along the sides. There were security cameras mounted above the door and the two corners. Justin assumed there would be others. They stood in front of the church for a moment then Darryl suggested they keep walking because they would look suspicious. They returned to his house. Justin said,

"With all that security, it would be hard to set it on fire."

Darryl answered with enthusiasm,

"It would be hard. I'd go for a back window at night. They have wire grills on them so I can't get in, I'd have to pour in as much petrol as I could quickly to set it alight. Lights would go on, perhaps alarms would go off and it wouldn't be long before someone from security or neighbours came along. The church has carpets and drapes so if I could get enough petrol in quickly, it should go off like a bomb."

"Would you turn yourself in if you got away with it?

"Yes, I would. I'd be on film anyway. I'd rather be an honest arsonist making a point, like Gerard did, than a vandal."

Justin knew where to go from there,

"OK. Let's imagine you've done it. You've emptied your can of petrol through the window, a security guard's coming and you've just thrown a lighted rag into the church. Whoosh, crackle, crackle, bang!"

Justin threw up his arms to demonstrate the explosion. Darryl liked it and laughed.

"Now you wait for the police to arrive, the security guard doesn't have a key and you happily listen to the fire roaring through the church. I'm not sure what happens next, I suppose the police take you away, you have an unpleasant night and the next morning Melanie bails you out. How would you feel then?"

"I think I'd be feeling satisfied about wrecking the church."

"And what next, what would it be like at home during the next few days?"

Darryl slumped at the thought. He said,

"Facing the music. Melanie would be horrified. I'd tidy up work things I had to do. Try to explain things to Melanie."

"Do you think that would be the end of your church-burning thoughts?"

"I hope so. You'd think so wouldn't you? I've thought about that, what if I just wanted to go and burn another church?"

Justin said,

"I don't know anything about your wife, but I can see you're worried about her reaction. What I've observed about spouse behaviour is that they might get upset and angry about little things but if something big happens they are usually supportive. Can you see your wife rallying to support you?

"I've thought about that a lot too and I really don't know what she'd do."

Darryl started shedding tears, but he didn't seem embarrassed. Justin continued,

"What if you went away somewhere after you were bailed, kept out of Melanie's way while she dealt with it, spoke to her on the phone?"

"Yeah, I could do that. We've got a place at Mogg's Creek."

"So, you're at Mogg's Creek. I suppose your court case could take months to come around. At Mogg's Creek you do lots of walks on the beach, talk to you wife on the phone, read *War and Peace* and every other book you've ever wanted to read."

Darryl smiled at the thought, then looked serious and said,

"I think I'd have to stay away from Melanie while she decided what she'd do."

"She's really important to you, isn't she?

'She's everything to me."

At that point, Darryl covered his face with his hands and

sobbed. Justin felt uncomfortable and waited. After a few minutes, he spoke again.

"Imagine this, a different scenario. A few weeks before you burned the church down, you tell Melanie all about how Father Stephen abused you and how it has damaged you. You ask her if she has noticed that you've been a bit strange lately. You explain that it's because of what Gerard did, that it has stirred everything up for you. How do you think she'd handle that?

Darryl wiped his face with his handkerchief then blew his nose. Looking out through the window he said,

"I think she'd be OK. She'd probably say she always thought something like that had happened to me."

"And if you'd told her, it would be less of a shock when you burnt the church down. You don't think she'd become a church-burning crusader too, do you?"

Darryl smiled,

"Definitely not, she has been disgusted by the revelations about the paedophile priests though."

Some threshold had been reached, an obstacle overcome. Justin felt emotionally drained and suspected that Darryl did too. Justin said,

"I'm not a counsellor Darryl. I'm not even sure why Peter asked me to visit you, but I'm glad I have. I think, like me, you don't want to see psychologists. I'm damaged, all of Father Stephen's victims are damaged in different ways. I'm not here to talk you out of burning the church. In fact, if you do it and need to go and hibernate at Mogg's Creek, I'll come and visit, we could go for walks and play five hundred."

Darryl laughed. Justin continued,

"I admire Gerard. When I got over the shock of watching his video I thought 'Great. Now something might happen'. I haven't had the drive to kill a priest or burn a church. That's not me, I haven't got it in me. In fact, I feel a bit of a coward when I compare myself with Gerard. How did you feel when you heard that Father Stephen was dead?"

"Good at first, but then it didn't seem to matter. He was so old he was going to die anyway. His death didn't take away the damage. But I'm glad that there are a lot of rapist priests out here now feeling scared shitless."

"Yeah, I thought the same thing. I remembered something I read about executions in the USA. In cases where someone was being executed for murder, they were inviting members of the family of the murder victims to watch the execution. They thought it would help with their grieving or their closure or something. It didn't help at all, the family members just said, 'He's gone, he's not suffering any more, but we still are'. I think they abandoned the program.

Anyway, I must go now. I'll phone tomorrow and I want to keep in contact, whatever happens."

Darryl shook his hand. Justin felt tears coming to his eyes. He said,

"You're a good bloke Darryl."

Justin phoned Darryl the next night. Melanie was home and he didn't want to speak for long. He said that he was thinking about telling Melanie about the abuse. He paused then said, with a spark of humour in his voice,

"On a scale of ten for my pre-occupation with burning a church; I've dropped from nine to six since your visit."

Justin was pleased to hear that. Perhaps he hadn't been completely honest with Darryl; he really didn't want him to try to burn the church. He didn't think his plan would succeed and it would just be a futile and humiliating gesture.

20

For Justin, returning to his flat after walking the Major Mitchell Trail was like moving to a new home; the flat hadn't changed, he had. He had a restless energy that altered every aspect of his previous life. He was playing his viola again, and enjoying it but he no longer felt immersed in the music. Instead of playing for two to three hours, he would stop after about half an hour. He would watch news programs on his computer and sit in coffee shops reading newspapers. He was exploring Melbourne and seeing it with new vision. He was more sensitive to the nuances of architecture, variations in the expression of wealth and the ethnicity of the people he encountered. He found this stimulating and was puzzled by the experience but happy to embrace it. He wondered if it was a result of his months of wandering in the mainly rural landscapes of the Major Mitchell Trail. Quite simply, he loved Melbourne, his home, his city.

He searched for his old flame, Morag McGuiness, on the internet and found her. She still lived on South Uist and there were several references to her role on the committee of the Highlander and Islander Games Society, for which she had been the president in 2009. Justin looked at photos of committee members with their names printed below and was confused at first because he didn't recognise her. Then he noticed that she had become fat, very fat, and the facial features he remembered were now buried in jowls and a double chin. He wasn't repulsed by this, he wanted to know the pathway her life had taken since he knew her eighteen years before.

He found her email address and started to compose a letter to her, giving her a brief description of his life. It became too long, so he abandoned the attempt at an email and started writing a long letter which he would send as an email attachment. It became a long process; he returned to bits he had written, expanded some, and recorded the emotional contexts of others. He was still writing after three weeks, spending most of his days either writing or having long walks during which he thought about what he would write next. The letter was a detailed description of the childhood abuse he had suffered and the way that it had influenced or determined the various phases of his life. He recognised that he had embarked on a therapeutic process, either that, or he was just stirring up a muddy pool that was better left undisturbed. When he eventually finished, he had a thirty-thousand word essay and a tremendous sense of satisfaction. How could he impose such a literary assault on Morag? After another week of hesitating, he sent the letter with an introductory email which amounted to an apology. He knew this would be a bizarre and probably unwelcome thing to receive but he rationalised that she was the trigger, it wouldn't have been written but for her, he owed it to her.

Justin had several phone conversations with Darryl, who was agonising over how he would talk to his wife Melanie. They discussed the different approaches he was considering and Justin offered to role-play Melanie for him so he could try out these different approaches. It was an extraordinary experience for both of them; it had Darryl in tears at one stage but they finished the session collapsing with laughter. As Darryl made his confessions, Justin would act a role as Melanie-the-tearful, Melanie-the compassionate, Melanie-the-cold-and-angry, or Melanie-the-downright-furious. Before Justin left, they celebrated with one of Darryl's best wines.

Three nights later, Darryl phoned to tell Justin he had had his talk with Melanie and it had gone very well. He didn't give Justin any details and Justin didn't ask. He said that he still thought about burning the church but the feeling had become distant, easier to control. Like 'bouncing a ball' he said.

Darryl asked Justin to talk with a friend of his named Declan, another victim of Father Stephen. Peter McBride phoned him again and asked if he would take on the counselling of two other men who had been seeing Gerard before he went to jail.

Justin arranged to visit Declan on a Saturday afternoon when his wife and grown children would be away. It took him over three hours to walk to Declan's home in the suburb of Wantirna South. He had never been there before and he enjoyed the walk. Wantirna South lay in the great wedge of outer urban development in Melbourne's south-east. From the appearance of the houses, Justin thought the suburb was built in the 1980s. As he walked along the street where Declan lived he noticed that the whole street was full of parked cars and thought there must have been a party somewhere.

Declan greeted him warmly and spoke readily about his abuse and the ways he believed it had affected his life. His main concern was the way he communicated with his wife. He described his unhappiness with the way they were drifting apart since his wife returned to full-time work and blamed himself. Justin's impression was that Declan was an insightful and emotionally intelligent man who believed his problems were the result of his never telling his wife about his childhood sexual abuse, a pattern which Justin found to be common in the men he spoke with. Justin was out of his depth when it came to marital counselling but did his best to be a good listener.

In the study where they sat, there were hundreds of cameras on shelves around the walls. Justin commented on these and Declan proudly described how he had been collecting cameras for fifty years and had some old and rare models. He spent the next hour showing Justin his favourites, opening them to demonstrate the evolution of camera technology. Justin genuinely enjoyed this but decided afterwards that it had been a mistake to spend so much time on Declan's hobby. It was a good way to establish friendship but it was an easy distraction and possibly stopped Declan from giving more time to what was most important for him.

When it was time for Justin to leave, Declan walked outside with him and asked where he had parked his car. He was amazed that Justin had walked and, because it had started to rain, insisted on driving him to the nearest station which was ten kilometres away. Justin commented on the way the street was parked out and asked where the party was. Declan's answer left him appalled with the disastrous planning of the suburb. He said,

"The street's always like that. The estate was built in 1989 and filled with young couples who went on to have the average two children each. Now, the kids have grown up and most of them are living at home and working or at Uni. There's no public transport so every household has four cars, for the parents and grown up kids. That's why the street is always full of parked cars. The drive from here to Carlton, where I work, takes an hour and a quarter. In the past, I would drive to a station and leave my car there to catch the train in, but so did everyone else in the area, so the residents near the station got annoyed and two-hour-parking-only signs went up. Then I drove to a station further out until the signs went up again. I went through that four times before I gave up and now I drive all the way to work."

*****

A meeting was held to establish the committee for Frank's victim support program. Justin and Peter were there and two women, Helen, from Broken Rights and Joan, a barrister whom Michael had approached to join the committee. Frank would not be a part of the committee because, for several reasons, he wanted to remain independent of its decision making. He would provide the money only and had ten million dollars ready for the committee to start with. Joan was able to describe the process of establishing the committee as a legal entity and she said they would need an accountant, preferably one who would serve on the committee. Justin said he would ask Darryl if he would join. When they had finished their official business, Justin had a long conversation with Helen. She, and the other members of the Broken Rites Council, all loved and missed Gerard. Some members were devastated by his behaviour, others, she thought, were "secretly doing star jumps" and Justin got the impression that she was one of them. Gerard had broken fundamental rules of Broken Rites and they should have officially expelled him but had in fact 'retired' him. They were relieved that he had found out Father Stephen's address independently of Broken Rites, otherwise their organisation would have been compromised.

The following night Frank appeared on the news leading a demonstration outside a court in Perth. A paedophile priest was on trial but the demonstrators didn't target the priest, they surrounded the defence barrister chanting, "Respect the victim".

*****

Justin received an email from the detective Craig Theophanous asking to call him. Justin phoned and Craig explained that it was just a courtesy call because he knew that Finn Magee was a friend of his. Finn had been found dead in a lane off Grey Street in St Kilda. Homicide had been called in, hence Craig's involvement, because he had a head injury and there was lots of blood. However, it turned out to be an accidental death. Finn had fallen off a wall and had several injuries resulting from the fall as well as the fatal head injury. No one knew why he had climbed up onto the wall.

Justin was upset and wrote down the name of the funeral director that Craig gave him. He then went on to have a conversation with Craig, a rewarding conversation that confirmed his belief that he was a very decent person. Justin explained how everyone was surprised that Gerard had murdered Father Stephen but in retrospect, recognised that he had the determination to do such a thing. Craig asked after the other men who had attended Justin's meeting. Justin discussed them, then went on to describe the informal counselling work he had been doing. Craig was interested and spoke of his personal devastation as he learned the extent of damage caused by the paedophile priests.

Justin phoned the funeral director and was, at first, upset by the response he received. The woman who spoke with him said there was not going to be a funeral. Mr Magee's body would be cremated and a family member was going to collect the ashes. For reasons of confidentiality she could not disclose the name of the family member. Justin didn't understand; he had never heard of someone not having a funeral. The woman asked him about his relationship with the deceased and softened her tone when he explained that he was an old school friend who had recently reconnected with Finn. She then went on to explain that what often happens with people "living in Mr Magee's circumstances" is that they have become alienated from their friends and family and go to, what is still called, "a pauper's grave". These are subsidised by the government but the funeral directors still make a loss on them so they are shared around. In Finn's case, a family member had agreed to pay but wanted as little involvement (and Justin concluded, minimal cost) as possible. Justin thanked the funeral director and tried to find a relative of Finn's to talk to, but couldn't.

That was a dreadful experience for Justin. He had never shown much interest in funerals in the past because he took them for granted but he couldn't let Finn go without doing something to mark his death. He looked in a drawer where he kept things from his childhood and found a ruler which Finn had given him. It was a souvenir wooden ruler with pictures from the Gold Coast which Finn had given to him when he returned from a holiday in Queensland. They must have been about twelve years old at the time. Justin carried the ruler around with him for the rest of the day.

*****

Three weeks after he sent his essay, Morag replied to Justin by email. She wrote,

My goodness Justin, what a story. I have read it three times now and it is the most moving thing I have ever read. I feel honoured that you chose to send it to me. Thank you.

Where have the years gone?

I read about your friend Gerard and the impact he has had all around the world. I am glad to say that we have been blessed with

good priests in the Outer Hebrides.

No work of literature from me, just a wee paragraph about my life. I've been on South Uist since you left, is it eighteen years ago? I enjoy the rhythms and relationships of island life and can't see myself ever leaving. Struan continued his heavy drinking ways but at least he treated me better. I suppose our relationship was more like that of a diligent parent and a wayward child, than a married couple. He died of liver disease seven years ago and I have been on my own since then. I work at the post office, which is a busy place now that everyone buys things on-line. I am very busy with committee work for the Highlander and Islander Games Association.

If you saw photos of me you will have noticed that I have long passed, what is euphemistically known as, "cuddly" and my hips and knees are wearing out. Your long letter has made me think about my own life and the way it has been dominated by alcoholic men – psychological issues there I am sure.

Are you still interested in architecture and design? I've a notion to invite you to afternoon tea at a special place in Glasgow where I occasionally go on Committee business. The tea rooms were designed by Charles Rennie McIntosh who is quite famous over here now. He designed the interior completely, down to the spoons and tea cups.

God bless you Justin.

The more Justin thought about the letter, the more he liked it. He was glad that she wanted to see him. He recognised that the invitation to the tea rooms was because she didn't want him to turn up on South Uist where he would be remembered, and their past history was known. He asked himself, what could he want from meeting her? He couldn't come up with a satisfactory answer but accepted that it was the sort of question that the passage of time would answer. He would communicate with her again by email.

He found images of the tea rooms on the internet and looked at other works of Charles Rennie McIntosh. He was fascinated.

*****

Darryl agreed to join the committee. He had thought about it for a week then accepted, saying, with his dry humour,

"That means I won't be able to burn any churches for a while."

Justin had carefully explained when inviting him that he was not trying to be coercive, that the offer was not a way to keep him away from the petrol cans but still, it worried him that he might be seen as being manipulative. He wasn't surprised when he had his recurring dream about the burning church that night because he had gone to bed thinking about Darryl. As he lay in bed the next morning thinking about his dream, he had an idea, a wonderful idea which delighted him with its purity and simplicity. It was an obvious next step, a natural progression in the changes he was going through at the moment and a confirmation that he was on the right path.

21

Richard O'Mara, at Colac Real Estate, took the call from the Melbourne man who wanted to look at the church for sale at Barwon Downs. He was surprised and pleased. Surprised because it had been on the market for three years and no one had looked at it for over a year, pleased because of a conversation he had with some other real estate agents the night before. He was describing the potential for Barwon Downs and believed it would be "discovered" and take off. The nearby towns of Birregurra, Forrest and Deans Marsh were all doing well. There were now good restaurants at Birregurra and Forrest which were drawing people from everywhere. Deans Marsh had its regular musical events at Martian's Café and Forrest was a centre for mountain bike rides. Melbourne people were making "Green Changes" and moving to all three towns and this was reflected in the turn-over and house prices. Since Barwon Down's store had closed, the only thing it had going for it was Clarice's, but it was crying out for some tourist attracting development in its main street, on the road to Apollo Bay.

The man sounded enthusiastic, he had a sister living in Barwon Downs and he had seen the church from the distance. That was a good sign because most people were put off by the colour. In fact, during the recent spate of church burnings, one of the Barwon Downs locals had said to him,

"I wish they'd come and burn our church."

The Melbourne man said he wasn't sure how he would use the church, he might even demolish it. Did it have a heritage overlay? (no, it didn't). Could Richard bring him some information about the demolition process?

He arranged to meet the man, Justin Collins, the next afternoon.

*****

Justin had been working hard, spending time with the numerous men who had been referred to him. He enjoyed this work and was sure he was doing something useful. The men he dealt with were all different, he had to depend on his instincts and follow their leads. He felt that he was on the safest ground, and less likely to make mistakes, by just letting them tell their stories. Some of the men focussed on what Justin considered to be secondary problems; the treatment they had had, compensation issues and what the government was doing. With them, he resisted trying to draw them out on their human relationships because the psychologists had probably already done that. Instead, he just tried to have fun with them. He didn't have any particular agenda. Because of this, he found himself in novel situations, going fishing or to sporting events or pubs. He was drinking more beer than he had since his youth.

Justin had created an imaginary model for the way people were affected by abuse in their childhood, a model based on architecture. The damage done depended on the type of "building" you were in the first place. If you were a skyscraper and your foundations were damaged, sooner or later you collapsed; Kevin and Finn were examples of skyscrapers. Darryl was a solidly built house with an annoying crack in it which couldn't be fixed but which didn't threaten the structural integrity of the building. When he applied his model to himself, he saw himself as a palace that had been abandoned and forgotten and became covered in thick brambles, and now someone was cutting away the brambles.

On the train to Birregurra, Justin had a few phone calls to make but by the time the train reached Moriac, he could relax and enjoy the landscape. It was early March and the Western District was a bleached yellow against the dazzling blue of the sky.

Maureen met Justin at the station. He hadn't seen her since Christmas Day but their relationship had changed, become closer, since he returned from the Major Mitchell Trail. Having a phone helped. Maureen said she could feel the changes going on in him.

At the station, Maureen told him what had happened at Siobhan's house,

"Do you remember how Chris' weeping cherry was stolen? Well, he's bought another one, and he's put a chain around it! Siobhan says it's an enormous chain which is bolted to the house. All the neighbours are talking about it, Siobhan's very embarrassed."

They had lunch with Jacques, then had time for a short walk in the forest before meeting Richard at 2 o'clock. It was a still, hot day, more summer than autumn but the nights were drawing in and there was the sense that the seasonal change was underway. For Maureen, this was the best time of the year. She described the forest at this time as being exhausted and waiting for the change; the branches of the trees looked limp, the dry leaves crackled under their feet and there were no flowers in bloom. The birds were silent and the only sign of life was the brown butterflies that they disturbed as they walked. Maureen commented,

"They're Common Brown Butterflies. The males and females look quite different, the females are mostly brown with a big target spot on their wings and the males have a black-veined pattern. At this time of year, you only see the females."

"Why's that?" asked Justin.

"I think the males are all dead. By February their wings are looking ragged, then they're all gone. The males and the females have different seasons. The males arrive in November and fly in circles around each other. Perhaps they're fighting and establishing their territories. Then the females arrive in January and for the next two months you see males and females, then the males die off and then by the end of April, the females are gone."

Justin and Maureen walked the short distance to the scarlet church on its bare paddock just above the town. There was no one about. The exhausted ambience of the forest seemed to have spread over the whole landscape and they were hot by the time they arrived. Richard arrived at the same time as them in a shiny Holden. He was wearing a white shirt and a tie and they felt sorry for him, that he felt the need to wear the tie in that heat.

The church was set on a small block surrounded by farm land that merged with the forest. The grass around the church had not been mowed for some time and was now a mottled mass of dry, collapsing tussocks. You would have expected there to be an ancient peppercorn or a remnant eucalypt nearby but, apart from a disused toilet, the church stood starkly in the middle of the block. It was a traditional design with the gable end towards the road. It had five windows along each side but none of them contained stained glass. As they walked towards it, Richard cheerfully explained that it was built in the 1930s and ceased to function as a church in the 1970s. It was deconsecrated then sold in 1990. That owner did nothing with it and it was sold again four years ago to the current owners. They restumped and painted it and had plans to turn it into their home but then they divorced.

The church sat on a gentle slope and the front of the church was elevated to allow for this slope. Richard took them up some wooden stairs and unlocked the large front doors for them to enter. It was quite bare inside with no furnishings and only a few light fittings. The rear of the church, where the altar and pulpit must have once been, was raised by one step to create a low platform. Maureen and Justin moved around the old church, inspecting it in a manner which they expected they were meant to in the presence of a real estate agent. Maureen commented,

"The glass windows are all intact."

Justin said,

"The floor boards are good. It looks as though they replaced some."

"Yes," said Richard. "They did a good job but only got as far as the basic shell. The power can be reconnected but there's no plumbing."

They wandered outside and walked around the church. Justin noted that there was a reasonable space underneath the church, the sides were covered with wooden slats and there was a trapdoor to the underneath. He opened the trap door and looked in.

They walked back to Richards's car where he gave Justin a folder with information about the property and information about demolition. He said,

"For a building that has not been used for more than a year, getting a demolition order is usually a quick process, taking a few weeks. Getting a building permit takes longer, depending on what you want to do but, because there are no immediate neighbouring houses, that shouldn't be a problem."

Justin thanked Richard, told him he liked the place and said that he would be in contact within the next few days. Richard drove back to Colac feeling good, he liked Justin and could tell that Justin liked what he saw, you can usually tell straight away if a client likes a place. He was proud of the way he had used the word 'deconsecrated', it was a new word for him, he had looked it up in the dictionary.

That evening, Justin discussed his plans with Maureen and Jacques; he wanted to buy the church and burn it as a type of healing ritual. He described how he got the idea from their winter solstice bonfire and from conversations with his friend Darryl. He had Daryl in mind in particular but also knew several other men who would probably be interested. He too would like to burn a church, it might even help to stop his recurring dream of the burning church.

Maureen and Jacques were surprised but enthusiastic and wondered if it could be done to complement their annual winter solstice celebration. Jacques, who was in the local fire brigade, said it would be permissible during the burning off season. That was usually at the end of April but might be a bit later this year because of the dry season. They wondered what the locals would think. Most of them thought that, since it had been painted scarlet, it was an eyesore but there would probably be some who wouldn't like the idea because it had been a church.

They stayed up late that night, drinking beer and talking. None of them wanted to leave and break up the feeling of connection they had. It was a hot, moonlit night and the animals were restless; they heard possums fighting, a koala was grunting and a boobook owl hooting. Inside the house, they were bothered by mosquitoes. Justin told Maureen how much he admired her relationship with the forest and the knowledge she had gained by spending so much time there. He voiced the idea that he was developing a similar connection with his environment, the totally urban environment of Melbourne. He also spoke of the change in his attitude towards playing his viola. In the past, it been all about striving for "deep resonance". He found this hard to explain but said that it was an almost hypnotic state he sometimes achieved when he had mastered a piece of music so that the playing of it was almost automatic and then he could dwell on approaching the perfect resonance of the bow on the strings. When that happened, the music seemed to "penetrate to the deepest part of my brain". He wasn't trying to do that now and his viola practice was a lighter experience. Maureen seized upon this to say that he needed to perform with others, to be giving with his music.

As he lay in bed that night, Justin worried about his plan for buying and burning the church. It was a mad idea, and if it didn't come about, he would be left with a useless piece of real estate. The money wasn't a problem for him but he didn't want to waste it. As much as he loved Maureen, there was something in him that rebelled against her enthusiasm for drawing him out, getting him involved. He reconciled that he was experiencing feelings that he didn't have when he lived as a hermit, but now that he was 'out of his cave' he would be subject to these 'real world' feelings.

By the next morning, Justin had made up his mind that he would buy the scarlet church. Maureen drove him into Colac and accompanied him while he made the arrangements. First, he went to see Richard in his office and signed the necessary forms, then went to the bank to get a bank cheque for the deposit. He wanted the shortest possible settlement period and this was arranged for one month. Next, they walked to the Colac Otway Shire Offices and got an application form for demolition. There was time before he caught a train to Melbourne so they went to a café for coffee.

It was a perfect March morning, it would be hot again in the afternoon but the air had cooled overnight and the sky was clear. Justin was filled with the sense that history was being made, something special was going to happen and the process had started that morning. Colac, on an ordinary working day, was crackling with significance for him. He observed his surroundings which had taken on the intensity of his inner processes. He found delight in the movement of people and cars, the sun on windows, the breeze through leaves. There was an unusual smell hanging over the town, a muddy, salty smell. Maureen explained how Lake Colac, out of view to the north, had gone dry recently and that accounted for the smell. Even this, which could have been described as an unpleasant smell, resounded in Justin's altered perception as something meaningful and magical. His mood fluctuated during the train journey home, he even had a moment of despair as the train passed the You Yangs, thinking that no one would be interested in coming to Barwon Downs for the church burning, but by the time he returned home, he was energised again. He planned a potential date. It should be on a Sunday, it had to be on a Sunday, the day for going to church. Hopefully, a Sunday closest to the winter solstice, giving it some ritual, pagan significance, like Maureen's bonfire. That would be late June. He would need to decorate the church, restore it to look like a real, active church. That meant he would have to purchase some pews, the stations of the cross to put on the walls, an altar, a pulpit, candle sticks and candles, vases. Should he repaint the church to make it look more conventional? He wanted to seek out and buy all these furnishings straight away but persuaded himself to calm down and wait for settlement and the demolition order.

22

In late March, Frank Rowe was in the news again. He had paid for the distribution of letters to houses in the neighbourhoods of thirty-two barristers living throughout Australia. These were barristers, who had during the last decade, defended paedophile priests in court. The letter read,

Your neighbour (the barristers name) defended the paedophile priest (priest's name) in court during (the year). Here follows a part of the transcript of the his/her cross-examination of the victim ...

The extracts were quite shocking to read because of the sneering tone, or the sarcasm which the barristers had used in their mocking of the victims.

The barristers, who were already jittery because another solicitors' offices had been set on fire, were outraged. They clamped an injunction to stop him distributing more of the letters and cried foul, that the court records were being quoted out of context. This is where Frank demonstrated his skills in dealing with the legal fraternity. He anticipated the argument of context and on the day of the distribution of the letters he wrote to the barristers, stating

I understand that my letter, although accurately quoting you, might be considered to be out of context. There is only one way to deal with this issue of context and that is to show the readers the full transcript of your cross-examination or, if you think it necessary, the full trial. Would you like me to send to all the recipients of my letter the full transcript of the trial to correct any misunderstanding?

He appeared on the television news and read one of these letters in response to the reporter's questions about the upset barristers. Throughout the interview, he repeatedly dropped his mantra "respect the victim" which had now become a popular catch-phrase with anyone talking about trials. When the reporter, half-heartedly presented the lawyers' view that it was a necessary part of our justice system for barristers to challenge witnesses, he gave, what became a much-quoted reply that,

"The brutal way they treat victims is unacceptable and needs to change. We don't burn witches any more, do we?"

*****

Justin received the demolition permit two days after settlement and only then did he start to discuss his plans with other people. He was nervous when he told Darryl, but he was delighted with the idea. Of course he wanted to be involved. He understood immediately Justin's concept of it being therapeutic and was moved by the expense Justin was prepared to outlay for his plan.

He said,

"I don't know if it will stop me wanting to burn St Brigid's, but I don't care if it doesn't, I want to see your church burn."

He discussed with Darryl the decorations for the interior of the church. They both thought it was important that there were the stations of the cross, which in their minds, distinguished Catholic churches from other denominations. Once Justin started searching for church decorations, he was surprised to find how much was available, a reflection of the number of churches which had closed in recent years.

Justin's church was a small country church and not wide enough for two rows of pews, so he bought eight pews to go in a single row. They were the type he wanted with guttering at the back to hold hymn books and looked as if they would have seated six or seven people. The second-hand dealer who sold them to Justin was delighted to get rid of them and sold them for a price that seemed to lack respect for the quality of the woodwork. It was less than the cost of transporting them to Barwon Downs. He looked at several sets of stations of the cross and chose the most expensive because of the beautiful wood carving. The antique dealer loved them and didn't want to part with them, or perhaps he was just a clever salesman. They were nineteenth century and had been carved by craftsmen in the Tyrol. He couldn't bear to tell the dealer what was going to happen to them when he paid the $20,000 that they cost. He transported them back to his flat in three large suitcases.

Justin had fun scouring second-shops for suitable decorations such as candlesticks and framed prints of Madonnas. He couldn't resist buying some kitsch prints of Jesus with his heart exposed because they had fascinated him as a child. They weren't really suitable as church decorations but he had places in mind for them inside the door at the back of the church. He bought an oak table for the altar and a beautiful new altar cloth with gilt threads from a shop that sold ecclesiastic supplies. Darryl wanted to have in the church a statue of Mary with her sky-blue gown and insisted on paying for it himself.

Buying a crucified Jesus was difficult and it was one of the last things he did. There were plenty available but it was a such a central feature of Christian faith that he couldn't escape a sense of shame in buying it for his purpose. When he had finally chosen one and was carrying it from the shop, his perspective changed. As an object, horizontal in his arms, it became an ugly image, a man being tortured to death. It was strange that he had never thought of it that way before.

Justin tentatively raised his plan with the men he was counselling. They were surprised but most were enthusiastic and wanted to come. Remembering the touching scene at Maureen's bonfire the previous winter solstice where her friend disposed of his medical records in the flames, he suggested that they bring something of their own, something of personal significance which they would like to symbolically dispose of in the burning church. This became a very emotional process, with many of the men wanting to explain to him what objects they were going to bring, and why. They also asked if they could bring friends or relatives. Justin hadn't expected this but he couldn't think of any reasons for restricting people. As word got around other people wanted to see Justin for counselling.

Justin invited Peter, Glen, Pat, Michael and Frank. Peter, Glen and Pat agreed to come straight away. Michael discussed the invitation at length with Justin on the phone, but the whole conversation was really a process of persuading himself to come and Justin smiled as he listened. Frank's response was thoughtful and apologetic, he couldn't come. He explained that all his work battling the lawyers involved presenting an image that he was opposed to the violent acts that were advocated by Gerard and he couldn't be seen at a church burning, even if it was legal and therapeutic. Justin assured him that he understood. Two days later he phoned and said,

"Bugger it Justin, I'm coming. I love the idea of what you are doing and I want to be in it, for myself and to support you."

Justin tried to keep track of the number of people who would attend. By late April he thought there would be sixty to seventy. Everyone in Barwon Downs knew about the plans and Maureen and Jacques had been carefully explaining the nature of Justin's work with traumatised men. The fire was meant to be therapeutic. The questions the locals asked were, 'Is he going to rebuild on the site?' and 'Can we come too?' Justin said,

"Tell them, yes, and yes."

At this time, Justin started performing regularly with Maureen at Clarice's. He would learn the tunes Maureen wanted him to play, travel to Birregurra by train where Maureen would pick him up on Fridays, then practice at her place prior to their performances on the Friday and Saturday nights. The tunes Maureen wanted Justin to learn were Celtic and folk tunes, which were mostly repetitive and easy for him to learn, the challenge for him was the tempo of some of the reels and jigs. At their performances, Justin found beauty in his role of complementing Maureen's singing and harp playing. They retained their instinct for connecting and Justin was able to match the varying moods of her songs. She would occasionally nod or smile for him to drop out or play alone. They didn't need to follow a program of tunes because of their talents in complementing each other and Maureen's ability to judge the moods of the audience. With time, Justin came to share this skill and knew which tune Maureen would select.

He began to recognise the regulars, the locals who came most weekends, as distinct from the weekenders who might have been to one of the good local restaurants for a long lunch and were ready to be entertained. He had conversations with the locals during breaks. They were interested in the plans to burn the church, which they spoke of as "our church", they understood the therapeutic nature of the plan and also knew that Justin had been sexually abused by the murdered priest, the same one who abused his friend Gerard Connolly. They considered this too private a matter to raise with him, instead, they raised practical issues, such as the church's terrible colour, how well it would burn and the local rainfall in June.

There was one moment, brief but frightening for Justin, when he thought that he had grossly offended a man with his plan to burn the church. The man was what he would describe as an old local, rather than one of the more recent green-change, urban-raised locals. He was a middle-aged man who was overweight and bearded, looking like the stereotype of a bikie. He struck up a conversation with Justin and said,

"I'm going to miss that church. My parents were married there and I was baptised there."

That was the moment Justin felt his heart sink. The church really was a place of local significance, a place of memories and meaningful life events. Suddenly his whole plan seemed brutal, insensitive and irreverent. He experienced the panicky sensation he had in his childhood when he got into trouble. It was a fleeting moment, the man went on to say,

"If it rains a lot the week before, it might be hard to get the fire going. I could bring around a trailer load of dry stuff, to put underneath the church to help get it going."

Never the less, that jolted Justin's confidence. He had initiated something which had grown more than he expected and now he probably couldn't stop the process, even if he wanted to. It was out of his control. Having set a date and a light-up time, he had no control over how the people behaved on the day. Would there be any aggression or difficult emotional behaviour? He had a sleepless night that night. As a hermit, he never had these sorts of problems, the loss of control that comes from dealing with people. He questioned his own need to have control and discovered patterns in his past life, patterns he had never noted before, of avoiding or leaving situations when he didn't feel in control. Was that another part of his damage?

Justin didn't invite John Holian to the burning, he didn't think it necessary for him to come but John heard about it and wanted to come. He regarded himself as a good Catholic who wanted to improve the church, to drag it into the twenty-first century. He had unresolved anger to do with his decision to leave the priesthood and wanted to burn in the church something that expressed his hostility towards the priesthood's vow of chastity.

John asked Justin if he would meet with a friend of his, a Catholic priest,

"One of the good ones," John said

The priest, Father Michael Worsek, had heard from John about the plan to burn a church and wanted to discuss it with him. Justin was nervous about this but had recovered somewhat from his doubts and felt sure he could courteously present his case to a priest.

Father Michael visited Justin at his flat. Justin had expected that he would be wearing some form of priestly dress, a collar or at least a crucifix, but he was dressed casually in slacks and an open-necked shirt. This correctly gave Justin the impression that he had not come on official business. He was youngish, probably in his mid-thirties, and brought with him such a sense of goodwill and kindliness that had Justin smiling more than usual.

Justin welcomed him and took him into the living room, noticing how bare it looked in the context of having a guest.

Father Michael wanted to be called Michael and, very early in the conversation said,

"I imagine you are surprised by my visit and I'd like to say straight away that I like the idea of the church burning that you are planning."

He explained how John Holian had described his plan and how excited he was about attending. He was nervous about visiting Justin and wanted to give a long explanation, but the main purpose of his visit was to ask permission to attend the church-burning himself. Justin must have looked surprised and Michael continued,

"I will understand if you don't want me there, but if I was to come, I wouldn't be in uniform and I wouldn't make myself known as a priest. I would be attending in the spirit of dealing with my own personal issues, for therapeutic reasons."

He was uncomfortable and Justin wanted to reassure him. He said,

"It's strange how my plan for the church-burning keeps changing. I was getting worried about the way it had slipped out of my control, but now I've accepted it's not my project, it's for anyone who wishes to come …"

He paused as if looking for the right words.

"I was going to say, for anyone who wishes to come in the right spirit, but I'm not even sure what that means anymore."

He smiled, and continued,

"You've surprised me, but you are welcome to come. Could you help me understand why you want to come to such an event, which must seem hostile to the Catholic Church."

Michael then gave his long explanation. Firstly, he saw himself as a devout Catholic and he worked hard to be a good parish priest. He loved his flock (that was the word he used) and he obeyed his vows, including the chastity vow. Although his faith was firm and he had no intention of leaving the Church, the murder of Father Stephen and its aftermath had accentuated some doubts which he had. He was disappointed by the governance of the church and appalled by the way the paedophile priests had been moved around. He was confident that wouldn't happen again, however he wasn't convinced that the problem of paedophile priests was solved. He believed that chastity was an on-going cause of dysfunction within the priesthood and that the hierarchy of the Church was too rigid and slow in changing with social conditions. Within Australia, there was a spirit of reform which unfortunately was not being expressed because of the influence of powerful figures such as Cardinal Drumm on the conservative side of the Church.

He then went on to describe what he had learnt about vocations, the drive that leads young men and women to become priests and nuns. In his case, he developed a religious fervour when he was fourteen years old. This stayed with him and he never doubted that he had a vocation and that he would become a priest. What he didn't understand as a teenager was the nature of our sexuality "and by the way, I'm strictly heterosexual", and how it was suppressed by his passion for religion but would never go away. He had a better understanding now and he battled with his sex-drive, a battle he was winning so far, but in retrospect, be believed that young men shouldn't enter the priesthood the way he did. It should only happen when men were older and had a better understanding of themselves. The other thing he had learnt about vocations is that many teenage boys mistakenly believe their lack of interest in girls means that they have a vocation. It is only later that they realise they are homosexual. This means that there is a higher proportion of homosexual men in the priesthood than the general population. These men have an even greater difficulty than him in dealing with their sexuality because of the Church's hostility towards homosexuality.

Michael suddenly looked weary and lowered his head. Justin felt a shift in his role to that of a father figure. He said,

"I understand. Thank you, you've told me something important, something I needed to know. What do you want from attending the church burning?"

"Good question. I'm not sure. At first, I was thinking that I wanted to witness what the other people attending were seeking, a learning experience for me, something that would make me a better priest. Now, I think it is more personal than that. I think that I need to witness an act of violence against the Church, and you are providing that in a symbolic form."

Justin asked,

"Do you think it might be too shocking for you? I've been working hard to make it look like a real Catholic church. Inside there's a Christ on the cross, a Madonna and the stations of the cross around the walls."

Michael looked up and smiled.

"John told me about that. That's good. It should be as real as possible. The church has been deconsecrated, so at a spiritual level, the building and everything in it is just a pile of stuff. I couldn't go if it was a consecrated church."

Justin was amused by this concept but it was reassuring for him that it could be seen that way by a priest. Although it was inevitable, he had never had any intention of offending people of faith. He continued,

"You probably know that I've invited people to bring objects to burn in the church, objects that have symbolic meaning for them. Will you want to bring something?"

"I don't think so, your church already has the symbolism which I want. They tell me it's painted red. Is that right?"

"Yes. The previous owners did that. The locals hate the colour."

"Well that suits me. You never see a red church because the colour is too strongly associated with lust and sexuality. The colour of the church will represent, for me, the corrupted sexuality of Catholicism. I don't need to bring anything."

Michael stayed for a cup of coffee and spoke, in a lighter vein, of his childhood in the western suburbs of Melbourne where he grew up as the son of Polish immigrants. As he was leaving, Justin emphasised how welcome he would be at the church burning and assured him that he would not identify him to anyone as a priest. He asked Michael,

"Will you get into trouble with the Church for attending?"

"Yes. I'll tell my bishop, but after the event. I'm sure he'll disapprove."

Justin had been struggling with the choice of whether or not to paint the church. He liked the idea of painting it a high-gloss white, making it a shining, beautiful building, enhancing the power of the image of its burning by giving it a pure and innocent colour. His main concern was how the locals would feel about the colour change, because when it was an active church it had been white. After hearing Michael's thoughts on the colour of the church he decided he would leave it as the scarlet church, if only for Michael.

23

Gerard had tried to anticipate what it would be like in Remand. He expected to feel physically threatened, experience hostility from the guards and then settle into a boring routine. He wasn't far off the mark, but the guards were more courteous than he expected and in fact seemed to admire him. They made sure he received newspapers with reports of the national and international responses to his video.

The other prisoners were a mixed lot, mostly angry young men. Some of them were withdrawing from drugs and seeing doctors to manage this but they were unpredictable and often shouted. He saw several fights which would break out for no apparent reason but he was never physically attacked himself. There was a posture which it was wise to adopt, a head down posture so that you didn't accidently stare at someone who was paranoid. Many of the young men, especially the drug addicts, were totally self-absorbed but the older prisoners in particular wanted to talk with him about his crimes. His age and the crimes he had committed gave him a type of prestige.

The food was stodgy and institutional and there was too much of it. Gerard made the best use of his exercise time to try to physically exhaust himself. If he played solitaire, he would usually be approached by other prisoners, as bored as he was, who would ask to play card games with him and that became the basis of his social life in Remand.

Bail became a pre-occupation for some of the prisoners, not for Gerard because, as a murderer, he was not eligible. Prisoners who learnt that their spouses or families were not prepared to post bail would yell and kick the walls.

Gerard had a brief and anticlimactic appearance before a magistrate after a month then returned to Remand to wait for his trial at the Supreme Court. He knew that this would be a frustrating wait and had been as cooperative as possible with the police to try to shorten this time.

He was delighted that his advocacy had resulted in priest-slayings and arson attacks and especially pleased that they were happening overseas. He felt it important that he maintained a low-key image and never gave the guards any reason to think he was gloating, so he kept his excitement to himself. He shamed himself about being excited, because he saw this as egotistical and reminded himself that any response to his advocacy would probably be short-lived. The Catholic Church wasn't going to change, its response would just be more management, more money spent on public relations. He had recognised all along that the best chance for meaningful change was in Australia's justice system.

Both his sons visited him and during these visits he could hardly contain his joy. They were embarrassed and he found himself discussing practical things with them, such as the management of his finances. He did however tell both of them that he loved them, he couldn't remember the last time he had done that.

Gerard had chosen in advance a few barristers who he would like to defend him. He got his first choice, James Belves. He had never met James, but he had learned of his work in defence by word of mouth and had read the transcripts of some of his trials. At his first briefing, he presented to Gerard the line of defence which he thought they should pursue. He would emphasise the damage that had been done to Gerard, the alcoholism, the failed marriage, the failure to reach his potential in terms of scholastic achievement and income. He would then explain how Gerard's work with Broken Rites had led Gerard to believe that he had to strike a blow as an individual. Gerard was now shocked by the response to his crimes and his advocacy for violence and regretted his conduct. The prosecution would describe the cold-blooded nature of the murder of Father Stephen, but their response would be to speak of Gerard's compassion in ensuring that there was no physical or mental suffering.

Gerard accepted some of this but rejected James' idea of expressing regret. He didn't regret his conduct, his crimes were an ideological statement and to deny this would make him look like a mentally disturbed, common criminal. If he pretended regret the prosecution would ridicule him.

At a later briefing, James argued again that Gerard should express some regret. His view was that there was lots of public support for Gerard and that the magistrate would be keen to find reasons to be lenient. Gerard should be humble, the damaged individual pushed to extreme behaviour which he now regretted. When Gerard again tried to argue his case, James presented the scenario of his prison sentence,

"Imagine this, you have been in jail for five years. Your five minutes of fame in 2016 are long past and the world has forgotten you. The paedophile priest issue has been dealt with and no one wants to think about it anymore. At this time, you could be facing another five or more years in jail or you could be counting the days until you are out. It all depends upon you expressing regret and providing the magistrate with a reason to give you a short sentence."

That image struck home with Gerard and he decided to change his defence. In the years of planning the murder and arson, he had written himself off after his acts. He expected to spend the rest of his life in jail and had even considered committing suicide after lighting the fires and distributing the video. He knew that everything was out of his control once he made his symbolic statement. In practice, he wanted to stay alive, to read about the progress in his war against the Catholic Church and celebrate the little victories. With the prospect of a shorter sentence there was more work that he could do.

In the weeks before the trial, he came to a compromise with James about expressing regret. This also meant that he couldn't use the court as a platform for advocating more violence against the Church, and abandoning the speech he had been planning for years at what he had expected to be his last appearance before the public.

Gerard had some unexpected help before his trial by some publicity about Father Stephen. An investigative team had researched Father Stephen's life and presented it on a television report. As well as his crimes, they reported that a total of twenty-three of his victims had committed suicide, up to forty-five years after the abuse. They also found that eight of his victims had died of drug overdoses and a further three died prematurely of unexplained causes. This was the first time that concrete figures of the morbidity of childhood sexual abuse had been presented to the public and, as one of the newspapers put it, "Was Father Stephen O'Dwyer a mass murderer?"

Following the report, Terry Lynch came out publicly advocating a short sentence for Gerard. He described his murder of Father Stephen as "despatching a mass murderer" and described Gerard as a damaged but dignified man, a man who was no risk to the public. He went on to describe how we send our soldiers overseas to kill people, then reward them with medals. Gerard deserved our respect.

Lynch was roundly criticised for comparing Gerard with soldiers and was forced to soften his support for Gerard, making it clear that he wasn't advocating vigilante action. Never the less, he garnered lots of support for Gerard and there was a large crowd to cheer him when he finally went to court in May.

There was much media interest in the trial and possibly because of this, the prosecution was fairly subdued. Gerard found the barrister to be far less challenging than he expected. The judge carefully examined the most damning evidence against him, photographs of the word 'PEDOPHILE' cut into Father Stephen's abdomen but then Gerard responded with his explanation that,

"It was terribly important to me that Father Stephen did not suffer physically or emotionally. One moment he was a man looking inside his electricity box, the next moment he was deeply unconscious then dead."

On the question of regret, he made a wordy, qualified statement about regretting the circumstances that led to his crime and how, since committing the crimes, he thought the situation had drifted completely out of control in a way he hadn't anticipated. He then made a statement which caused momentary consternation in the court room. He said,

"There is one thing that I deeply regret. I cheated a keen Hawthorn supporter of seeing his team win its third Grand Final in a row."

The prosecution barrister saw this as a statement of appalling black humour and disrespectfully cynical, but with Gerard in the dock looking humble and sincere the judge, a Hawthorn supporter, saw it differently. This statement made headlines in the Herald Sun Newspaper and struck a popular note with the Australian public.

Gerard had to wait three weeks before the judge handed down his verdict. He was to serve eight years imprisonment with a non-parole period of five years. Many people thought this sentence was too lenient but most thought it was excessive. He was able to serve concurrently the sentence he received in a later trial for the arson attacks.

*****

Justin wrote to Morag after her initial response. She wrote back a week later and from then on, email letters passed between them about once per week. Justin wrote long email letters, longer than most people write but nothing like the essay that he first sent. Morag wrote letters that became progressively longer, as if she was gaining confidence in writing. Justin wrote personal letters about his counselling work and his plans for burning the church. He had no inhibitions about describing his doubts and his bursts of euphoria. He realised that, by anyone's judgement, this was a strange correspondence but his confessional essay had made him feel able to write anything he wanted. Morag's letters were polite responses and descriptions of her life on South Uist, something Justin had asked her to write about. Even though Justin was free with descriptions of his emotional states, they could still be described as impersonal because he never referred to his past relationship with Morag or the possibility of ever seeing her in future. Likewise, Morag avoided any reference to their relationship or memories of their time on the island together. The tone of her letters was supportive, approving and even motherly at times with phrases such as,

You must look after yourself when you are having such a turbulent time. Are you getting enough sleep?

As the days shortened and the low angle of the sun announced the onset of winter, Justin wondered about the routine of their unusual correspondence. From his point of view, he had a pen pal who was prepared to respond sympathetically to his written ventilations. Did he want more? Did he want to see Morag, have a relationship with her? These questions made him realise that his sexuality had been locked away, like so many other aspects of himself, during his years as a hermit. Was he a suppressed heterosexual or simply asexual? Was that the reason he had wanted to communicate with Morag in the first place? And what of Morag, why was she so tolerant and respectful of his letters? He re-read her letters looking for clues. Apart from the invitation to afternoon tea in Glasgow, there was no suggestion that she wanted to see him. Was there an element of mild amusement in her letters with statements such as,

My goodness, another confession!

What extraordinary ideas will you come up with next?

It was with these thoughts in mind that Justin went for a long walk that took him north of the Yarra and into Fitzroy. He walked the length of Brunswick Street, twice, so that he could enjoy both sides of the street. Like Chapel Street, it was one of Melbourne's exciting, youthful streets but with subtle differences; Brunswick Street was less hedonistic and more intellectually bohemian with good bookshops and pubs that advertised poetry readings. It was a street near a university.

In Brunswick Street, Justin saw a young man wearing a top with the Yin and Yang symbol on it. He loved the symbol, the two opposites intertwined to create a perfect circle, complementary tadpole shapes representing just about anything you wanted them to represent. For the rest of the walk he played with the symbol in his mind finding opposite matches within himself such as solitude and sociability, youth and maturity, introspection and extroversion. He pictured the dividing line between the two halves and pushed it mentally towards one side of the circle. That was Morag and himself; since they were lovers, she had become fatter and he had become thinner, however they still fitted within the perfect containing circle. It was an image that lingered and gave him an inexpressible but satisfying answer to his questions.

By the time he reached home, he decided that he wanted to alter, to progress in some way, the communications he was having with Morag. He would be provocative, write something that would project them to a different level or possibly put an end to the communication altogether. He couldn't think of an outcome he wanted, other than breaking the comfortable routine they had established. He thought for several hours about what he would write and opted for simplicity. He wrote,

Morag. I have been thinking about our correspondence. Am I being a pest? Am I exploiting your good nature and putting you in the uncomfortable and unwanted situation of being a counsellor while I thrash around emptying my bag of accumulated garbage?

24

In June, Justin found himself busy with his plans for the church burning. The weather had turned wet and cold and Barwon Downs, being at the foot of the Otways, was wetter and colder than Melbourne. Justin and Jacques spent time removing the wooden slats from around the base of the scarlet church so that they could put combustible material underneath, just in case it was raining on the day of the burning. People kept phoning Justin to ask him if they could come and they usually wanted to have long phone conversations to explain. Michael Worsek had found two more priests who wanted to come with him. Siobhan and Chris wanted to come and bring Byron and Chandler. That worried Justin, regardless of how uncomfortable it might make him feel, he had accepted everyone who was keen to come to the burning, but children were different. He had never thought of the church burning as a happy family gathering around a bonfire, it was a situation where people were coming to express anguish and anger, violence even, and he was not sure how this would manifest itself. He asked Maureen why Siobhan and family wanted to come. She said,

"I think they just want to know more about their crazy Uncle Justin and be a part of your life."

Craig Theophanous wanted to come. He surprised Justin with his long explanation, not about childhood sexual abuse, but about power relationships in our society and how this was expressed in the political process and in law. As he listened to Craig, Justin was conscious that he was putting up barriers. Craig was intelligent and making sense and yet Justin was bracketing his ideas as 'ideological stuff' and dismissing it. This is what he did, and had been doing for a long time, but he hadn't always been like that. He could trace back this pattern of thinking to his late twenties, when he was disillusioned and left Australia. He remembered how, at university, he would often buy the Trotskyites' newspapers, read them and feel inspired by the alternative views they offered. He would consider going to their meetings but then change his mind, finding fault in the strident tone of their articles or making some other excuse. He delved into his memory of these times; reading the articles made him feel exhilarated and motivated, but behind these feelings there was anger, anger at the injustices of the world economic order.

That was it. It was anger he was dealing with at the time, or not dealing with.

His pattern of motivation then rejection, which evolved to automatic rejection, was bound up with the feeling of anger.

He didn't recognise that at the time, but it was important. Was that how most people responded to anger? Was his response, and the various pathways his response sent him down, something exceptional, something he should now confront?

He tried to re-experience the anger he had felt as a young man, repackage it as 'motivation for change'. He went over Craig's arguments, making himself agree with them to test his inner response. It was true, Melbourne society, possibly the whole of his culture was riddled with the power politics and abuses of power which enabled priests to rape children. The same abuses of power would apply to all churches and would have been happening forever. He must ask Peter how long priests had been abusing children in Australia. Melbourne wasn't a clean-slate city, it was founded with a rotten core of institutions such as its founding churches. And there would have been other rotten cores, town planning was an obvious one. Everyone knew that Melbourne had never had rational town planning, the city lunged ever outward without proper infrastructure on the basis of corrupt deals between politicians and developers. It probably had been like that since John Batman first cheated the aborigines and planned a city on the Yarra. How many other dimensions of intrinsic rottenness did Melbourne have?

Justin held on to these feelings for the rest of the day. Why? He didn't know, he just knew it was something he had to go through. He ended the day with a stomach ache and heartburn, unaccustomed physiological responses to the anger.

*****

As the count of the expected number attending the church burning passed one hundred and fifty, Justin had more moments of anxiety and more troubled nights. He kept reminding himself that the problem was his own sense of lack of control, which was something he had to accept. This was what life was about.

*****

Morag replied to Justin's email ten days later. He was glad to see the email in his inbox and relieved because he had felt uncomfortable since sending it. He had come to see the question he asked her as coercive, as if he was asking for praise. She wrote,

Hello Justin. Summer solstice is approaching and our evenings are stretching out until after 11 o'clock now. I am enjoying evening walks down to the cove, something I won't be able to do when it gets warmer because the midges will be biting. I have had some lovely sightings of a family of otters.

Your question is an important one and I have put some thought into my reply. I love your letters and very much want them to continue. I will try to explain myself clearly.

You write beautifully. Regardless of the subject, I savour your use of language and the expressions which make your writing sparkle. I love your wit and your ability to express the complex range of emotions you are experiencing.

I admire you as a person who is going through something of great personal importance and importance for other people. I believe you are making history and I am very, very privileged to be treated to such a close account of what you are doing.

Your letters have become terribly important for me personally in ways that I won't be able to express because I don't really understand the changes I am going through, and I certainly don't have your ability to express myself, but I'll try.

A few months ago, I saw myself as a person content with her lot, but with a very limited future. I am morbidly obese with diabetes, heart disease and arthritis (consequences of my obesity). I was expecting to die prematurely, or to be too ill to work or attend committee meetings in the near future. Since your first letter, I have lost twenty-nine pounds. I can walk much further and have dramatically reduced my need for insulin. I am still obese but now I can look at myself in the mirror without feelings of revulsion and I feel wonderful when people complement me on my weight-loss. I have overcome some of my resistance to discussing my difficult childhood and relationship problems and now I am seeing the psychologist who visits the island once each month. I have a long way to go but I am filled with hope for the future.

There, I've said it. I have been afraid that if I mentioned my personal life you would stop writing to me. I don't have any romantic illusions Justin, I expect to live out my days on South Uist and you have a special attachment for your city of Melbourne. You also now have a very important role in caring for people in Melbourne. I do, however, want to tell you that I love your letters and I humbly request that you continue writing to me.

Thankyou Justin, regardless of what happens in the future, I want you to know how much you have helped me.

Her letter moved Justin to tears, it wasn't what he had been expecting at all. Within a few minutes of reading it he felt a familiar resistance rising within. For decades, he had mistrusted any sort of flattery, another pattern of thinking and feeling which had become ingrained. This time however, he was able to open himself up to her heart-felt gratitude and he bathed in the glow of pleasure that came with reading her letter. It took him two days before he felt ready to reply, a reply that had to be honest, simple and respectful. He wrote,

Thankyou Morag, your letter brought me to tears and I have felt wonderful since reading it. Let me now formally accept your invitation to afternoon tea in Glasgow. I will arrange a date with you when my work here has settled down. I am about to get very busy but I look forward to describing the church burning to you.

*****

Frank phoned Justin and spoke for much longer than usual. Instead of his gruff, blunt statements then his need to do something else, he spoke at length about the work he was doing for the victims of priest abuse. He had re-written his will so that most of his assets would go to the committee for legal support, of which Justin was a member. Some of his money would go to, what he called his "attack force", the organisation he had founded, now with the official name of *Respect the Victim*. From its base in Perth, he had established branches in all states with the purpose of "making life hell" for any barrister who treated badly in the courtroom a victim of sexual abuse. He said he was concerned that his two daughters would challenge his will, so he was transferring another fifty million dollars to the account that Daryl had established for the committee.

Justin couldn't help remembering the tough and dynamic schoolboy and the aggressive footballer as Frank spoke. Frank was on a mission and approaching his tasks with the enthusiasm and energy he showed in his childhood.

Frank went on to describe the way he totally rejected St Crispins, the Catholic Church and Melbourne when he moved to Perth aged eighteen. At first, he rejected his family too but reconnected with them after seven years and had good relationships with his parents and sisters. He was looking forward to coming to the church burning and wanted to bring something to burn but had long ago discarded everything to do with St Crispins. He had however found his deceased mother's rosary beads, the last vestige of his connection with the Catholic Church and was bringing them to burn.

It was only four days later that Justin received the news that Frank had died of a massive heart attack. He wondered if Frank had guessed he didn't have long to live and that was the reason behind the phone call and the talk of financial arrangements. He was sad but proud of Frank who had done so much since the meeting last winter. Justin couldn't help comparing himself with Frank and Gerard, two individuals who had made powerful statements and done things, as ways of dealing with their childhood sexual abuse. His actions were insignificant compared with theirs but they were all doing things in character, things that they could do.

Justin flew to Perth for the funeral with Peter and Michael. It was a big funeral with lots of press coverage, held at a suburban public hall. Business colleagues and the local member of parliament spoke in praise of him portraying him as saintly, the tough guy who stood up for society's victims. After the service, a tall, thin woman, who looked in her sixties, came up and introduced herself to Justin as Frank's secretary. She gave him an envelope which Frank had mysteriously asked her to give to Justin if he wasn't able to make his planned trip to Melbourne in late June. It was a plain envelope which felt lumpy. On it, Frank had written,

Justin, if I don't make it you'll know what to do with this.

Justin opened the envelope and found that it contained nothing but a set of rosary beads.

As he waited at the airport with Michael and Peter, the three of them talked about Frank and Gerard. They wished that Gerard could be there with them. Michael had gone through a process of change in his attitudes towards the Catholic Church and the legal profession. He even said,

"I shouldn't say this but I admire Gerard for what he did."

He was keen to talk and continued, opening up in a manner that surprised them. He said,

"I believe I have described to you my creeping disillusionment with the Catholic Church. I raised with my Parish Council the idea of reaching out to the victims of paedophile priests. As I expected, I was rebuffed; the Council's view was that it should be dealt with at the diocesan level with legal consultation. I had made my point and resigned from the Council, something which I feel good about.

Not only have I been questioning the role of the Church in my life, but also my career and even my marriage. I have had a successful career but now, approaching my retirement, the wealth and position in society which I aspired to have lost their gloss for me. I now see that I have been a small cog in large machine, running smoothly as long as I conformed but now, with a few chips off my cog wheel, the machine works against me. My wife Anne has been supportive of me to a certain extent since I told her about my abuse at the hands Father Stephen, but became upset when I suggested that we tell our children. Her view is that she married a man with whom she shared certain beliefs and values and we have raised our children based on those values. I agree with her on that and I accept that I must not inflict upon her my new beliefs. Now, I only go to mass when it is deemed important for appearances sake and I conform with the family expressions of religion which I did in the past."

He hadn't yet asked his wife if she would come to the church burning, but Peter's ex-wife was coming with him. Peter had been quiet for most of the day but he spoke with ease when Justin asked him,

"How long has it been going on Peter? Have priests been abusing children throughout Australian history?

"Ah. A good question," said Peter.

"I'm sure they have, but it is difficult to find conclusive records. It is only in recent times that the criminal behaviour of priests has been reported to the police and they sometimes colluded with the Church anyway. There are church records, but they are difficult to obtain and, call me paranoid if you like, but I suspect that many of the records of priests' sexual behaviour have been destroyed. This might have been initiated by Bishops working within their own dioceses or the orders might have come from further up the hierarchy.

We have a few glimpses from the historic record. You know that Mary McKillop became Australia's first saint in 2010? Prior to that, the details of her life were put under the microscope. She was briefly excommunicated in 1871 and, much to the embarrassment of the Catholic Church, it was because her nuns exposed a paedophile priest. There was an Irish priest, Father Patrick Keating, who was abusing children at Kapunda in South Australia. The nuns working there complained to his immediate superior, Father Charles Horan, but he told them to mind their own business. So they complained through other channels, the vicar general in Adelaide investigated, found Father Keating guilty and sent him back to Ireland. He wasn't defrocked, he returned to Ireland to work as a parish priest and no doubt abused Irish children.

Father Horan was furious and vowed to destroy Mary McKillop's order of nuns, the Sisters of Joseph. He worked on Bishop Shield, the Bishop of Adelaide who ex-communicated Mary for insubordination but reinstated her five months later."

Peter broke off from his story and gave Justin a wry smile.

"It has been said that Mary McKillop should become the patron saint of whistle-blowers, but I'm sure that the public image machine of the Church would never permit that.

The writer Lindsay Russell caused a scandal when she took Father Michael Quinn to court for breach of promise in 1910. He was packed off to Queensland after that.

The Bishops have always been dealing with the sexual behaviour of priests, but it has usually been their heterosexual relationships with adult women. Until recent times, the power relations were such that children were never believed so paedophilia didn't reach a level of public consciousness. This worries me because, even if priests stop abusing children in Australia and the western world, they still have the power and the prestige in South America and Africa to continue getting away with it there.

I have a PhD student who is working on the history of paedophile priests in Australia. She is scouring court records and police reports. A useful way to identify the guilty priests is to look at the records of where they have lived. In the cases of victims who have lodged complaints, she tracks the priests and identifies where they have worked previously. The paedophile priests always have records of frequent moves."

*****

On the flight home Justin thought about Frank, trying to understand the life he had lived. His death was premature, like Finn's. Could his death be described as indirectly caused by Father

Stephen? Of the twelve boys in their drama class, six were now dead. Was anyone keeping track of these deaths? The Catholic Church certainly wasn't.

25

On the Thursday before the church burning, Justin caught the train as usual from Southern Cross Station for the journey to Birregurra. He had come to enjoy this routine; the rhythmic sounds of the train, the familiarity of the landscapes and the mental ticking-off of the stations. It was a restful, soothing routine. Even the minor human dramas of the boarding and departures of passengers was somehow soothing, brief flurries of activity while everyone observed each other, made their judgments and then, snail-like, withdrew back into the shells of their own private worlds. Today however, the journey was different, it wasn't routine because the impending church burning loomed large. Its inevitability was like a crusher at the end of a conveyor belt for Justin. He was so overwhelmed by the voiced and implied expectations of all the people who planned to come that he was losing sight of his role. He knew that he didn't actually have to do much and that he wasn't responsible for other peoples' expectations and tried to focus on his own needs, reminding himself that the whole business stemmed from a subconscious message, the dream of a burning church. The event might be therapeutic for him. Dealing with other people and their needs was something he was sensitive to because he had separated himself from it for so long, something he would have to get used to.

He distracted himself by looking more closely at the other passengers. Until Geelong there were all sorts, the most interesting was a young woman, speaking on her mobile phone to a man with whom she was sharing the custody of their child. She gave blunt, unhelpful answers to his appeals for more time with his daughter. Hearing her short answers between long silences was like having tiny glimpses of a prolonged human drama that went back many years and would continue for many years into the future.

After Geelong, where most of the passengers left the train, the carriage seemed to breathe a sigh of relief. The serious business of the journey now declared itself, the delivery of country people from the alien environment of the city to the refuges of their homes. Most of the passengers would be returning to Colac or Warrnambool or the smaller towns scattered across the Western District. They all looked rural, from the way they dressed to the expansive ways they occupied their seats. Their accents were different, less restrained, less modified by the narrow demographics of urban living. The very fact that they were travelling by train and not car suggested lower socio-economic status. They expressed themselves without the hooded looks of urbanites when they spoke on their mobile phones and unselfconsciously yelled at their children. Justin wondered what they thought of him, would they comment when he left the train at Birregurra? He started a conversation with a boy who was travelling with his family and was disappointed when they left the train at 'Winch', his name for Winchelsea.

Maureen met Justin at the Birregurra Station and as she drove Justin along the, now very familiar, road from the Birregurra Station to Barwon Downs, the landscape seemed more intense; the swollen clouds looked about to burst and the low-angled sunlight picked out the shed roofs and smears of water lying in the low areas. The cows seemed to be purposefully placed in the paddocks, as if they were waiting for something. He knew what features would appear with every bend in the road, features such as stacked round bales, a sign advertising eggs for sale and the cluster if teasels that Maureen loved. It was with a sense of relief from the tension of anticipation that he arrived at Barwon Downs.

As they passed the church, they saw a man getting into his car, a mud-spattered ute with an empty trailer attached. The gate to the church block was open and the car was parked close to the church. Justin wondered what the man was doing on his property. Maureen laughed and said,

"That's Jim Farelly. He said he would put some more dry wood under the church. I wonder if there is any room left. Lots of them have done that Justin. I've been surprised by how involved the locals are and now they're worried that rain might spoil the burning so they have been stacking dry stuff under the church."

That evening, Clarice's was busier than usual, Justin noticed the hum as they approached the door. It was an unsettling, demanding sound. He wondered if it was really any different from the usual bustle or was the collective sounds of a large group of locals different from that of the Friday and Saturday night mobs. Jacques had stocked plenty of beer for tonight, which he was going to sell at cost price, a gesture of goodwill and gratitude for this, the locals night of support for Maureen and Justin.

It was too much for him; the sea of smiling faces, the happy interjections and later, the enthusiastic dancing. Justin concentrated on his viola paying, focussing intently on Maureen and wriggling to ease the tension in his back and shoulder muscles. Most people would have judged his performance as excellent but he felt wooden, detached from the spirit of communion that Maureen was sharing with the crowd, she was loving it. He remembered times during his twenties when he felt like this, similar situations when he was performing with Maureen. When he eventually told Maureen that he wasn't going to perform any more he had many reasons but it all came down to this sense of distance and separation from the audience. He wondered if it was possible for him to ever overcome the feeling and enjoy performing as much as Maureen.

People wanted to complement him, to shake his hand and tell him how much they were looking forward to the burning. They speculated about the weather and decided that the fire would still go off like a bomb even if it was raining. Justin's face ached from his forced smiles and was relieved when their breaks were over and he could return to performing. By the time they finished, he and Maureen were exhausted from all the jigs and reels they had played and the room was hazy from the dust that had been stirred up by the dancing.

That night, Justin woke from a deep sleep in panic. His mind must have been processing the arrangements for the church burning and he realised that he did not have public liability insurance for the church block. He sat up in bed and thought through what had happened. When he bought the church, he had thought of insurance but dismissed the idea because he would shortly destroy it. Now, he realised that with hundreds of people on the block around the burning church, there was the risk of someone getting burnt or injured. In his panicky state, he thought he would have to travel to Melbourne and spend the day looking for an insurer. He couldn't get back to sleep but eventually settled down enough to rationalise that he could deal with the issue over the phone. He rose early and made a phone call at 9am and very quickly solved the problem by a brief conversation with a helpful and reassuring young woman. He didn't describe the planned ritualistic burning of the church but made the point that "a lot of wood will be burnt during the demolition", and the liability insurance covered that.

Maureen joined him and commented on how anxious he looked. She too had slept poorly and thought she had been having some of her twin telepathy. Justin explained his anxiety about the public liability and went on to explain the waves of anxiety that he was subject to. He felt much better for articulating his worries and Maureen was a sympathetic listener. Jacques joined them and they had breakfast together, then Maureen invited him to go for a walk with them to look for fungi.

It was a still, heavily-overcast day. They rugged up warmly and put on water-proof coats because it looked about to rain. Their breath fogged and Jacques said that meant that the temperature was less than seven degrees. The mood of the forest matched the bleak weather with its oppressive stillness and dripping leaves. Despite the gloom, Maureen was animated, in her element. It had been a particularly good year for fungi, she said,

"On my walk two days ago, I identified eighty different varieties, more than I have ever counted before. It's a good omen."

She flashed a smile at Justin when she said that. She continued,

"It's been a particularly good year for the Cortinars and my favourites, the Hygrocybes. They're beautiful little, waxy, brightly coloured ones."

They walked slowly, Justin matching their methodical, head-down gait. He found great pleasure in Maureen's looks of delight when she found interesting fungi. She loved to rediscover fungi growing in the same places she had found them in previous years and said that this was reassuring for her, witnessing a regeneration which made her feel a part of the forest. She showed him her favourites, small Hygrocybes coloured mauve, white and yellow and an enormous Cortinar, a dazzling shade of colour somewhere between red and orange. Amongst the grass at the side of the track she found two varieties of greenhood orchids, inconspicuous green orchids which Justin would never have noticed himself. Maureen said,

"To me they represent 'change of shift' in the forest. The fungi have reached their peak by late June and will decline from now on, but the greenhoods are the first of the orchids to appear. The orchid season will peak in October and then they too disappear, except for the long-lasting hyacinth orchids which will dot the forest with their pink flowers through the summer."

They walked deep into the forest, to a primeval area of tree ferns and maiden hair ferns. They saw beautiful little migrant robins, the males with bright orange chests. Jacques identified them as flame robins and scarlet robins and pointed out the subtle differences that distinguished them.

They arrived back at the house damp but invigorated and had soup for lunch with home-baked sour dough bread. Maureen and Justin practiced some tunes together until Justin felt tired and went to bed for a few hours to catch up on sleep. Their performance at Clarice's that night was more like the usual routine and didn't cause Justin the anxiety he had felt on the Thursday night. The audience was quiet, attentive but less engaged than the locals and Justin enjoyed the opportunity to perform a greater variety of tunes and songs, including the haunting Irish songs that he and Maureen loved so much.

Justin had a second night of poor sleep. This time, it took him ages to fall asleep because he couldn't stop thinking about Morag. The thought of seeing her, of keeping the appointment with her at the Glasgow tea rooms filled him with dread. What would it be like for him? Did he feel any attraction for her? He didn't think so, but he knew about the unpredictability of meeting former lovers and how it could stir up all sorts of passions. Would he like to be with her on South Uist? He was almost certain that part of his life was over and his future was in Melbourne. Would he find her physically repulsive, or boring, and have to act a part in order to be polite? And what would it be like for Morag? Would seeing him be disappointing? Was the energy behind her change of outlook and weight-loss based on some sort of illusory connection with him and would the image be shattered when she saw him in the flesh? He didn't need to make any decisions, or think about her at all but he couldn't still his wandering mind.

On the Saturday, he spent more time rehearsing with Maureen and had another afternoon nap. He received many phone calls, last minute requests from strangers who had heard about the planned church burning and wanted to attend. He tried to sound cheerful and welcoming as he listened to their nervous enquiries. The Saturday night performance was another good one and seemed to pass quickly with Maureen and Justin concentrating more on the performance of the new tunes than the audience, a quiet lot, most of whom were digesting the all-afternoon degustations they had consumed at the restaurant nearby.

On the Sunday morning, Justin woke to the sounds of currawongs calling in the forest. It was an jarring sound but one of the many things which he had come to associate with all the pleasant human and environmental aspects of Maureen's home and which made it feel so cosy for him now. As the thin light of the winter dawn peeped around the edge of his blind. he was pleased to think that he had slept right through the night for a change. There were no other birds calling, that meant that it must be raining but he couldn't hear any rain on the metal roof so it was probably just a soft drizzle. His sense of calm ended when he remembered that this was the big day. He had a new thought, a new thing to worry about. What if someone wanted to sabotage the burning? What if a local, angry about the burning of the church, decided to do an early morning raid and set the church on fire before anyone arrived? A stupid idea, but rather than lie in bed and worry about it, Justin got up, dressed and walked to the church.

It was very cold but had stopped raining. Barwon Downs was lost under heavy fog. The sounds of his footsteps and the smells of wood smoke from the town's slow combustion heaters were the sensations he noticed. At the church block, he unlocked and opened the large gate, then the church door and went inside. There was no one about. Alone in the church, he was able to separate himself from all the work he had done decorating the building in the months beforehand and see it for what it was, a fair imitation of a real country Catholic Church. He rediscovered the respect and reverence that he must have acquired during his childhood for churches. He walked slowly around the interior, touching the beautiful stations of the cross, the Madonna and the crucified Christ. He needed to do this, to view his creation in a different light before he threw the whole scene over to the myriad expectations of the people who would come that day. He locked the church door and went back to Maureen's house.

He ate his breakfast alone, glad that Maureen and Jacques had not risen. He wanted to return to the church as quickly as possible, this time as the host, the compere of an extraordinary event. Thinking he might be there all day, he took a bag with him containing a bottle of water, newspaper, matches and the objects he needed for his own and Frank's rituals.

Back at the church, he took three photographs from his bag and pinned them to a side wall between two of the stations of the cross. They were photographs taken when he was a student at St Crispins, two of them were formal photographs showing dozens of boys and several priests, including Father Stephen. The third photograph was an informal one which had been taken by a parent, it showed Justin and the other eleven boys from his drama class standing with a smiling Father Stephen. He took a felt pen from his bag and drew crosses on the chests of the six boys from that class who were now dead.

Next, he had to deal with Frank's rosary beads. So far, he hadn't been able to decide how to use them in a way that would match the spirit of Frank's angry and complete rejection of the Catholic Church. He sat in the front pew and gazed around the church. He thought of cutting the string and throwing the rosary beads all around the church. An angry gesture but somehow not conspicuous enough for Frank. It should be more central and visible. He took the crucified Christ down from the wall and put the rosary beads around its neck. Too tame, too decorative. He tied the rosary into a noose and put it around the Christ's neck. The image was disturbing, he needed to pause, then he looped the rosary tightly around the neck, there was plenty of length so he kept winding the rosary chain around the Christ's mouth, then nose, then eyes until the whole chain was used up and he locked it in place by tying it behind the head. Justin's hands were shaking and he felt short of breath, like the Christ, he felt he was being choked, smothered, suffocated. He put the figure on the ground and looked away but still felt breathless. He walked out of the church and stood at the entrance, taking deep breaths. The breathlessness subsided but, frightened by the intensity of the experience he sat on the steps and curled himself into a ball. He stayed in that position for several minutes until a car pulled up in front of the church. It was one of Maureen's neighbours and he called from the driver's window,

"Hi Justin. The big day! I'm going shopping but will be back for the fire. I'm looking forward to it."

Justin stood and smiled, the neighbour drove away. Justin went back into the church, picked up the crucified Christ and replaced it on the wall, trying not to look at its face.

26

The first people arrived soon after 10am, two cars with four men who were strangers to Justin. They knew who Justin was because they had spoken with him on the phone but, amongst the scores of people who had phoned, he couldn't recall them. They wandered around the church looking intently at Justin's photos and the crucified Christ with its wrapped face. That was uncomfortable for Justin, especially when they wanted him to explain why the Christ's head was wrapped. They returned to their cars then took into the church the things they had brought with them, two of them had photographs, some framed, some unframed. One had some sporting trophies he had won at his school, he mentioned the name of the Catholic boarding school he had attended. One had a painting which he had done himself, a large expressionist painting with lots of black and red paint and what could have been a human figure surrounded by spikes. The painter asked Justin if he could hammer a nail into the wall to mount his painting. Justin agreed but then realised he didn't have a hammer, but the man had brought his own and mounted his painting beside the crucified Christ. Another of the men asked if he could write on the wall beside the photographs he had tacked up. Justin granted permission, amused at his proprietorial role. The man then wrote a long personal story about his sexual abuse at school and the ways the abuse had affected him.

As he was writing, a steady trickle of people arrived. Justin greeted them at the door then they entered the church. They were mostly men but there were some woman and family groups with teenaged children. They all moved around the church inspecting the decorations and the objects that others had brought, then placed their own objects, although not everyone had brought things.

Photographs were the most common things that people wanted to display and school and childhood photographs were popular. Many people wrote stories on the walls beside their photographs and Justin wondered if they had planned to do that or had they got the idea from observing those who arrived earlier. There were vases of flowers with cards attached and candlesticks to hold candles, which they lit. One woman brought an incense holder and lit the incense. A man pinned up sheet music with the songs which, he explained to Justin, were the songs he sang when he was a choir boy at school.

Many people brought objects connected with their Catholic childhoods; bibles, prayer books, rosary beads and pieces of school uniforms. One man had pushed a knife through a bible and with the protruding end of the knife he attached the bible to the church wall. There were many paintings and statues of Jesus and a few images of the Madonna. Some of these were intact, some had been defaced in various ways, the cape of one of the Madonnas had been carefully painted bright red. Most of these objects were placed on the altar and, when that filled, on the floor around it.

By 11 o'clock the church was packed with people doing their rounds of inspection, then placing their objects. A man Justin didn't know came with an axe. He looked angry at first and Justin was concerned. He spoke with the man who had painted on the axe handle 'FUCK YOU McARDLE'.

When Justin asked him what he wanted to do he became tearful and said,

"I wanted to smash something, but there are too many people in there."

Justin took him into the church and said,

"You can smash the altar if you like, we can remove the things on it first. Or would you like to smash the Madonna?"

The man thought for a moment then smiled and said,

"No. I don't need to do that now. I'll just lean it against the altar."

Pat and Glen arrived together and Justin was delighted to see them. They had brought paint jars and brushes and asked if they could paint some writing on the outside church wall. They looked around the inside of the church then went outside to the back wall of the church.

Three men arrived with a life-sized dummy dressed as a priest. It had a noose around its neck and the name 'Ridsdale' written across the face. There was some discussion about where they would hang it, but they decided they would prefer to attach it to the outside of the church so that they could see it burn. They had brought a ladder with them so that they could mount it.

By 11.30 Justin had lost count but there were hundreds of people on the church property. From where he stood beside the door he could see that cars were parked the full length of the main street and around the corner of the approach to Barwon Downs. Peter arrived, with Moira and Michael. They inspected the church then had a brief conversation with Justin. Peter said,

"This is amazing Justin, there is so much being expressed in there. I only brought a candle, to light for my lost childhood. I'm glad you put up that photo of the drama class, I destroyed mine years ago. I visited Gerard recently. He asked me to put something in the church for him. Guess what?"

"What?"

"A short piece of metal pipe. He didn't explain why but it must have something to do with murdering Father Stephen. By the way, he was delighted to hear about what you are doing here today. He wants to see you."

That was wonderful news for Justin. He knew that he should visit Gerard but had been putting it off because he thought that Gerard might disapprove of the church burning, as a gesture which he might see as undermining his aggressive approach to the Catholic Church.

He spoke briefly with Michael and mischievously asked him if he had invited his wife Anne. He replied in a similar vein and a wicked smile with,

"I asked her, and she didn't want to come. When I get home, she will want to know all about this, and I'm not going to tell her!"

Later arrivals found the church so filled with people and objects that they attached their things to the outside of the church and there were dozens of people writing on the church walls. Justin walked to the back of the church to see what Glen and Pat had done. They had painted 'FUCK YOU FATHER STEPHEN' in large letters then given their paint and brushes to others who had written similar things about other priests. There are least twenty 'fuck you's' with various priests' names following. Justin was at first shocked but then accepting. This was what it was all about, they had created a wall of anger and had been discrete enough to do it at the back, out of view of the road. It reminded Justin of the behaviour of women who wanted to sunbath topless and the way they would position themselves at the peripheries of the crowds of people at popular beaches, away from the family areas in the centre.

Darryl arrived with Declan and both their wives. Darryl gave Justin a big hug and said,

"You've done it Justin. This is fantastic. I didn't bring anything, I didn't need to. I just want to see it burn."

John Holian was in the crowd with Craig Theophanus and several friends. Father Michael Worsek was with a group of men whom Justin assumed to be priests, in their civilian clothes. People were taking photos and some were filming the scene. Justin was concerned that this might cause problems for Father Michael but, like so many things today, it was completely beyond his control. The locals came late during the morning. They looked around the church, inside and out, and moved amongst the crowd of outsiders awed by the strangeness of it all and the strength of the unfamiliar feelings that were being expressed. Some of them nodded to Justin but weren't inclined to speak with him, they drifted to the peripheries of the church block and stood in groups, waiting. Maureen arrived with Jacques, Siobhan, Chris and their children, Byron and Chandler. She hugged Justin and said,

"I didn't realise this would be so big. Be proud of yourself."

At noon, with people still arriving, Justin felt the expectation of the crowd building. He hadn't actually planned where to start the fire, but the crowd had formed an arc around the western side of the church, the vacant side of the church block, so that defined the place. As soon as some later arrivals had spent their time inside the church, he asked everyone inside the church to leave. This was a slow process but when the church was empty, he locked the church door. The time was 12.15.

He walked to the western side of the church and stood roughly at the middle of the church wall. Above and slightly to his right was the dummy priest, hanging limply against the church by its noose. There were photographs and hand-writing all along the church wall. He turned to face the crowd which had become quite still. Someone coughed, then the crowd was completely silent. Justin felt uncomfortable as the object of such intense expectation. They wanted him to say something, make a speech. Of course, why hadn't he thought of that? How stupid of him. They had all put as much thought and energy into planning their attendance here as he had. Most of them had travelled a long way. They wanted, needed a few words of ritual before the burning. Justin had never been comfortable speaking to groups and could barely control his rising sense of panic. He struggled out with,

"Thanks for coming here today."

There were a few smiles and nods, then silence. The sun appeared from behind a cloud and cast its weak mid-winter light on the faces in the crowd, faces filled with anticipation. It gave him enough confidence to continue,

"I hadn't planned to give a speech today and I didn't realise how many would be coming."

He paused, trying to plan the words for the inclusive idea which had come to him.

"This is a very powerful experience for me. Something happened to me in the church this morning. I don't really understand it, but it was important and I think it's going to make a difference for me. And now you've all come and put your own things in the church, and had your own experiences."

He looked around at the crowd smiling, they smiled back.

"It's been wonderful to see you doing that, to look at what you've brought and to read what you've written. Witnessing that has made me realise that I'm not alone."

His voice was wavering, he was overwhelmed from the

intensity of the affinity he felt with the crowd. He paused than said in a louder voice,

"We're not alone."

It seemed to him that people were responding with silent movements of their lips, as they might respond in church. He drew a deep breath then said,

"OK. It's time to light the fire."

He took the matches and paper from his bag and was about to turn to light the fire when he noticed Byron and Chandler holding their parents' hands. They looked frightened.

Justin walked over to them and asked if they would help him start the fire. They looked at him impassively, then Chandler smiled and walked towards him. Byron turned and pushed his face into his mother's side and, not wanting to embarrass him, Justin took Chandler's hand and walked with her towards the church wall. As they reached it, Byron ran over to join them. There was some laughter at this, a subtle easing of the tension.

Justin squatted beside the church where there was some light kindling of small tree branches protruding. From this position, he could see that the whole underneath of the church was packed with dry, flammable material, not only branches, but cardboard boxes and scrunched-up newspaper. He later learned that one of the locals had placed, what he called 'bombs' under the church, bundles of newspaper around packets of fire-lighters. He made a ball of newspaper, pushed it in amongst the kindling and put a lighted match to it. It flared and the flames spread slowly through the kindling. Next, he made two more balls of newspaper, pushed them under the church and asked Byron and Chandler to light them. They froze and he suspected that neither of them had ever struck a match before. He coaxed Chandler up close to a ball of newspaper, struck a match and guided her hand to hold the match. She dropped the match which fizzled on the ground. He tried again, this time with her hand close to the newspaper. In the few seconds that she managed to hold the match, the newspaper caught alight. Byron held his match rigidly but managed to light his piece of newspaper first time. They stepped away as the burning kindling spread out to both sides.

The fire spread quickly under the church. Justin and the children moved back to join the crowd watching, wondering if he should say anything about standing clear but it seemed unnecessary, and he hoped his role was over now, he wanted to blend in. The crackling of the burning kindling was surprisingly loud, there was lots of smoke, but fortunately there was a breeze coming from the west which blew it away from the crowd.

The red paint on the lower edges of the church started to blister and blacken then small tongues of flame flitted up from underneath. Heat rising up the side of the church made the attached photographs discolour and move, a few fell to the ground. The crowd made slight movements, seemingly as a single entity which needed to stretch and readjust itself to the changing scene. With a roar, a flame moved rapidly up the side of the church wall, at the front end, and very quickly a single plume of flame was reaching higher than the top of the metal roof. The crowd was well back but still some people moved further away.

Justin turned to look at the intently watching faces. A window broke and falling shards echoed from within the church. Another flame burst upwards from near where the priest dummy was hanging. Photos flared and twisted and the dummy started to move in the hot updraft. All attention was on the dummy now, the crowd was witnessing something it had never seen before, something which it knew was irreverent, subversive, dangerous, but something which it badly wanted to see. The dummy priest's robe ignited and quickly dissolved into black smoke, obscenely exposing the dummy's bare legs and torso, shocking in their pallor. The exposed body blackened and cracked, the rope caught fire, a hand fell off. The rope broke and the dummy dropped to the ground with a thud, breaking into pieces. The crowd made a collective noise of appreciation. The shattering of the priest dummy altered the unity of the crowd, individuals asserted their presence with gasps and tears and friends rallied to support them. The spectacle took on a more serious tone and the chill rippled through the crowd.

The church had become a wall of flames and weatherboards peeled away from the grips of exhausted nails exposing the conflagration now happening within the church. The heat was at its most intense and the crowd had eased itself back as far as the flimsy fence on the block's western edge. Part of the roof buckled and collapsed. The rear wall fell outwards with a whoomph, throwing out sparks and burning timbers. In a moment of panic, Justin worried that the western wall would fall towards the crowd, showering it with sparks. The collapse was in fact a graceful inward diminution, a gentle settling of twisted metal roofing on a web of burning diagonal spars. The crowd craned to look for familiar objects in the dying church. A station of the cross stood out defiantly on a still-vertical burning beam, clear sky behind it framing a burning cross. A woman near Justin crossed herself at the sight. The front door stood longer than the walls and when it too fell and crashed down the stairs and the crowd knew the show had passed its peak.

As the heat receded, the crowd disengaged to fill the open space closer to the where the wall had been. Some men picked up half-burnt pieces of timber and threw them into the fire, raising local flares and towers of sparks. People started talking, some even turned their backs to the fire. They came up to Justin to talk and to thank him. Some shook his hand, some hugged him, many of them were crying. He didn't know what to say to these people but didn't feel pressure to say anything. He could see clusters of people talking and although he couldn't hear what they said, their postures suggested the profound emotions they were expressing. Some people were filming the fire and also the crowd, an intrusion into these private dramas which Justin hated to see. Father Michael Wosek and his friends thanked Justin and slipped away. Justin spoke with John Holian and Craig Theophanous, both of whom were blinking back tears. They said trivial things which belied the depths of their experiences, Justin understood this and found himself moving his arms to express things he couldn't put into words. Peter joined Justin and was more articulate but in a way that seemed as if he was covering up his true feelings. He said he would be leaving soon because he 'had to get Moira back to Melbourne'. Justin asked him,

"Peter, have you thought of writing a book on the history of abusive priests in Australia? You know you're the right one to do it."

Peter grimaced and answered,

"I've been doing it for years, I'm procrastinating. I need to finish the book and get it published before the Royal Commission releases its recommendations. You have inspired me to do it, you and Gerard and Frank. You three have done things."

Justin felt like hugging him, but as if to pre-empt him, Peter thrust forward his hand to shake.

Many people were leaving now and the main street was busy with the sounds of cars extracting themselves from awkward parking places. Maureen and family joined Justin, Byron and Chandler were the most animated he had ever seen them and Siobhan thanked him for getting them involved with the lighting of the fire. Jacques had two things to report to Justin; the water tank from the town's public toilet had been emptied by the unprecedented number of visitors, and he had heard that several car loads of people wanting to attend the church burning hadn't made it because they had mistakenly gone to Barwon Heads instead of Barwon Downs. Jacques laughed about this because people often confused Barwon Downs with Barwon Heads but it was something that saddened Justin and disturbed him for the rest of the day.

A hard core of about fifty stayed around the fire until well after dark, a fairly even mixture of locals and visitors. They talked, made friends and spent a lot of time just staring into the fire. Eskies appeared and beer and snacks were passed around. Some men became practical about managing the fire, removing and stacking pieces of roofing metal and kicking outlying pieces of wood into the middle of the fire. Justin discovered that he had one more role, to stay at the fire until everyone else had left. There was a practical reason, to make sure that the fire was safe, but there was also another reason the nature of which he couldn't really define. It was a bit like the captain of a sinking ship being the last to leave, or like a Japanese boss being seen to be the last person to leave work in the evening. It was after midnight when he left and walked the short distance to Maureen's home. The fire was still smoking, he knew it could smoulder for days, but it was safe and more rain was predicted anyway.

The church burning was reported on the news and several copies of amateur film were shown with the reports. During the next few weeks, the church burning was discussed on talk-back radio and television talks shows and panels. Journalists wanted to talk with Justin and have him on their shows but he refused all invitations and in fact went into hiding, not answering his phone for any unfamiliar numbers. John Holian became the person whom the press sought out about the church burning because he had been there and because he spoke confidently and intelligently about all aspects of the damage caused by childhood sexual abuse. Justin's name often came up with honour and respect as the man who had provided the church for the burning.

27

During the weeks after the burning, Justin was very busy with his informal counselling work, he had anticipated that he would be. He had learned what to expect because of what happened whenever the Royal Commission into institutional responses to childhood sexual abuse released its reports, it stirred up the victims in unpredictable ways. For some, it was the first step on a pathway that lead to acknowledgement, then a degree of resolution and acceptance. Others had to avoid seeing newspapers or watch the news on television because of the anxiety they experienced once the lid was lifted on their repression of bad memories. The Royal Commission had established that seven percent of Catholic priests had been abusing children during the previous fifty years, so there were thousands of damaged adults, most of whom hadn't begun to discuss their trauma.

Justin didn't know the best approach to dealing with these damaged people. He had spoken with men and women who said they had resolved their problems through counselling, but there were many more who hadn't. From his own work, he was certain that it was useful for the victims to speak with someone who could listen without judgement to their personal stories which were enmeshed with guilt, shame and self-loathing. Linking them with other victims also seemed to be useful. Beyond that, Justin was unsure about the potential the victims had for better lives and suspected that the older they were, the less hope there was.

Justin made the arrangements to visit Gerard in Barwon Prison. He had never been to a prison before.

He was very nervous on the day of his visit, about the process of going to a prison but also nervous about seeing Gerard. He had missed opportunities of establishing a friendship with Gerard and still blamed himself for not seeing Gerard before Christmas.

The prison was as bleak and uninviting as he expected it would be. Could there be such thing as a welcoming prison? After walking through an outer gate, he went past a cluster of smoking women to a door signed VISITORS WAIT HERE. He entered the room which was bare except for rows of plastic chairs, there was a heavy steel door at one end and an office facing the room with a raised steel shutter. A middle-aged woman wearing a prison guards' uniform was seated there. She checked the details of his visit arrangements and asked him if he had visited a prisoner there before. Because he hadn't, she explained the procedure in a monotonous voice as she must have many times before. She gave him a numbered card and told him to wait until called.

There were three other people seated in the room and the smokers outside the room were also waiting to visit. There was only one other man, an elderly man and all the other visitors were women. He didn't know if it was a sheer coincidence but there was an obvious class difference between the four of them in the room and the smokers outside whom he could see through a window. Inside, were the old man and two middle-age women, all were smartly dressed. He assumed they were visiting their sons. The smokers ranged in age from teens to late middle-age, some were very thin and some were morbidly obese. Several of the younger women were heavily made-up. They were all intent on their smoking and none of them was speaking. Justin found a seat separate from the other three in the room, who were all seated in different parts of the room themselves. Because they were avoiding eye-contact with him, he assumed they didn't want to talk. Who wants to talk about the reason a loved one is in jail?

He waited a long time while other visitors' numbers were called and they passed through the steel door. He wished he had brought a book to read. When he was called, he walked to the steel door, which opened automatically for him. An un-smiling guard met him and asked him to empty his pockets, then took the few things he had and put them in a numbered box which he placed on a shelf. He gave Justin a plastic tag with a number on it which matched the number on his box. Then the guard asked Justin to stand with his feet on foot markers which were painted on the floor. This made him stand with his legs apart. Then he had to raise his arms and the guard gave him a very thorough pat down. There was a female guard at the desk, he assumed that she did the pat downs for the female visitors. Then he walked through a metal detector to a smaller room with plastic chairs. He didn't have to wait long when a guard there said,

"You can see prisoner Connolly now. Proceed to the last table and sit facing him. Don't leave your chair until the end of the visit."

The guard escorted him through a door to the visiting room and stood on the inside of the door. The visiting room had five small tables running down its middle with chairs on either side. There was another guard standing at the far end near another door. There were people seated at each table, the prisoners in their uniforms on the right side and visitors facing them at the first four tables. He could see Gerard at the fifth table and walked towards him on the visitors' side of the room. He felt very self-conscious as he walked that short distance, it reminded him of the day he graduated from university when he walked onto the stage to collect his degree.

Gerard rose from his seat to greet Justin and leant forward to shake his hand. He must have sensed Justin's nervousness because he smiled and said,

"We're allowed to shake hands here. It's great to see you Justin."

They shook hands. As they did so, Justin was aware of two dimensions to that encounter, factors which reminded, renewed and updated the relationship at a very primal level. Justin was much taller than Gerard, but the grip of Gerard's handshake was much more confident than Justin's. He had another of his memories of an incident on the football field from their school days; he was under pressure, facing a wall of opponents when Gerard appeared near his side, Justin handballed the football to him and he successfully raced away.

Justin tried to move the chair back in order to sit on it, but found it was bolted to the floor. Gerard commented,

"They do that to stop you from throwing it."

His tone changed,

"I suppose this is your first visit to a prison?"

"Yes, it is. Do I look a bit bewildered?"

"You're OK. The guards are reasonable people, just forget your surroundings. I love having visitors."

His smile generated such warmth that Justin felt inclined to look away, but he held Gerard's gaze and smiled back. He said,

"I'm sorry it's taken so long. I wanted to see you before Christmas."

"Ah," said Gerard. "Things changed at Christmas, didn't they. I've been wanting to apologise to you for the aftermath of the murder."

He dropped 'the murder' lightly, as if he had been mentioning 'afternoon tea' or 'washing the dishes'. Justin felt an inner tightening but resolved to accept the normality of the conversation. Gerard continued,

"You probably had a hard time with the police because you and the others who were at Peter's place, would all have been suspects. I knew that would happen. I'm sorry."

Justin felt the magnanimity that a sincere and unexpected apology creates. He no longer felt nervous.

"It was OK, I had a cast-iron alibi. I must have led them on a merry dance though because I was on a long walk around the Western District. They caught up with me at Ararat."

He laughed,

"In the meantime, they'd been through my flat and my computer, which was a bit embarrassing."

By his own description, the incident became humorous in retrospect. Gerard looked as if he was trying not to laugh. He said,

"Have you seen any more of Brian Hannay or Craig Theophanous?"

"I've seen Craig, I've come to like him. He was at the burning," Justin said.

Gerard said,

"I like them both. Hannay is tough, he put me through the wringer, but I was more worried by Theophanous. I had the feeling he was psychoanalysing me and would trip me up with something I hadn't thought of.

There was something else I wanted to say, not so much an apology, but an explanation. It was at that meeting that I got Father Stephen's address. Don't blame yourself about that because I was already committed to killing a convicted rapist priest. If it hadn't been Father Stephen, it would have been Father Joseph Knebel. I actually tried to kill him the previous Christmas, I broke into his house at Dandenong and waited there all day for him, but he didn't come home! It was farcical."

Gerard's comical expression invited a smile but Justin couldn't manage that, he just looked surprised. Gerard looked thoughtful, then changed the topic,

"I loved your idea about having a public church burning, I wish I could have been there. It was a brilliant idea Justin, I've spent years thinking about what I could do, but I never thought of that. It was a beautiful idea because it created publicity but also because I'm sure it has been therapeutic for a lot of people. All my ideas have essentially been destructive. What made you think of it? Was it your recurring dream?"

"No," said Justin, and described Darryl's pre-occupation with burning a church.

"But the idea was there. I'm hoping that the whole process has been therapeutic for me too."

"Have you stopped having the dream?" Gerard asked.

Justin smiled and said,

"I haven't had any since the burning, but it's early days. If I can get through a year without the dream, I'll start to believe that something has shifted in my subconscious."

Gerard asked Justin to describe the burning, which he did in detail. He was pleased that John Holian, whom he knew, attended. He was also pleased to hear that some priests went incognito. He said,

"There are some good priests, but the best ones leave. Sooner or later, they realise that the Church is a power abusing machine and that it's not going to change. We know the type of priest that ends up in the Vatican from the example of our own Cardinal Drumm, the backward-looking, authoritarian traditionalists.

I'm surprised that Craig Theophanous was there. Why was that?"

Justin answered,

"I think he is a very intelligent man and the abuse of power by the Church has been an eye-opener for him. He's questioning how society works. Peter was at the burning. He put a piece of steel pipe in the church for you."

Gerard lost his look of confidence at that and almost looked embarrassed. He said,

"Yes. That's the Catholic coming out in me, the spiritual disposal of the murder weapon. You know, I've never regretted killing Father Stephen, but that's a cerebral thing. On the other hand, I've always thought of myself as a basically decent man and I'm sometimes shocked when I remember that I'm a murderer. Perhaps I have a soul after all."

They were both quiet for a moment. Justin wanted to say something gentle, something reassuring but decided that it was more important to wait for Gerard to speak, in case he had something more profound to say on the topic. Gerard looked up and spoke,

"I'm glad Peter was there, he's a lovely man. He's been writing a book about sexually abusive priests for ages. It's an important book but I wish he'd finish it."

Justin said,

"He knows that. He told me that we've inspired him to get it finished."

Justin looked around the visitors' room. He had almost forgotten where he was. He asked Gerard,

"How do you find being in here?"

Gerard answered,

"It's OK. I'm surprised by how quickly I've gotten used to it. I expected to be here forever, and in fact, an earlier draft of my plan was to kill myself after I'd distributed the video. I might be out of here in five years so life looks much brighter. The guards are OK, they treat me well and some have told me they admire me for killing a rapist priest. The other prisoners are mostly OK. The ones taking drugs are unpredictable, I keep away from them. Many of the younger ones treat me as a sort of father figure, they come and talk to me about their messy lives and often end up in tears. I've learnt a lot about humanity in here, I'd say that everyone in jail has had some sort of trauma in their childhood, and more often than not, sexual abuse. Once the damage has happened, they don't acquire the skills, such as self-discipline, which come with a stable childhood. It's as if they stop developing emotionally and behave impulsively, which leads to drug use and crime. I can relate that pattern to myself and why I screwed up as a young man. Society judges people by their actions and a common attitude towards prisoners is that they had choice, they didn't have to break the law. Judges show a bit of discernment when they take law-breakers' pasts into account but journalists and politicians pan them for doing that. Anyway, our prisons will continue to fill as long as children are abused."

Another moment of silence. Gerard must have thought he was being too morbid because he continued cheerily,

"And I'm going to study law. I've got the time and motivation to get through the course. I can't be admitted to the bar but I can be more useful to Broken Rites with a knowledge of legal processes. Isn't it great what Frank did. He's given victims the clout to take on the Church and I love his 'Respect the Victim' organisation. I can't help comparing his legal support service and Respect the Victim to a cashed-up Sinn Fein and its militant wing, the IRA."

Justin too liked the concept. He said,

"That's great that you'll be studying law. You must already know a lot about the law with regard to paedophile priests."

Gerard said,

"Yes, and it's a depressing world slanted heavily in favour of the Church."

Justin enjoyed being a witness to Gerard's enthusiasm and commitment, and reflected on his own lack of confidence. He said,

"Gerard, it's great to see you are so confident, so certain about what you are doing and where your life is going. I've been wracked with doubts during the last few months. I've had more sleepless nights than I can remember, agonising over what I'm doing."

He paused, surprised so see that Gerard was smiling, then he started laughing. He said,

"I'm sorry Justin, I shouldn't laugh and I do take you seriously. It's because I've lived with doubt for years, mulling over things I might or might not do and no one to discuss my ideas with. I murdered a man! Can you imagine all the doubts and fears I had planning that? The point is, I did it. And you did what you planned. You overcame your doubts and did something wonderful."

Gerard reached across the table and put his hand on top of Justin's.

"Be proud of yourself Justin. Everyone who does something alone, or something unique has doubts."

Gerard gave Justin's hand a squeeze then sat back in his chair. Justin was deeply moved. He felt the relief that Gerard offered, through the touch of his hand as much as from what he said. Justin said,

"Thanks Gerard. I'm glad I came to see you. During the last year I've been emerging from the shell of my previous life and it has been difficult. Dealing with people has caused me a lot of anxiety but I know now that I can gain a lot of strength from talking to others, people such as you. What happens now Gerard? I'm worried that after the drama and publicity everything will go back to the way it was before and the victims of priests will be forgotten about."

Gerard thought about his response for a few moments.

"On the short term, it depends on how the media treats it. You and Frank, and me in my own destructive manner, have caused a lot of publicity. As more and more cases go to court, I hope they will refer to your church burning and my attacks. More victims of rapist priests will come forward now, I know this for a fact from my friends at Broken Rites, so there should be a steady stream of publicity. I hope that *Respect the Victim* publicises the abusive tactics of the Church's barristers and disgraces them in the eyes of the public.

On the longer term, the recommendations of the Royal Commission into institutional responses to child sexual abuse will be very important. The public has been horrified by what the Royal Commission has revealed and people will be wanting the government to act on these recommendations. The Catholic

Church will continue in its usual way of protecting its power and wealth. That's something you can be sure of and they will undoubtedly oppose the recommendations and employ spin doctors to disguise their motives. I'm hoping that the Royal Commission will recommend the mandatory reporting of confessions by priests of sexual abuse. There was the incredible case of Father Michael McArdle who abused hundreds of boys and girls over a period of twenty years. He apparently confessed what he was doing on about one and a half thousand occasions to thirty different priests and none of them did anything to stop him. The Church will claim it is its right to keep secret what happens in confession.

The churches don't pay any taxes, that's one of the reasons they are so wealthy. I'd like to see a recommendation that they are taxed or, better still, pay for the cost to society of the rapist priests or ministers from the other churches. They should pay for the counselling for the victims and their families, funeral costs for all the suicides, compensation packages for damaged lives and loss of earning capacity and the cost of the trials and imprisonment of the priests. A figure of about fifty million dollars per rapist priest would be realistic and that would send a rocket up the church and make them want to stop priests raping children.

Historically, our political parties have been very soft on the Catholic Church and sadly, they will probably try to water down the recommendations when it comes to acts of parliament. This is when I am hoping that public opinion will force the pollies to do the right thing. The ugly face of traditional Catholicism has been exposed during the last few years. The Abbott/Hockey cabinet had the most church-going Catholics Australia has ever seen and it was a pretty inhumane cabinet. Also, we've got the smouldering issue of equal marriage which has annoyed most Australians, so there is a real ground swell for the rejection of traditional religious values being expressed in government.

With regards to the ways the courts function. I think there was a slow change happening in the way that victims are regarded as witnesses and treated badly. Publicity and *Respect the Victim* are speeding up the process.

And don't forget all the individuals like you who are chipping away with their work, helping the victims in whatever ways they can."

At that moment, one of the guards approached Justin and Gerard and, very politely, said that their visiting time would finish in five minutes. Gerard had finished his speculations and they wanted to spend the remaining time enjoying the warmth of their time together. Justin told Gerard that he would be back to visit him soon. As he was about to leave Gerard said,

"There's something else I wanted to tell you, and I hope you'll forgive the Christian analogy. When I heard the news, and read about your church burning. I absolutely loved it, it's the best I've felt since coming here. I had this idea that I had played the role of John the Baptist, to your Jesus."

28

After visiting Gerard, Justin felt excited in a way that he hadn't felt since his youth. He was brimming with ideas and the knowledge that he had the time and energy to pursue whatever pathways he chose. Visions flashed though his mind of what he could do and everything he thought of involved people. He could study psychology and obtain the qualifications he needed to do better counselling. He felt confident that he had the human skills and depth of insight which his previous life had given him. He could spend more time playing his viola with people, either with Maureen or a string quartet. He liked the idea of learning new tunes, meeting in peoples' homes to rehearse, then performing serious classical music to an appreciative audience.

Or he could do something completely different such as studying design, or architecture, or town planning. These were things for which he had had an amateur's passion all his life. Perhaps he could plan the house which he intended to have built on the now-bare church block at Barwon Downs. His thoughts spun wildly on the potential for this building. It should be a show-piece, a memorial to the church burning and a tribute to all the victims of childhood sexual abuse. He pictured a red-painted building with a tower symbolising a flame. He could become an architect and design the building himself.

No, he couldn't. Justin laughed at the way his thoughts were ticking over. It would take too long to become an architect who could design such a building, but he could work with an architect to build it, in the very near future. It would put Barwon Downs on the map.

What a change he had been though during the last year, when some strange impulse led him to Windsor, where he had his chance meeting with Peter. Now, he had a circle of friends and family with whom he wanted to spend time and he also had the energy to do new things, energy that was directed outwards. He wondered, would it all fizzle out? Would he retreat to his flat and his former way of life, He knew that his anxiety would be an issue. Should he see a psychologist? His instinct was, not yet.

For hours, he rode this wave of exhilaration that the awareness of his potential gave him, trying to hold onto it, pushing himself for more ideas. He planned to let his ideas coalesce then he would discuss them with Maureen. He wondered if she was experiencing his excitement. But regardless of what he would do during the next few years, there was something important that he had to do first.

*****

Justin enjoyed exploring Glasgow the morning after his arrival. He liked the grandeur of its monumental buildings, similar to Melbourne's but on a bigger scale. He wondered if that was because of its longer history as a commercial centre without the benefits of space and modern transport which allowed Melbourne to spread out. It was a warm summer's day with lots of shoppers in the streets and buskers performing, which gave the city centre a youthfulness and vibrancy. He walked for hours, preferring immersion than visiting the sites of historic interest which the tourists sought out.

He found the Willow Tea Rooms, where he would be meeting Morag that afternoon. He wanted to be sure of where it was so that he knew exactly how long it would take him to walk there from the cheap hotel where he was staying. As the time for their 3 o'clock meeting approached, he was amused to register how anxious he was. He wanted to arrive at the appropriate time. He suspected that Morag would be punctual and didn't want to arrive before her, in case she had a favourite place in mind where they should sit and needed to negotiate that before Justin arrived. He walked slowly to the Rooms in Sauchiehall Street, paused to admire the curved exterior, then entered at 3.02pm.

He still didn't know what Morag meant to him. She was certainly now a friend, a close friend, someone he could write to with honesty about his most important thoughts and feelings. He didn't think he wanted to have a relationship with her and tried to anticipate all the possible feelings that meeting her might generate. He was sure his future was in Melbourne and he couldn't imagine Morag in Melbourne. He couldn't bear the thought of sharing his flat with anyone.

Morag too anticipated their rendezvous with uncertainty. She had been looking forward to meeting Justin since receiving his email a month before but had lost her confidence in the last few days. Her weight loss had left her with sagging skin which embarrassed her. She could disguise her arms and legs in a voluminous dress but not her jowls and drooping double chin. She looked at herself in the mirror and touched her chin, resolving to keep her head still so that it wouldn't wobble but knowing that in practice that wouldn't be possible. The day was going to be hot and humid and that would make her sweat in her long-sleeved dress. This worried her so much that she caught a taxi the short distance from her hotel to the Tea Rooms rather than walk. She also worried about the arrival time. She knew the Tea Rooms well and wanted to get a table near the rail on the mezzanine floor with a good view throughout the building. She planned to get to the building by 2.50pm but was in fact seated by 2.45pm.

When Justin entered the Tea Rooms, he was struck by the sense of light and space created by the central light well and the mezzanine. The colours he noticed next, harmonious blends of black, white and shades of pink, fractured into fragments by panels and furniture. With a growing sense of delight, he discovered repeating patterns of lines and squares in the walls, the chairs and the screens. There were squares made up of cut out smaller squares in the backs of the chairs and a forest of vertical lines in the tall, straight backs of the chairs, the slats of the mezzanine rails and the stained glass. He found classical arts and crafts patterns in glass and metal evoking a bygone era and momentarily lost himself in the visual feast.

The spell was broken by Morag, standing beside her chair above him on the mezzanine and waving to him. He found his way up the stairs to join her, reminding himself to show no reaction to her size. Her eyes and her smile were the same and in her brief greeting he recalled his love of the islander accent, the purer Scottish accent of people whose first language is Gaelic. He kissed her lightly on the cheek and they sat at their table with its crisp white linen tablecloth. He said,

"Morag. This place is magnificent. I'm so glad you arranged for us to meet here."

Justin gazed around the room and Morag pointed out all the distinctive features of Charles Rennie McIntosh's designs. This led to her describing other places around Glasgow which contained his work. Justin was gushing in his enthusiasm, which was genuine, but by the time the waitress came to take their order, he wanted a change of tone. It was as if they were both trying to avoid the tension that anticipating the meeting had provoked. He said,

"I've been nervous about meeting you Morag, but it's been easy."

Morag looked down, drawing strength, then said,

"I was nervous too."

Justin continued,

"We've communicated well with our emails. I was worried that we might lose something face-to-face, but I'm glad to say that hasn't happened."

They were both quiet. It had turned serious too quickly. Morag looked down and Justin found himself taking the lead.

"You must have been surprised to hear from me. You must have thought I was mad."

He smiled and Morag rallied,

"I was shocked and surprised, but I didn't think you were mad. I was honoured, flattered that someone on the other side of the world would send me such an epistle."

They found their level and spoke at length about their lives and Justin's emergence, leading up to the church burning. Justin was conscious of how harsh his Australian accent was in contrast with Morag's Scottish accent with its gentle lilts. He didn't like her obesity and noticed the dress which was meant to hide and her need to wipe the sweat from her brow but concentrated on her eyes which hadn't changed. Morag thought Justin was gorgeous; thinner and grey with shorter hair but now with beautiful smile wrinkles around his eyes. He was better looking now, if that was possible, than when she last saw him. She insisted that Justin try one of the Tea Room's caramel short cakes, she wouldn't of course have one and that lead to some conversation about her health and her weight loss. She said,

"I'm now only three quarters of the person I used to be, literally!"

They talked about the changes that had occurred on South Uist and the people Justin had come to know when he was there but both of them avoided references to themselves as a couple during that time. Justin however, had something to say, something he had been planning for the last month,

"I owe you an apology Morag. I neglected you, I wasn't giving enough of myself when I was with you. It's been a pattern in my life and I don't want to be like that anymore. I can understand it better now that I've acknowledged how much I was damaged."

Morag nodded but was so moved that she couldn't put into words what she wanted to say.

They spoke of their plans for the near future. Justin was going to travel to Derbyshire and do the Pennine Way walk but before he left Glasgow he would visit, at Morag's suggestion, the recreated rooms of Charles Rennie McIntosh's house. He would spend a few days in London then return to Australia. Morag asked him about Melbourne and he found himself free-wheeling on Melbourne's history, politics, architecture and the attractive inner suburban streets which he loved. He spoke without interruption for about half an hour then stopped, thinking he was being boring. Morag protested,

"It's just the sort of thing an island lassie wants to hear about."

They spoke for nearly three hours and even when there seemed to be a natural lull in their conversation, neither of them knew how to let go. Justin offered to take Morag out for dinner that night but no, she was catching the last plane back to South Uist. Justin wasn't disappointed, he had enjoyed his time with

Morag but was feeling the need to be alone. They promised each other that they would continue to communicate by email.

Justin had bought a present for Morag, but since buying it, he had worried about the appropriateness of giving it to her. He had visited a shop in Melbourne which sold Australiana, thinking to buy her an Australian animal trinket. There he found a beautiful display of Australian opal jewellery and couldn't resist buying an opal pendant. It was a simple, small pendant mounted on Sterling silver but it was the colour that attracted him, unlike the other multi-coloured opals, this one was mainly blue with a few flecks of red and gold at the edges. The shade of blue was the same as Morag's eyes and his eyes. He remembered the day that they put their heads together and looked closely into a mirror to determine that their eyes were exactly the same shade of light blue.

When they were about to leave the Tea Rooms, Justin decided to give Morag the pendant on its chain. She said,

"Oh thank you Justin. It's beautiful."

Justin reached out and put his hand on top of hers and gave it a gentle squeeze. As they left Morag became anxious that Justin might want to give her a hug because she was clammy with sweat. He didn't, he gave her a quick peck of a kiss and walked away.

Morag didn't fly to South Uist that night, she had booked her flight for the next morning. She had planned to tell Justin she was returning that night if he wanted to prolong their time together. Even as she made that decision she recognised that she was doing what she always did, regulating and controlling the way she interacted with people. It had been a wonderful meeting but as the evening passed, she became upset with herself, she had let herself down. She should have been more flexible about the time they spent together and not let him get away with that apology, she should have apologised for the way she treated him all those years ago. She surprised herself by crying, something she hadn't done for decades.

29

Justin enjoyed walking the Pennine Way, he found the walking easy and didn't mind the showery weather. He encountered other walkers all along the Way but, to his surprise, he enjoyed the social life of the walk. The walkers were from all around the world, but mostly middle-aged middle-class English people who were open to good quality conversation with a touch of formality. This worked well on the track and in the dining rooms of the hostels and pubs where the walkers met in the evenings. Justin found that he would adjust the pace of his walking to accommodate the people he wanted to talk with, or on a few occasions, to get away from people he wanted to avoid. The walkers brought a strong sense of fellowship to the evening dinners where they discussed their adventures of the days' walks.

Justin was more open about his life than he was used to being, for example he would tell some of the Australians he met about the church burning. All the Australians knew about the church burning because it had been widely reported, as did some of the English and German walkers he spoke with. Discussing the church burning always led to conversations about the damage done by childhood sexual abuse and his own unusual life. He was flattered by the widespread knowledge about the church burning and felt that he was educating people.

Justin liked the women he met; there were many travelling in small groups and a few travelling alone. They were all strong and independent women who might be muddy and sweaty on the walk but always managed to scrub up well for dinner. Groups of women tended to adopt him at the evening meals and he enjoyed the motherly frisson of their interest in him. He gained confidence in talking with women as the walk progressed and would walk and dine alone with some of the single women. It was in this way that he met Deirdre, a divorced architect from Geelong. They found plenty of common ground and Deirdre was excited by Justin's concept of a symbolic building on the site of the burnt church, Deirdre was nursing a swollen knee and walking slowly but Justin slowed his pace in order to walk with her. Even when they weren't talking, he felt comfortable in her presence.

Justin told Deirdre about his meeting with Morag and even though he was at pains to describe the meeting in almost spiritual terms, as a part of his recovery process, his description came out sounding sordid to his own ears. That night, as he went over what he had said, he was distressed to think that Deirdre might have reinterpreted his story as, 'You visited an old flame hoping to rekindle the relationship but when you found she was fat and ugly you lost interest'. After a restless night, he concluded that perhaps that was the best explanation after all.

He regretted that he had met Deirdre only three days before the end of the walk and decided that he would ask to see her again back in Australia. Before he could, she took the initiative and asked him. They agreed to meet for lunch in Geelong.

Justin spent four days in London before returning to Australia. He felt uncomfortable in the crowds and wanted to get back to Melbourne to get on with things. He visited a few places he wanted to see such as the Victoria and Albert Museum but didn't enjoy being a tourist on his own.

Mrs Weissmann made a fuss of him when he arrived home, then gave him a list of jobs she would like him to do for her, he had anticipated that. There were dozens of emails for him to read but he was too tired to face them all that night. He read the ones from Peter and Morag. Peter wrote,

Hope you had a great trip, give me a call when you get home and let's meet for lunch. You'll be pleased to hear that I have finished my book and found a publisher. There is some editing to do and some legal checking, but it should be out by December.

Justin phoned him straight away, congratulated him and arranged the meeting.

Morag's email was short but intense and filled Justin's thoughts for several days afterwards, during which time he read it several times. He was buoyed by its spirit of connection and the message of real support he had given her. Her revelation left him wondering what might have been, what direction their lives together could have taken. The ambiguity of the feelings she expressed made him anxious but at the same time confirmed his belief that all human relationships were messy, fragile, changeable but worthwhile. He decided to give his reply lots of thought before responding with the delicacy that was necessary. Her email read,

Hello Justin

I hope you had an uneventful journey home, it must be tiring, flying for so long. I've never flown for more than 2 hours, that was when I flew to France as a teenager. Did you enjoy the Pennine Way? I imagine you would have found it quite crowded after your walk around Victoria. Did you meet any English walkers wearing long red socks and knee-length trousers? You'd never see a Scot dressed like that!

It was wonderful to meet you at the Willow Tea Rooms. I keep thinking about our meeting and what I like most, is just how easy it was. Witnessing your appreciation of the Charles Rennie McIntosh designs was delightful for me. You too have inspired me by the way you described Melbourne (I was going to say 'by your love of Melbourne' but it's more complicated than that, isn't it?). I have always liked Australian films, but since hearing you describe your Melbourne I have been tracking down and watching films which are set in Melbourne. I have watched, The Castle, On The Beach, Death In Brunswick, Animal Kingdom and Three Dollars. Now I am watching the dark series, The Slap.

More serious now.

You apologised for the way you treated me when we were together. I was furious with myself afterwards for letting you get away with that. 'You always treated me well' I thought. 'I was the one who behaved badly, and it was me who ended the relationship' On reflection, I think I understand the importance for you of making that apology, it was part of your 'recovery' for want of a better word. So, thank you, apology accepted. Now please accept my apology. I was controlling and never gave of myself as I should have. I have a better understanding of myself now and why I have sabotaged the meaningful relationships of my life.

Which leads me to the hardest part, I now want to be completely open and honest with you, the way you have been with me since your first email.

You know about my alcoholic father and husband. It was worse than that. My father sexually abused me from the ages of 12 to 14. My mother knew, but she was too weak and disempowered to do anything about it. Within my marriage there was rape as well as the other physical violence. With the help of my psychologist, I have come to an understanding of the way these experiences shaped me and what I can do now to improve my self-image and the way I relate to people. Your indirect influence has been very important, possibly more important than what I have done with my psychologist.

There, I've told you.

I often think about the different journeys you and I are on. You are a long way ahead of me; you are healthy and gorgeous (I told you I was going to be honest). You have tremendous potential, and the time to do what you want to do. You are giving back and helping others and that is where your strength lies. You will probably meet some wonderful woman now to make your life complete and that is as it should be. I am still losing weight, although at a much slower rate now. To compensate, I walk long distances, often into the night. I have been given the nickname, 'The Midnight Rambler' and kind souls who find me wandering around the middle of the island will offer to drive me home to Lochboisdale. My health is improving all the time. With the weight loss, my body has become a bag of sagging flesh. There are operations to remove the stretched skin but they are expensive and at present I feel that I don't deserve that. Perhaps I will in future. Just as important, are the steps I am taking to look after myself mentally and improve the ways I relate to people, a long process, to do with learning to trust. I am also dealing with my self-esteem issues and the way I am attracted to alcoholics.

So here we are, 2 damaged people on opposite sides of the world, walking our separate pathways. I imagine that, like me, you do not know where your path will lead and if, at our age, we can make the changes necessary to fulfil our potentials as human beings.

Enough of that, I want to finish lighter. I love the pendant you gave me. I put it on the night we met and I don't think I will ever take it off. The opal is the blue of my eyes, the blue of your eyes. Every day, I have little daydreams about the pendant. I picture you finding it in a shop and what you express on your face when you see it, I wonder what thoughts passed through your mind when you decided to buy it for me. I see you taking it from its box and admiring it, having doubts about whether or not to give it to me, and I wonder how you felt when you gave it to me. I am forever fondling my pendant Justin and looking at it around my neck in the mirror. It always makes me happy.

Best wishes
Your strange, saggy, struggling but optimistic pen pal
Morag

ACKNOWLEDGEMENTS

I would like to thank all the friends, patients and colleagues who have given me the ideas for this story. Thanks also to Jenny Briers for her support and proof-reading and the team at Ilura Design for helping to prepare the book for publication.

ABOUT THE AUTHOR

Tim Lowe is a general practitioner who has worked with homeless patients, and patients with mental health and addiction problems.

Church Burning is his third novel. His first, *Equinox of Tears,* was published in 2003, and his second, *The Arab Club: Four Women and a Man,* in 2014.